W9-AUM-283

The Snaky Yellow Fingers of

DR. FU MANCHU held a needle syringe. He made a quick injection and studied the motionless man before him. Then, with a delicate atomizer, Dr. Fu Manchu shot sprays up the left and right nostrils of the unconscious victim.

Ten seconds later Herman Grosset sat suddenly upright, staring wildly ahead. His gaze was caught and held by green, compelling eyes only inches from his own.

"You understand—" the strange voice spoke slowly: "The word of command is 'Asia!'"

"I understand," Grosset replied.

"The word," Dr. Fu Manchu intoned hypnotically, is 'Asia.'"

"Asia," Grosset echoed.

"Until you hear that word—" the voice seemed to come from the depths of a green lake—"forget, forget all that you have to do."

"I have forgotten."

"But when you hear the word. . . . ?"

"I shall kill!"

PRESIDENT FU MANCHU

Sax Rohmer

PYRAMID BOOKS ▲ NEW YORK

PRESIDENT FU MANCHU

A PYRAMID BOOK

Published by arrangement with Doubleday and Company, Inc.

Doubleday edition published 1936

Pyramid edition published, December 1963
    Second printing, December 1969

Copyright, 1936, by Sax Rohmer

All Rights Reserved

Printed in the United States of America

PYRAMID BOOKS are published by Pyramid Publications, Inc.
444 Madison Avenue, New York, New York 10022, U.S.A.

PRESIDENT FU MANCHU

1 *THE ABBOT OF HOLY THORN*

THREE CARS drew up, the leading car abreast of a great bronze door bearing a design representing the beautiful agonized face of the Savior, a crown of thorns crushed down upon His brow. A man jumped out and ran to this door. Ten men alighted behind him. The wind howled around the tall tower and a carpet of snow was beginning to form upon the ground. Four guards, appearing as if by magic out of white shadows, lined up before the door.

"Stayton!" came sharply. "Stand aside."

One of the guards stepped forward—peered. A tall, slightly built man who had been in the leading car was the speaker. He had a mass of black, untidy hair, and his face, though that of one not yet west of thirty, was grim and square jawed. He was immediately recognized.

"All right, Captain."

The man addressed as captain turned to the party and issued rapid orders in a low tone. The leader, muffled up in a leather, fur-collared topcoat, his face indistinguishable beneath the brim of a soft felt hat already dusted with snow, rang a bell beside the bronze door.

It opened so suddenly that one might have supposed the opener to have been waiting inside for this purpose; a short, elegant young man, almost feminine in the nicety of his attire.

The new arrival stepped in and quickly shut out the storm, closing the bronze door behind him. In a little lobby communicating with a large square room equipped as an up-to-date office, but at this late hour deserted, he stood staring at the person who had admitted him.

A churchlike lamp, hung from a bracket on the wall, now cast its golden light upon the face of the man wearing the leather coat. He had removed his hat, revealing a head of crisp, graying hair. His features were angular to the point of gauntness, and his eyes had the penetrating quality of armored steel, while his complexion seemed strangely out of keeping with the climate, being sun-baked to a sort of coffee color.

"Are you James Richet?" he snapped.

The elegant young man inclined his glossy head.

"At your service."

"Lead me to Abbot Donegal. I am expected."

Richet perceptibly hesitated; whereupon, plunging his hand with an irritable, nervous movement into some pocket beneath the leather topcoat, the visitor produced a card and handed it to Richet. One glance he gave at it, bowed again in a manner that was almost Oriental and indicated the open gate of an elevator.

A few moments later:

"Federal Agent 56," Richet announced in his silky tones.

The visitor entered a softly lighted study, the view from its windows indicating that it was situated at the very top of the tall tower. From a chair beside a book-laden desk the sole occupant of the room—who had apparently been staring out at the wintry prospect far below—stood up, turned. Mr. Richet, making his queer bow, retired and closed the door.

Federal Agent 56 unceremoniously cast his wet topcoat upon the floor, dropping his hat on top of it. He was now revealed as a tall, lean man, dressed in a tweed suit which had seen long service. He advanced with outstretched hand to meet the occupant of the study—a slightly built priest, with the keen, ascetic features sometimes met with in men from the south of Ireland and thick, graying hair; a man normally actuated by a healthy sense of humor, but tonight with an oddly haunted expression in his clear eyes.

"Thank God, Father, I see you well."

"Thank God, indeed." He glanced at the card which Richet had laid upon his desk even as he grasped the extended hand. "I am naturally prepared for interference with my work, but this thing . . ."

The newcomer, still holding the priest's hand, stared fixedly, searchingly, into his eyes.

"You don't know it all," he said rapidly.

"This imprisonment——"

"A necessity, believe me. I have covered seven hundred miles by air since you broke off in the middle of your radio address this evening."

He turned abruptly and began to pace up and down that

book-lined room with its sacred pictures and ornaments, these seeming strangely at variance with the large and orderly office below. Pulling a very charred briar pipe from the pocket of his tweed jacket he began to load it from a pouch at least as venerable as the pipe. The Abbot Donegal dropped back into his chair, running his fingers through his hair, and:

"There is one favor I would ask," he said, "before we proceed any further. It is difficult to talk to an anonymous man."

He stared down at the card upon his desk. This card bore the printed words:

FEDERAL AGENT 56

But across the bottom right-hand corner was the signature of the President of the United States.

Federal Agent 56 smiled, a quick, revealing smile which lifted a burden of years from the man.

"I agree," he snapped in his rapid, staccato fashion. "Smith is a not uncommon name. Suppose we say Smith."

The rising blizzard began to howl around the tower as though many wailing demons clamored for admittance. A veil of snow swept across uncurtained windows, dimming distant lights. Dom Patrick Donegal lighted a cigarette; his hands were not entirely steady.

"If you know what really happened to me tonight, Mr. Smith," he said, his rich, orator's voice lowered almost to a murmur, "for heaven's sake tell me. I have been deluged with telephone messages and telegrams, but in accordance with your instructions—or" (he glanced at the restlessly promenading figure) "should I say orders—I have answered none of them."

Smith, pipe alight, paused, staring down at the priest.

"You were brought straight back after your collapse?"

"I was. They would have taken me home, but mysterious instructions from Washington resulted in my being brought here. I came to my senses in the small bedroom which adjoins this study."

"Your last memory being?"

"Of standing before the microphone, my notes in my hand."

"Quite," said Smith, beginning to walk up and down again. "Your words, as I recollect them, were: 'But if the Constitution is to be preserved, if even a hollow shell of Liberty is to remain to us, there is one evil in this country which must be eradicated, torn up by its evil roots, utterly destroyed. . . .' Then came silence, a confusion of voices, and an announce-

9

ment that you had been seized with sudden illness. Does your memory, Father, go as far as these words?"

"Not quite," the priest answered wearily, resting his head upon his hand and making a palpable effort to concentrate. "I began to lose my grip of the situation some time earlier in the address. I experienced most singular sensations. I could not co-ordinate my ideas, and the studio in which I was speaking alternately contracted and enlarged. At one moment the ceiling appeared to become black and to be descending upon me. At another, I thought that I stood in the base of an immeasurably lofty tower." His voice grew in power as he spoke, his Irish brogue became more pronounced. "Following these dreadful sensations came an overpowering numbness of mind and body. I remember no more."

"Who attended you?" snapped Smith.

"My own physician, Dr. Reilly."

"No one but Dr. Reilly, your secretary, Mr. Richet, and I suppose the driver of the car in which you returned, came up here?"

"No one, Mr. Smith. Such, I am given to understand, were the explicit and authoritative orders given a few minutes after the occurrence."

Smith stopped on the other side of the desk, staring down at the abbot.

"Your manuscript has not been recovered?" he asked slowly.

"I regret to say, no. Definitely, it was left behind in the studio."

"On the contrary," snapped Smith angrily, "definitely it was not! The place has been searched from wall to wall by those who know their business. No, Father Abbot, your manuscript is not there. I *must* know what it contained—and from what source this missing information came to you."

The ever-rising wind in its fury shook the Tower of the Holy Thorn, shrieking angrily around that lofty room in which two men faced a problem destined in its outcome to affect the whole nation. The priest, a rapid, heavy smoker, lighted another cigarette.

"I cannot make out," he said—and now a natural habit of authority began to assert itself in his voice—"I cannot make out why you attach such importance to my notes for this speech, nor why my sudden illness, naturally disturbing to myself, should result in this sensational federal action. Really, my friend—" he leaned back in his chair, staring up at the tanned, eager face of his visitor—"in effect, I am a prisoner here. This, I may say, is intolerable. I await your explanation, Mr. Smith."

Smith bent forward, resting nervous brown hands on the priest's desk and staring intently into those upturned, observant eyes.

"What was the nature of the warning you were about to give to the nation?" he demanded. "What is this evil growth which must be uprooted and destroyed?"

These words produced a marked change in the bearing of the Abbot Donegal. They seemed to bring recognition of something he would willingly have forgotten. Again he ran his fingers through his hair, now almost distractedly.

"God help me," he said, in a very low voice, "I don't know!"

He suddenly stood up; his glance was wild.

"I cannot remember. My mind is a complete blank upon this subject—upon everything relating to it. I think some lesion must have occurred in my brain. Dr. Reilly, although reticent, holds, I believe, the same opinion."

"Nothing of the kind," snapped Smith, "but that manuscript has to be found! There's life or death in it."

He ceased speaking abruptly and seemed to be listening to the voice of the storm. Then, ignoring the priest, he suddenly sprang across the room and threw the door wide open.

Mr. Richet stood bowing on the threshold.

2 A CHINESE HEAD

IN AN APARTMENT having a curiously pointed ceiling (one might have imagined it to be situated in the crest of a minaret) a strange figure was seated at a long, narrow table. Light, amber light, came through four near-Gothic windows set so high that only a giant could have looked out of them. The man, whose age might have been anything from sixty to seventy—he had a luxurious growth of snow-white hair—was heavily built, wearing a dilapidated woolen dressing gown; and his long sensitive fingers were nicotine-stained, since he continuously smoked Egyptian cigarettes. An open tin of these stood near his hand, and he lighted one from the stump of another—smoking, smoking, incessantly smoking.

Upon the table before him were seven telephones, one or other of them almost always in action. When two purred into life simultaneously, the smoker would place one to his right ear, the other to his left. He never replied to incoming messages, nor did he make notes.

In the brief intervals he pursued what one might have supposed to be his real calling. Upon a large wooden pedestal was set a block of modeling clay, and beside the pedestal lay implements of the modeler's art. This singular old man, the amazing frontal development of his splendid skull indicating great mathematical powers, worked patiently upon a life-sized head of an imposing but sinister Chinaman.

In one of those rare intervals he was working delicately upon the high, imperious nose of the clay head, when a muffled bell sounded and the amber light disappeared from the four Gothic windows, plunging the room into complete darkness.

For a moment there was no sound; the tip of a burning cigarette glowed in the darkness. Then a voice spoke, an unforgettable voice, by which gutturals were oddly stressed but every word was given its precise syllabic value.

"Have you a later report," said this voice, "from Base 8?"

The man at the long table replied, speaking with German intonations.

"The man known as Federal Agent 56 arrived at broadcasting station twenty minutes after midnight. Police still searching there. Report just to hand from Number 38 states that this agent, accompanied by Captain Mark Hepburn, U. S. Army Medical Corps, assigned to Detached Officers' List, and a party of nine men arrived Tower of the Holy Thorn at twelve-thirty-two, relieving federals already on duty. Agent 56 last reported in conference with Abbot Donegal. The whole area closely covered. No further news in this report."

"The Number responsible for the manuscript?"

"Has not yet reported."

"The last report from Numbers covering Weaver's Farm?"

"Received at 11.07. Dr. Orwin Prescott is still in retirement there. No change has been made in his plans regarding the debate at Carnegie Hall. This report from Number 35."

The muffled bell rang. Amber light appeared again in the windows; and the sculptor returned lovingly to his task of modeling a Chinaman's head.

3 *ABOVE THE BLIZZARD*

In Dom Patrick Donegal's study at the top of the Tower of the Holy Thorn James Richet faced Federal Officer 56. Some of his silky suavity seemed to have deserted him.

"I quite understand your—unexpected—appearance, Mr. Richet," said Smith, staring coldly at the secretary. "You have greatly assisted us. Let me check what you have told me. You believe (the abbot unfortunately having no memory of the episode) that certain material for the latter part of his address was provided early on Saturday morning during a private interview in this room between the Father and Dr. Orwin Prescott?"

"I believe so, although I was not actually present."

There was something furtive in Richet's manner; a nervous tremor in his voice.

"Dr. Prescott, as a candidate for the Presidency, no doubt had political reasons for not divulging these facts himself." Smith turned to Abbot Donegal. "It has always been your custom, Father, to prepare your sermons and speeches in this room, the material being looked up by Mr. Richet?"

"That is so."

"The situation becomes plainer." He turned to Richet. "I think we may assume" he went on, "that the latter part of the address, the part which was never delivered, was in Dom Patrick's own handwriting. You yourself, I understand, typed out the earlier pages."

"I did. I have shown you a duplicate."

"Quite," snapped Smith; "the final paragraph ends with the words 'torn up by its evil roots, utterly destroyed.'"

"There was no more. The abbot informed me that he intended to finish the notes later. In fact, he did so. For when I accompanied him to the broadcasting station he said that his notes were complete."

"And after his—seizure?"

"I returned almost immediately to the studio. But the manuscript was not on the desk."

"Thank you. That is perfectly clear. We need detain you no longer."

The secretary, whose forehead glistened with nervous perspiration, went out, closing the door silently behind him. Abbot Donegal looked up almost pathetically at Smith.

"I never thought," said he, "I should live to find myself so helpless. Can you imagine that I remember nothing whatever of Dr. Prescott's calling upon me? Except for that vague, awful moment when I faced the microphone and realized that my mental powers were deserting me, I have no recollection of anything that happened for some forty-eight hours before! Yet it seems that Prescott was here and that he gave me vital information. What can it have been? Great heavens—" he stood up, agitatedly—"*what* can it have been? Do you really believe that I am a victim, not of a failure in my health, but of an attempt to suppress this information?"

"Not an attempt, Father," snapped Smith, "a success! You are lucky to be alive!"

"But who can have done this thing, and how did he do it?"

"The first question I can answer; the second I might answer if I could recover the missing manuscript. Probably it's destroyed. We have a thousand-to-one chance. We are indebted to a phone call, which fortunately came through direct to you, for knowledge of Dr. Prescott's whereabouts."

"Why do you say 'which fortunately came through'? You surely have no doubts about Richet?"

"How long with you?" snapped Smith.

"Nearly a year."

"Nationality?"

"American."

"I mean pedigree."

"That I cannot tell you."

"There's color somewhere. I can't place its exact shade. But one thing is clear: Dr. Prescott is in great danger. So are you."

The abbot arrested Smith's restless promenade, laying a hand upon his shoulder.

"There is only one other candidate in the running for dictatorship, Mr. Smith—Harvey Bragg. Yet I find it hard to believe that he . . . You are not accusing *Harvey Bragg?*"

"Harvey Bragg!" Smith laughed shortly. "Popularly known as 'Bluebeard,' I believe? My dear Dom Patrick, Harvey Bragg is a small pawn in a big game."

"Yet—he may be President, or Dictator."

Smith turned, staring in his piercing way into the priest's eyes.

"He almost certainly *will* be Dictator!"

Only the mad howling of the blizzard disturbed a silence

which fell upon those words—"He almost certainly *will* be Dictator."

Then the priest whose burning rhetoric, like that of Peter the Hermit, had roused a nation, found voice; he spoke in very low tones:

"Why do you say he certainly will be Dictator?"

"I said *almost* certainly. His war-cry 'America for every man—every man for America' is flashing like a fiery cross through the country. Do you realize that in office Harvey Bragg has made remarkable promises?"

"He has carried them out! He controls enormous funds."

"He does! Have you any suspicion, Father, of the source of those funds?"

For one fleeting moment a haunted look came into the abbot's eyes. A furtive memory had presented itself, only to elude him.

"None," he replied wearily; "but his following today is greater than mine. Just as a priest and with no personal pretensions, I have tried—God knows I have tried—to keep the people sane, and clean. Machinery has made men mad. As machines reach nearer and nearer to the province of miracles, as Science mounts higher and higher—so Man sinks lower and lower. On the day that Machinery reaches up to the stars, Man, spiritually, will have sunk back to the primeval jungle."

He dropped into his chair.

Smith, resting a lean, nervous hand upon the desk, leaned across it, staring into the speaker's face.

"Harvey Bragg is a true product of his age," he said tensely —"and he is backed by *one man!* I have followed this man from Europe to Asia, from Asia to South America, from South to North. The resources of three European Powers and of the United States have been employed to head that man off. But he is here! In the political disruption of this country he sees his supreme opportunity."

"His name, Mr. Smith?"

"In your own interests, Father, I suggest it might be better that you don't know—yet."

Abbot Donegal challenged the steely eyes, read sincerity there, and nodded.

"I accept your suggestion, Mr. Smith. In the Church we are trained to recognize tacit understandings. You are not a private investigator instructed by the President, nor is 'Mr. Smith' your proper title. But I think we understand one another. . . . And you tell me that this man, whoever he may be, is backing Harvey Bragg?"

"I have only one thing to tell you: Stay up here at the top of your tower until you hear from *me!*"

"Remain a prisoner?"

Patrick Donegal stood up, suddenly aggressive, truculent.

"A prisoner, yes. I speak, Father, with respect and authority."

"You may speak, Mr. Smith, with the authority of Congress, of the President in person, buy my first duty is to God; my second to the State. I take the eight o'clock Mass in the morning."

For a moment their glances met and challenged; then:

"There may be times, Father, when you have a duty even higher than this," said Smith crisply.

"You cannot induce me, my friend, to close my eyes to a plain obligation. I do not doubt your sincerity. I have never met a man more honest or more capable. I cannot doubt my own danger. But in this matter I have made my choice."

For a moment longer Federal Agent 56 stared at the priest, his lean face very grim. Then, suddenly stooping, he picked up his leather topcoat and his hat from the floor and shot out his hand.

"Good night, Father Abbot," he snapped. "Don't ring. I should like to *walk* down, although that will take some time. Since you refuse my advice, I leave you in good hands."

"In the hands of God, Mr. Smith, as we all are."

2

Outside on the street, beyond the great bronze door with its figure of the thorn-tortured head, King Blizzard held high revel. Snow was spat into the suffering face when the door was opened, as though powers of evil ruled that night, pouring contumely, contempt, upon the gentle Teacher. Captain Mark Hepburn, U.S.M.C., was standing there. He had one glimpse of the olive face of James Richet, who ushered the visitor out, heard his silky "Good night, Mr. Smith"; then the bronze door was closed, and the wind shrieked in mocking laughter around the Tower of the Holy Thorn.

Dimly through the spate of snow watchful men might be seen.

"Listen, Hepburn," snapped Smith, "get this address: Weaver's Farm, Winton, Connecticut. Phone that Dr. Orwin Prescott is not to step outside for one moment until I arrive. Arrange that we get there—fast. Have the place protected. Flying hopeless tonight. Special train to Cleveland. Side anything in our way. Have a plane standing by. Advise the pilot

16

to look up emergency landings within easy radius of Weaver's Farm. If blizzard continues, arrange for special to run through to Buffalo. Advise Buffalo."

"Leave it to me."

"Cover the man James Richet. I want hourly reports sent to headquarters. This priest's life is valuable. See that he's protected day and night. Have this place covered from now on. Grab anybody—*anybody*—that comes out tonight."

"And where are you going, Chief?"

"I am going to glance over Dom Patrick's home quarters. Meet me at the station. . . ."

4. MRS. ADAIR

MARK HEPBURN drove back through a rising blizzard. The powers of his newly accredited chief, known to him simply as "Federal Agent 56," were peculiarly impressive.

Arrangements—"by order of Federal Agent 56"—had been made without a hitch. These had included sidetracking the Twentieth Century Limited and the dispatch of an army plane from Dayton to meet the special train.

Dimly he realized that issues greater than the fate of the Presidency were involved. This strange, imperious man, with his irritable, snappy manner, did not come under the jurisdiction of the U.S. Department of Justice; he was not even an American citizen. Yet he was highly empowered by the government. In some way the thing was international. Also, Hepburn liked and respected Federal Agent 56.

And the affection of Mark Hepburn was a thing hard to win. Three generations of Quaker ancestors form a stiff background; and not even a poetic strain which Mark had inherited from a half-Celtic mother could enable him to forget it. His only rebellion—a slender volume of verse in university days, *Green Lilies*—he had lived to repent. Medicine had called him (he was by nature a healer); then army work, with its promise of fresh fields; and now, the Secret Service, where in this crisis he knew he could be of use.

For in the bitter campaign to secure control of the country there had been more than one case of poisoning; and toxicology was Mark Hepburn's special province. Furthermore, his military experience made him valuable.

Around the Tower of the Holy Thorn the blizzard wrapped itself like a shroud. Only the windows at the very top showed any light. The tortured bronze door remained closed.

Stayton stepped forward out of a white mist as Hepburn sprang from his car.

"Anything to report, Stayton? I have only ten minutes."

"Not a soul has come out, Captain, and there doesn't seem to be anybody about in the neighborhood."

"Good enough. You will be relieved at daylight. Make your own arrangements."

Hepburn moved off into the storm.

Something in the wild howling of the wind, some message reaching him perhaps from those lighted windows at the top of the tower, seemed to be prompting his subconscious mind. He had done his job beyond reproach. Nevertheless, all was not well.

One foot on the running board of the car, he paused, staring up to where that high light glimmered through snow. He turned back and walked in the direction of the tower. Almost immediately he was challenged by a watchful agent, was recognized, and passed on. He found himself beside a wall of the building remote from the bronze door. Here there was no exit and he went unchallenged. He stood still, staring about him, his fur coat-collar turned up about his ears, the wind frolicking with his untidy wet black hair.

A slight sound came, only just audible above the shrieking of the blizzard, the opening of a window. . . . He crouched close against the wall.

"All clear. Good luck . . ."

James Richet!

Then someone dropped, falling lightly in the snow almost beside him. The window closed. Hepburn reached out a long, sinewy arm, grabbed and held his captive . . . and found himself looking down into the most beautiful eyes he had ever seen!

His prisoner was a girl, little above medium height, but slender, so that she appeared much taller. She was muffled up in a mink coat as a protection against that fierce wind; a Basque beret was crushed down upon curls which reminded him of polished mahogany. A leather satchel hung from one wrist, and she was so terrified that Hepburn could feel her heart beating as he held her in his bearlike grip.

He realized that he was staring dumbly into those uplifted

18

deep-blue eyes, that he was wondering if he had ever seen such long, curling lashes . . . when *duty, duty*—that slogan of Quaker ancestors—called to him sharply. He slightly relaxed his hold, but offered no chance of escape.

"I see," he said, and his dry, rather toneless voice revealed no emotion whatever. "This is interesting. Who are you and where are you going?"

His tones were coldly remorseless. His arm was like a band of steel. Rebellion died and fear grew in the captive. Now she was trembling. But he was forced to admire her courage, for when she replied she looked at him unflinchingly.

"My name is Adair—Mrs. Adair—and I belong to the staff of the Abbot Donegal. I have been working late, and although I know that there's some absurd order for no one to leave, I simply must go. It's ridiculous, and I won't submit to it. I insist upon being allowed to go home."

"Where is your home?"

"That can be no possible business of yours!" flared the prisoner, her eyes now flashing furiously. "If you like, call the abbot. He will vouch for what I say."

Mark Hepburn's square chin protruded from the upturned collar of his coat; his deep-set eyes never faltered in their regard.

"That can come later if necessary," he said, "but first——"

"But first, I shall freeze to death," said the girl indignantly.

"But first, what have you got in that satchel?"

"Private papers of Abbot Donegal's. I am working on them at home."

"In that case, give them to me."

"I won't! You have no right whatever to interfere with me. I have asked you to get in touch with the abbot."

Without relaxing his grip on his prisoner, Hepburn suddenly snatched the satchel, pulling the loop down over her little gloved hand and thrusting the satchel under his arm.

"I don't want to be harsh," he said, "but my job at the moment is more important than yours. This will be returned to you in an hour or less. Lieutenant Johnson will drive you home."

He began to lead her towards the spot where he knew the Secret Service cars were parked. He had determined to raise a minor hell with the said Lieutenant Johnson for omitting to post a man at this point, for as chief of staff to Federal Agent 56 he was personally responsible. He was by no means sure of himself. The girl embraced by his arm was the first really disturbing element which had ever crashed into

19

his Puritan life; she was too lovely to be real: the teaching of long-ago ancestors prompted that she was an instrument of the devil.

Reluctantly she submitted; for ten, twelve, fifteen paces. Then suddenly resisted, dragging at his arm.

"Please, please, for God's sake, listen to me!"

He pulled up. They were alone in that blinding blizzard, although ten or twelve men were posted at points around the Tower of the Holy Thorn. A freak of the storm cast an awning of snow from the lighted windows down to the spot upon which they stood, and in that dim reflected light Mark Hepburs saw the bewitching face uplifted to him.

She was smiling, this Mrs. Adair who belonged to Abbot Donegal's staff; a tremulous, pathetic smile, a smile which in happier hours had been one of exquisite but surely innocent coquetry. Now it told of bravely hidden tears.

Despite all his stoicism, Mark Hepburn's heart pulsed more rapidly. Some men, he thought, many, maybe, had worshiped those lips, dreamed of that beckoning smile . . . perhaps lost everything for it.

This woman was a revelation; to Mark Hepburn, a discovery. He was suspicious of the Irish. For this reason he had never wholly believed in the sincerity of Patrick Donegal. And Mrs. Adair was enveloped in that mystical halo which haunts yet protects the Celts. He did not believe in this mysticism, but he was not immune from its insidious charm. He hated hurting her; he found himself thinking of her as a beautiful, helpless moth torn by the wind from some green dell where fairies still hid in the bushes and the four-leaved shamrock grew.

He felt suddenly glad about, and not ashamed of, *Green Lilies*. Mrs. Adair, for one magical moment, had enabled him to recapture that long-lost mood. It was very odd, out there in the blizzard, with his racial distrust of pretty women and of all that belonged to Rome. . . .

It was this last thought—Rome—that steadied him. Here was some black plot against the Constitution. . . .

"I don't ask you, I *entreat* you to give me my papers and let me go my own way. I promise, faithfully, if you will tell me where to find you, that I will see you tomorrow and explain anything you want to know."

Hepburn did not look at her. His Quaker ancestors rallied around him. He squared his grim jaw.

"Lieutenant Johnson will drive you home," he said coldly, "and will bring you your satchel immediately I am satisfied that its contents are what you say they are."

In the amber-lighted room where the man with that wonderful mathematical brow sat at work upon the bust of a sinister Chinaman, one of the seven telephones buzzed. He laid down the modeling tool with which he had been working and took up the instrument. He listened.

"This is Number 12," said a woman's voice, "speaking from Base 8. In accordance with orders I managed to escape from the Tower of the Holy Thorn. Unfortunately I was captured by a federal agent—name unknown—at the moment that I reached the ground. I was taken under escort of a Lieutenant Johnson towards an address which I invented at random. A Z-car was covering me. Heavy snow gave me a chance. I managed to spring out and get to the Z-car. I regret that the federal agent secured the satchel containing the manuscript. There's nothing more to report. Standing by here awaiting orders."

The sculptor replaced the receiver and resumed his task. Twice again he was interrupted, listening to a report from California and to another from New York. He made no notes. He never replied. He merely went on with his seemingly endless task; for he was eternally smearing out the work which he had done, now an ear, now a curve of the brow, and patiently remodeling.

A bell rang, the light went out, and in the darkness that unforgettable, guttural voice spoke:

"Give me the latest report of Harvey Bragg's reception at the Hollywood Bowl."

"Last report received," the Teutonic voice replied, and a cigarette glowed in the darkness, "one hour and seventeen minutes ago. Pacific Coast time: twelve minutes after ten. Audience of twenty thousand people, as earlier reported. Harvey Bragg's slogan, 'America for every man—every man for America' was received without enthusiasm. His assurance, hitherto substantiated, that any reputable citizen who is destitute has only to apply to his office to secure immediate employment, went well. Report of end of speech not yet to hand. No other news from Hollywood Bowl. Report sent in by Number 49."

A moment of silence followed, silence so complete that the crackling of burning tobacco in an Egyptian cigarette might have been heard.

"The report of Number 12," said the guttural voice, "is overdue."

"I received a report from Number 12—" he glanced at an electric clock upon the table—"at 2.05 A.M."

Whereupon, word for word, this man of phenomenal memory repeated the message received from Base 8 exactly as it had been delivered.

A dim bell rang and the room became lighted again. The sculptor picked up a modeling tool.

5 *THE SPECIAL TRAIN*

THE SPECIAL TRAIN bored its way through mists of snow.

"They won't attempt to wreck us, Hepburn!" Federal Officer 56 smiled grimly and tapped the satchel which had belonged to Mrs. Adair. "*This* is our safeguard. But there may be an attempt of some other kind."

In the solitary car Smith sat facing Hepburn. Seven of the party which had taken command of the Tower of the Holy Thorn were distributed in chairs about them. Some smoked and were silent; others talked; others again neither smoked nor talked, but glanced furtively in the direction of Captain Hepburn and his mysterious superior.

"You have done a first-class job, Hepburn," said Smith. "I tricked the man Richet (who is some kind of half-caste) into an admission that this—" he tapped the satchel—"was material supplied by Dr. Prescott."

"I ordered Richet's arrest before I left."

"Good man."

The train roared through the night and Smith leaned forward, resting his hand upon Hepburn's shoulder.

"The enemy knows that Dr. Prescott has found out the truth! How Dr. Prescott found out *we* have got to learn. Clearly he is a brilliant man. I'm afraid, Hepburn—I am afraid——"

He gripped Hepburn's shoulder and his grip was like that of a vise.

"You have read this thing . . . and the part which is in Father Donegal's handwriting tells the story. How he was prevented from broadcasting that story I begin to suspect. Note this particularly, Hepburn: I observed that Dom Patrick, when looking over the typescript brought in by James Richet, moistened the tip of his thumb in turning over the pages. A habit. The point seems significant?"

"Not to me," Hepburn confessed, staring rather haggardly at the speaker.

"Ah! Think it over," said Smith; then: "I know why you are downcast. You lost the woman—but you got what we were really looking for. Here's the story of an outside organization aiming to secure control of the country. Don't worry about Mrs. Adair. It's only a question of time. We'll get her."

Mark Hepburn turned his head aside.

The contents of the satchel had proved to be the completed text of Abbot Donegal's address, the last five pages in the Father's untidy manuscript. But those last five pages revealed a plot which, if carried out, would place the United States under the domination of some shadowy being, unnamed, who apparently controlled inexhaustible supplies not only of capital but of men!

Following this revelation, his new chief, "Federal Officer 56," had given him his entire confidence. He had suspected, but now he knew, that a world drama was being fought out in the United States. A simple soul at heart, he was temporarily dazzled by recognition of the fact that he had been appointed chief of staff in an international crisis to Sir Denis Nayland Smith, Ex-Commissioner of Scotland Yard, created a baronet for his services not only to the British Empire but to the world.

And in a moment of weakness he had let the woman go who might be a link, an irreplaceable link, between their task and this thing which aimed to place the United States under alien domination!

In that hour of disillusionment he felt a double traitor; for this man, Nayland Smith, was so dead straight. . . .

An atmosphere of impending harm hovered over the party. Mark Hepburn was not alone in having seen the venomous blizzard spitting snow unto that bronze Face. Among the seven who accompanied them were members of the ancient faith upheld sturdily by the hand of Abbot Donegal; and these, particularly—touched, he told himself, by medieval superstition—doubted and wondered as they were blindly carried through the stormy night. They were ignorant of what underlay it all, and ignorance breeds fear. They knew that they were merely a bodyguard for Captain Hepburn and Federal Officer 56.

Suddenly, appallingly, brakes were applied, all but throwing the nine men out of their chairs. Nayland Smith came to his feet at a bound, clutching the side of the car.

"Hepburn!" he cried, "go forward with two men. This train can slow down but it must not stop!"

Mark Hepburn ran forward along the car, touching two of the seven on their shoulders as he passed. They followed him out. A flare spluttered through snowy mist, clearly visible from the off-side windows.

"Switch off the lights!"

The order came in a high-pitched, irritable voice.

A trainman appeared and the car was plunged in darkness. A second flare broke through the veil of snow. Federal Officer 56 was crouching by a window looking out, and now:

"Do you see!" he cried, and grabbed the arm of a man who was peering out beside him. "Do you see!"

As the train regained momentum, presumably under the urge of Hepburn, a group of men armed with machine guns became clearly visible beside the tracks.

The special was whirling through the night again when Hepburn came back. He was smiling his slow smile. Federal Agent 56 turned and stood up.

"This train won't stop," said Hepburn, "until we make Cleveland."

6 *AT WEAVER'S FARM*

"WHAT'S THIS?" muttered Nayland Smith hoarsely.

The car was pulled up. They were in sight of the woods skirting Weaver's Farm. Night had fallen, and although the violence of the storm had abated there was a great eerie darkness over the snow-covered landscape.

Parties of men carrying torches and hurricane lanterns moved like shadows through the trees!

Smith sprang out onto a faintly discernible track, Mark Hepburn close behind him. They began to run towards the woods, and presently a man who peered about among the silvered bushes turned.

"What has happened?" Smith demanded breathlessly.

The man, whose bearing suggested military training, hesitated, holding a hurricane lamp aloft and staring hard at the speaker. But something in Smith's authoritative manner brought a change of expression.

"We are federal agents," said Mark Hepburn. "What's going on here?"

"Dr. Orwin Prescott has disappeared!"

Nayland Smith clutched Hepburn's shoulder: Mark could feel how his fingers quivered.

"My God, Hepburn," he whispered, "we are too late!"

Clenching his fists, he turned and began to race back to the car. Mark Hepburn exchanged a few words with the man to whom they had spoken and then doubled after Nayland Smith.

They had been compelled by the violence of the blizzard to proceed by rail to Buffalo; the military plane had been forced down by heavy snow twenty miles from the landing place selected. At Buffalo they had had further bad news from Lieutenant Johnson.

Crowning the daring getaway of Mrs. Adair, James Richet, whose arrest had been ordered by Mark Hepburn, had vanished. . . .

And now they were plowing a way along the drive which led up to Weaver's Farm, a white frame house with green shutters, sitting far back from the road. A survival of Colonial New England, it had stood there, outpost of the white man's progress in days when the red man still hunted the woods and lakes, trading beads for venison and maple sugar. Successive generations had modernized it so that today it was a twentieth-century home equipped from cellar to garret with every possible domestic convenience.

The door was wide open; and in the vestibule, with its old prints and atmosphere of culture, a tall, singularly thin man stood on the mat talking to a little white-haired old lady. He held a very wide-brimmed hat in his hand and constantly stamped snow from his boots. His face was gloomily officious. Members of the domestic staff might dimly be seen peering down from an upper landing. Unrest, fear, reigned in this normally peaceful household.

The white-haired lady started nervously as Mark Hepburn stepped forward.

"I am Captain Hepburn," he said. "I think you are expecting me. Is this Miss Lakin?"

"I am glad you are here, Captain Hepburn," said the little lady, with a frightened smile. She held out a small, plump, but delicate hand. "I am Elsie Frayne, Sarah Lakin's friend and companion."

"I am afraid," Hepburn replied, "we come too late. This is Federal Officer Smith. We have met with every kind of obstacle on our way."

"Miss Frayne," rapped Smith in his staccato fashion, "I must put a call through immediately. Where is the telephone?"

Miss Frayne, suddenly quite at ease with these strange invaders out of the night, smiled wanly.

"I regret to say, Mr. Smith, that our telephone was cut off some hours ago."

"Ah!" murmured Smith, and began tugging at the lobe of his left ear, a habit which Hepburn had come to recognize as evidence of intense concentration. "That explains a lot." He stared about him, his disturbing glance finally focusing upon the face of the thin man.

"Who are you?" he snapped abruptly.

"I'm Deputy Sheriff Black," was the prompt but gloomy answer. "I have had orders to protect Weaver's Farm."

"I know it. They were my orders—and a pretty mess you've made of it."

The local officer bristled indignantly. He resented the irritable, peremptory manners of this G man; in fact Deputy Sheriff Black had never been in favor of federal interference with county matters.

"A man can only do his duty, Mr. Smith," he answered angrily, "and I have done mine. Dr. Prescott slipped out some time after dusk this evening. Nobody saw him go. Nobody knows why he went or where he went. I may add that although I may be responsible there are federal men on this job as well, and not one of them knows any more than I know."

"Where is Miss Lakin?"

"Out with a search party down at the lake."

"Sarah has such courage," murmured Miss Frayne. "I wouldn't go outside the house tonight for anything in the world."

Mark Hepburn turned to her.

"Is there any indication," he asked, "that Dr. Prescott went that way?"

"Mr. Walsh, a federal agent who arrived here two hours ago, discovered tracks leading in the direction of the lake."

"John Walsh is our man," said Hepburn, turning to Smith. "Do you want to make any inquiries here, or shall we head for the lake?"

Nayland Smith was staring abstractedly at Miss Frayne, and now:

"At what time, exactly," he asked, "was your telephone disconnected?"

"At five minutes after three," Deputy Sheriff Black's somber tones interpolated. "There are men at work now trying to trace the break."

"Who last saw Dr. Prescott?"

"Sarah," Miss Frayne replied—"that is, so far as we know."

"Where was he and what was he doing?"

"He was in the library writing letters."

"Were these letters posted?"

"No, Mr. Smith, they are still on the desk."

"Was it dark at this time?"

"Yes. Dr. Prescott—he is Miss Lakin's cousin, you know—had lighted the reading lamp, so Sarah told me."

"It was alight when I arrived," growled Deputy Sheriff Black.

"When did you arrive?" Smith asked.

"Twenty minutes after it was suspected Dr. Prescott had left the house."

"Where were you prior to that time?"

"Out in the road. I had been taking reports from the men on duty."

"Has anyone touched those letters since they were written?"

"No one, Mr. Smith," the gentle voice of Miss Frayne replied.

Nayland Smith turned to Deputy Sheriff Black.

"See that no one enters the library," he snapped, "until I return. I want to look over the room in which Dr. Prescott slept."

Deputy Sheriff Black nodded tersely and crossed the vestibule.

But even as Nayland Smith turned toward the stair, a deep feminine voice came out of the night beyond the entrance doors, which had not been closed. The remorseless wind was threatening to rise again, howling wanly through the woods like a phantom wolf pack. Flakes of fine snow fluttered in.

"He has been kidnaped, Mr. Walsh—because of what he knew. His tracks end on the shore of the lake. It's frozen over . . . but there are no more tracks."

And now the speaker came in, followed by two men carrying lanterns; a tall, imperious woman with iron-gray hair, aristocratic features, and deep-set flashing eyes. She paused, looking about her with a slow smile of inquiry. One of the two men saluted Hepburn.

"My name is Smith," said Federal Officer 56, "and this is Captain Hepburn. You are Miss Lakin, Dr. Orwin Prescott's cousin? It was my business, Miss Lakin, to protect him. I fear I have failed."

"I fear it also," she replied, watching him steadily with her fine grave eyes. "Orwin has gone. They have him. He came here for rest and security. He always came here before any important public engagement. Very soon now at Carnegie Hall is the debate with Harvey Bragg." (She was very impressive, this grande dame of Old America.) "He had learned something, Mr. Smith—heaven knows I wish I shared his knowledge—which would have sent Bluebeard back forever to his pinewoods."

"He had!" snapped Smith grimly.

He reached out a long, leather-clad arm and gripped Miss Lakin's shoulder. For a moment she was startled—this man's electric gestures were disturbing—then, meeting that penetrating stare, she smiled with sudden confidence.

"Don't despair, Miss Lakin. All is not lost. Others know what Dr. Prescott knew——"

At which moment somewhere a telephone bell rang!

"They've mended the line," came the gloomy voice of Deputy Sheriff Black, raised now on a note of excitement.

He appeared at a door on the right of the vestibule.

"All incoming calls are covered," snapped Smith, "as you were advised?"

"Yes."

"Who is calling?"

"I don't know," the deputy sheriff replied, "but it's someone asking for *Sir Denis Nayland Smith*."

He looked in bewilderment from face to face. Nayland Smith stared at Miss Lakin, smiled grimly and walked into a long, low library, a book-lined room with a great log fire burning at one end of it. The receiver of a telephone which stood upon a table near the fire was detached from its rest.

Someone closed the outer door, and a sudden silence came in that cozy room where the logs crackled. Sarah Lakin stood at the threshold, watching with calm, grave eyes. Mark Hepburn stared in over her shoulder.

"Yes," snapped Smith; "who is speaking?"

There was a momentary silence.

"Is it necessary, Sir Denis, for me to introduce myself?"

"Quite unnecessary, Dr. Fu Manchu! But it is strangely unlike you to show your hand so early in the game. You are outside familiar territory. So am I. But this time, Doctor, by God we shall break you."

"I trust not, Sir Denis; so much is at stake: the fate of this nation, perhaps of the world—and there are bunglers who

28

fail to appreciate my purpose. Dr. Orwin Prescott, for instance, has been very ill-advised."

Nayland Smith turned his head towards the door, nodding significantly to Mark Hepburn; some trick of the shaded lights made his lean, tanned face look very drawn, very tired.

"Since you have a certain manuscript in your possession, I assume it to be only a question of time for you to learn why the voice of the Holy Thorn became suddenly silent. In the Father's interests and in the interests of Dr. Prescott, I advise you to consider carefully your next step, Sir Denis——"

Nayland Smith's heart pulsed a fraction faster—Orwin Prescott was not dead!

"The abbot's eloquence is difficult to restrain—and I respect courage. But someday I may cry in the words of your English King—Henry the Second, was it not?—'Will no one rid me of this turbulent priest . . .' My cry would be answered—nor should I feel called upon to walk, a barefooted penitent, to pray at the Father Abbot's tomb beside his Tower of the Holy Thorn."

Nayland Smith made no reply. He sat there, motionless, listening.

"We enter upon the last phase, Sir Denis . . ."

The guttural voice ceased.

Smith replaced the receiver, sprang up, turned.

"That was a cut-in on the line," he snapped. "Quick, Hepburn! the nearest phone in the neighborhood: Check up that call if you can."

"Right." Mark Hepburn, his jaw grimly squared, buttoned up his coat.

Sarah Lakin watched Nayland Smith fascinatedly.

"Hell-for-leather, Hepburn! At any cost you *must* get through to Abbot Donegal tonight. Dr. Fu Manchu warns only *once*. . . ."

7 *SLEEPLESS UNDERWORLD*

MARK HEPBURN replaced a tiny phial of a very rare reagent on a shelf above his head and, turning, stooped and peered through a microscope at something resembling a fragment of gummy paper. For a while he studied this object and then stood upright, stretching his white-clad arms—he wore an overall—and yawning wearily. The small room in which he worked was fitted up as a laboratory. Save for a remote booming noise as of distant thunder, it was silent.

Hepburn lighted a cigarette and stared out of the closed window. The boom as of distant thunder was explained: it was caused by the ceaseless traffic in miles of busy streets.

Below him spread a night prospect of a large area of New York City. Half-right, framed by the window, the tallest building in the world reared its dizzy head to flying storm clouds. Here was a splash of red light; there, a blur of green. A train moved along its track far away to the left. Thousands of windows made illuminated geometrical patterns in the darkness. Tonight there was a damp mist, so that the flambeau upheld by the distant Statue of Liberty was not visible.

A slight sound in the little laboratory on the fortieth floor of the Regal-Athenian Tower brought Hepburn around in a flash.

He found himself looking into the dark, eager face of Nayland Smith.

"Good Lord, Sir Denis! you move like a cat——"

"I used my key. . . ."

"You startled me."

"Have you got it, Hepburn—have you got it?"

"Yes."

"What?" Nayland Smith's lean face, framed in the upturned fur collar of his topcoat, lighted enthusiastically. "First-class job. What is it?"

"I don't know what it is—that is to say I don't know from what source it's obtained. But it's a concoction used by certain tribes on the Upper Amazon, and I happened to remember that the Academy of Medicine had a specimen and borrowed it. The preparation on the MS., the envelopes and the stamps gives identical reaction. A lot of study has been devoted to this stuff, which has remarkable properties. But nobody has yet succeeded in tracing it to its origin."

"Is it called *kaapi?*"

"It is."

"I might have known!" snapped Nayland Smith. "He has used it before with notable results. But I must congratulate you. Hepburn: imagination is so rarely allied with exact scientific knowledge."

He peeled off the heavy topcoat and tossed it on a chair. Hepburn stared and smiled in his slow fashion.

Nayland Smith was dressed in police uniform!

"I was followed to headquarters," said Smith, detecting the

30

smile. "I can assure you I was not followed back. I left my cap (which didn't fit me) in the police car. Bought the coat—quite useful in this weather—at a big store with several entrances, and returned here in a taxicab."

Mark Hepburn leaned back on a glass-topped table which formed one of the appointments of the extemporized laboratory, staring in an abstracted way at Federal Officer 56.

"They must know you are here," he said, in his slow dry way.

"Undoubtedly! They know I am here. But it is to their advantage to see that I don't remain here."

Hepburn stared a while longer and then nodded.

"You think they would come right out into the open like that?"

Nayland Smith shot out his left arm, gripping the speaker's shoulder.

"Listen. You can hardly have forgotten the machine-gun party on the track when an attempt was made to hold up the special train? This evening I went out by a private entrance kindly placed at my disposal by the management. As I passed the corner of Forty-eighth Street, a car packed with gunmen was close behind me!"

"What!"

"The taxicab in which I was driving belonged to a group known as the Lotus Cabs. . . ."

"I know it. One of the biggest corporations of its kind in the States."

"It may be nothing to do with them, Hepburn. But the driver was in the pay of the other side."

"You are sure?"

"I am quite sure. I opened the door, which is in front in the Lotus Cabs, as you may remember, and crouched down beside the wheel. I said to the man, 'Drive like the devil! I am a federal agent and traffic rules don't apply at the moment.' "

"What did he do?"

"He pretended to obey but deliberately tried to stall me! In a jam, the gunmen close behind, I jumped out, wriggled clear of the pack, cut through to Sixth Avenue and chartered another cab."

He paused and drew a long breath. Pulling out the time-worn tobacco-pouch he began to load his briar.

"This stink-shop of yours is somewhat oppressive," he said. "Let's go into the sitting room."

He walked out to a larger room adjoining, Hepburn following. Over his shoulder:

31

"Both you and I have got to disappear!" he snapped.

As he spoke he turned, pipe and pouch in hand. Hepburn met the glance of piercing steely eyes and knew that Nayland Smith did not speak lightly.

"The biggest prize which any man every played for is at stake—the control of the United States of America. To his existing organization—the extent of which even I can only surmise—Dr. Fu Manchu has added the most highly efficient underworld which civilization has yet produced."

Nayland Smith, his pipe charged, automatically made to drop the pouch back into his coat pocket, was hampered by the uniform, and tossed the pouch irritably onto a chair. He took a box of matches from the marble mantelpiece and lighted his briar. Surrounded now by clouds of smoke he turned, staring at Hepburn.

"You are rounding up your Public Enemies," he went on, in his snappy, staccato fashion. "But the groups which they controlled remain in existence. Those underground murder gangs are still operative, only awaiting the hand of a master. That master is here . . . and he has assumed control. Our lives, Hepburn—" he snapped his fingers—"are not worth that! But let us review the position."

He began to walk up and down, smoking furiously.

"The manuscript of Abbot Donegal's uncompleted address was saturated with a preparation which you have identified, although its exact composition is unknown to you. His habit of wetting his thumb in turning over the pages (noted by a spy, almost certainly that James Richet, the secretary who has escaped us) resulted in his poisoning himself before he reached those revelations which Dr. Fu Manchu regarded as untimely. The abbot may or may not recover his memory of those pages, but in his own interests, and I think in the interests of this country, he has been bound to silence for a time. He is off the air. So much is clear, Hepburn?"

"Perfectly clear."

"The gum of those stamps and envelopes, reserved for Dr. Prescott's use at Weaver's Farm, had been similarly treated. Prescott seems to have left the house and proceeded in the direction of the lake. He was, of course, under the influence of the drug. He was carried, as our later investigations proved, around the bank to the north end of the lake, and from there to the road, where a car was waiting. Latest reports regarding this car should reach headquarters tonight. It was, as suspected, undoubtedly proceeding in the direction of New York."

"We have no clue to the person who tampered with the

stationery at Weaver's Farm," Hepburn's monotonous voice broke in.

"At the moment, none."

Nayland Smith moved restlessly in the direction of one of the windows.

"Somewhere below there," he went on, shooting out a pointing forefinger, "somewhere among those millions of lights, perhaps in sight from this very spot—Orwin Prescott is hidden!"

"I think you are right," said Mark Hepburn, quietly.

"I am all but certain! New York, and not Washington, would be Dr. Fu Manchu's selection as a base. He has been operating here, through chosen agents, for some months past. Others are flocking to him. I had news from Scotland Yard only this morning of one formidable old ruffian who has slipped through their nets for the twentieth time and is believed to be here. And Prescott will have been brought to the Doctor's headquarters. God knows what ordeal faces him— what choice he will be called upon to make! It is possible even that he may be given no choice!"

Nayland Smith clenched his fists and shook them desperately in the direction of the myriad dancing lights of New York City.

"Look!" he cried. "Do you see? The mist has lifted. There is the Statue of Liberty! Do you realize, Hepburn—" he turned, a man all but imperturbably moved now by the immensity of his task, "—do you realize what that figure will become if we fail?"

The wild light died from his eyes. He replaced his pipe and audibly gripped the stem between his small, even white teeth.

"We are not going to fail, Sir Denis," Hepburn replied in dry unmusical tones.

"Thank you," snapped Nayland Smith, and gripped his shoulder. "Dr. Fu Manchu being a Chinaman, in which quarter of the city should you think it most unlikely he would establish a base?"

"Chinatown."

Nayland Smith laughed gleefully.

"That is exactly how *he* will argue."

2

In a small room, amber lighted through high windows, a man worked patiently upon a clay model of a Chinese head. A distant bell sounded, and the room became plunged in darkness. Only the glowing end of a cigarette showed through this darkness. A high-pitched, guttural voice spoke.

"Give me the latest report from the Number responsible for covering Federal Officer 56 in New York."

"Only one other report to hand," the modeler replied immediately; "received at eight forty-five. Federal Officer 56 is occupying an apartment in the Regal-Athenian Tower. Federal Officer Captain Mark Hepburn is also located there, and engaged upon chemical experiments. A few minutes after eight o'clock, Federal Officer 56 left by a service door and engaged one of the Lotus Cabs. The driver notified the Number covering Lexington exits. A protection car was instructed, but 56 gave them the slip on the corner of Forty-eighth and reached Centre Street at eight thirty-five. Report concluded as follows: 'Presume he is still at police headquarters as no notification that he has left is to hand.'"

Following a few moments of silence:

"Inform me," the guttural voice continued, "directly any report is received from Number 38, now proceeding from Cleveland to New York City."

The distant bell rang again and amber light prevailed once more in the small, domed room. The white-haired intellectual sculptor blinked slightly as though this sudden illumination hurt his eyes. Then, taking up tortoise-shell rimmed spectacles which he had laid down at the moment that the light had become extinguished, he dropped the stump of an Egyptian cigarette in an ash tray, having ignited another from the burning end. Taking up a modeling tool he returned to his eternal task.

8 THE BLACK HAT

A LOTUS CAB, conspicuous by reason of its cream bodywork and pink line, drew up at the corner of Mulberry and Bayard streets. The passenger got out; a small man, very graceful of movement, dark, sleek, wearing a gray waterproof overcoat and a soft black hat. He stood for a moment beside the driver as he paid his fare, glancing back along the route they had followed.

His fare paid, he crossed Pell Street and began to walk east.

The driver turned his cab, but then made a detour, crossing Mott Street. He pulled up before Wu King's Bar and went in. He came out again inside three minutes and drove away.

Meanwhile, the man in the black hat continued to walk east. A trickle of rain was falling, and a bleak wind searched the Chinese quarter. He increased his pace. Bright lights shone out from stores and restaurants, but the inclement weather had driven the Asiatic population under cover. In those pedestrains who passed him in the drizzle the man in the black hat seemed to take no interest whatever. He walked on with an easy, swinging stride as one confident that no harm would come to him in Chinatown.

When he passed an open door, to his nostrils came a whiff of that queer commingling of incense and spice which distinguishes the quarter. The Chinaman is a law-abiding citizen. His laws may be different from those of the Western world, but to his own codes he conforms religiously. Only a country cousin on a sightseeing expedition could have detected anything mysterious about the streets through which the man in the black hat hurried. Even Deputy Inspector Gregory of the branch accountable for the good behavior of Chinatown had observed nothing mysterious in his patrol of the public resorts and private byways.

Except for a curious hush when he had stopped in at Wu King's Bar for a chat with the genial proprietor and a look around for a certain Celestial, there was nothing in the slightest degree suspicious in the behavior of the people of the Asiatic quarter. This impression of a hush which had fallen at the moment of his entrance he had been unable to confirm—it might have been imaginary. In any event Wu King's was the headquarters of the Hip Sing Tong, and if it meant anything it probably meant a brewing disturbance between rival Chinese societies.

He was still considering the impression which this hush, real or imaginary, had made upon his mind when, turning a corner, he all but bumped into the man with the black hat.

The black hat was lowered against the keen wind: the detective, wind behind him, was walking very upright. Then, in a flash, the black-hatted man had gone. Momentarily the idea crossed the detective's mind that he had not seen the man's face—it might have been the face of a Chinaman, and he was anxious to meet a certain Chinaman.

He turned for a moment, looking back.

The man in the black hat had disappeared.

It was a particularly foul night, and Gregory had more than carried out his instructions. He trudged on through the icy drizzle to make his report. Secret orders had been received from headquarters calling upon all officers to look out for a very old Chinaman known in London as Sam Pak, and now believed to be posing as a residing alien. His description was vividly etched upon the detective's mind. The man in the black hat could not possibly fill the part, for this Sam Pak was very old. What this very old man could be wanted for was not clear to the deputy inspector. Nevertheless, that momentary instinct would have served him well had he obeyed it. . . .

The man whose features he had failed to see turned the first corner behind the police officer. When Gregory looked back the man was watching. Seeing Gregory walk on, he pursued his way. This led him past the corner occupied by Wu King's Bar and right to the end of the block. Here the man in the black hat paused in shelter of a dark doorway, lighting a cigarette and shielding the light with an upraised hand. He then consulted a typewritten sheet which he drew from his raincoat pocket. Evidently satisfied that he had not misunderstood his instructions, he replaced the lighter and glanced swiftly right and left along the street. This inspection assured him that none of the few pedestrians in sight was Gregory (whom he had recognized for a police officer). He groped along the wall on his right, found and pressed a bell.

Then again he looked out cautiously. Only one traveler, a small, furtive Asiatic figure, was approaching in his direction. A slight sound told the man in the black hat that a door had opened. He turned, stepped forward and paused, seeking now with his left hand. He found a switch and depressed it. He heard the door close behind him. A moment more he waited, then, fumbling again in the darkness, he discovered a second switch, and light sprang up in the narrow passage in which he stood. The door which had opened to admit him was now shut. Another closed door was at the end of the passage. There was a bell-push beside it. He pressed the bell seven times—slowly. . . .

2

Deputy Inspector Gregory had not quite reached the end of the block, when heading towards him through the mist and rain he saw a tall, gaunt figure, that of a Salvation Army captain, gray mustached and bespectacled. He would have passed on, for the presence of Salvation Army officials in unlikely quarters and the most inclement weather was a sight familiar enough. But the tall man pulled up directly in his path, and:

"Excuse me if I am wrong," he said, speaking slowly and harshly, "but I think you are a police officer?"

Gregory glanced the speaker over and nodded.

"That's right," he replied. "What can I do for you?"

"I am looking," the harsh voice continued, "for a defaulter, a wayward brother who has fallen into sin. I saw him not five minutes ago, but lost him on the corner of Pell Street. As you were coming from that direction it is possible that you passed him."

"What's he like to look at?"

"He is a small man wearing a gray topcoat and a black soft hat. It is not our intention to charge him with his offense, but it is my duty to endeavor to overtake him."

"He passed me less than two minutes ago," Gregory replied sharply. "What's he listed for?"

"Converting money to his own uses; but no soul is beyond redemption."

The harsh, gloomy voice held that queer note of exaltation which Inspector Gregory had heard so often without being able to determine whether it indicated genuine piety or affectation.

"I'll step back with you," he said tersely. "I know the corner he went around, and I know who lives in every house on that street. We'd better hurry!"

He turned and hurried back against the biting wind, the tall Salvation Army official striding along beside him silently. They came to the corner on which Wu King's Bar was situated—the resort which Gregory had so recently visited; turning around it, they were temporarily sheltered from the icy blast.

"He may have gone into Wu's," said Gregory, as they looked along a deserted street, at one or two points of which lights shone out on the rain-drenched sidewalk. "Just stay here, and I'll check up."

He pushed open the door of the restaurant. To the nostrils of the Salvation Army official who stood outside was wafted a breath of that characteristic odor which belongs to every Chinatown in the world. In less than a minute the detective was out again.

"Not been in Wu's," he reported. "He must have gone in somewhere further along, otherwise there wouldn't be any object in going that way; unless he's out for a walk. There's no other joint open back there. Do you know of any connections he has in this quarter?"

"Probably many," the harsh voice replied, and there was sadness in the tone. "He's attached to our Chinatown branch. I'm obliged to you but will trouble you no further, except to ask that if ever you see this man, you will detain him."

Gregory nodded, turned, and started off.

"No trouble," he said. "Hope you find the guy."

The Salvation Army official walked to the end of the street, gloomily scrutinizing closed doors to right and left, seeming to note the names over the shops, the numbers, the Chinese signs. Then turning to the right again at the end of the block, he walked on through the rain for a considerable distance and finally entered an elevated railroad station. . . .

Salvation Army delegates from all over the United States were assembled in New York that week, and a group of the senior officials had been accommodated at the Regal-Athenian Hotel. Therefore, no one in the vast marble-pillared lobby of that palatial establishment was surprised to see the tall and gloomy captain walk in. No confrère was visible in the public rooms through which he passed: the last had retired fully an hour earlier. Entering a tower elevator:

"Thirty-three," he announced gloomily.

He stepped out on the thirty-third floor, where two deputies from neighboring States were sharing an apartment. He did not go to their apartment, however. He opened a door at the end of the long carpeted corridor and began to mount a stair. He met no one on his way, but at the fortieth floor he opened a door and peered out into another deserted carpeted corridor. . . .

Captain Mark Hepburn, pacing restlessly from room to room of the suite at the top of the tower, sometimes looking out of the window at rain-drenched New York below him, sometimes listening to the whine of the elevator, and sometimes exchanging glances with the equally restless Fey, Nayland Smith's man, who also wandered disconsolately about, suddenly paused in the little vestibule. He had heard quick footsteps.

A moment later the door opened, and a gloomy Salvation Army captain entered.

"Thank God! Sir Denis," said Hepburn and tried to repress the emotion he felt. "I was getting really worried."

The Salvation Army captain removed his cap, his spectacles, and, very gingerly, his gray mustache, revealing the gaunt, eager features of Nayland Smith.

"Thanks, Hepburn," he snapped. "I am sorry to have bothered you. But I was right."

"What!"

Fey appeared silently, his stoic face a mask.

"A whisky and soda, sir?" he suggested.

"Thanks, Fey, a stiff one."

A triumphant light danced in Smith's steely eyes, and:
"It looks as though you had some news," said Hepburn.

"I have." Nayland Smith extracted pipe and pouch from
the pocket of his uniform jacket. "My guess was right—a
pure guess, Hepburn, no more; but I was right. Can you
imagine whom I saw down there in Chinatown tonight?"

"Not——"

"No—my luck didn't go as far as that. But just as I was
turning out of Mott Street, right in the light from a restaurant,
I saw our friend James Richet—Abbot Donegal's ex-secretary!"

"Richet?"

"Exactly. One of the key men. Luck was with me. Then,
suddenly, it turned. Of all the unimaginable things, Hepburn
. . . a *real* Salvation Army officer came up to me! Following a
brief conversation he challenged me to establish my identity,
and I was forced to do so."

He pulled back the top of his tunic, revealing the gold
badge of a federal agent.

"A clumsy business, Hepburn. But what could I do? In
the meantime, I had lost my man. I met a detective officer
as I went racing around the corner. He was unmistakable.
I know a policeman, to whatever country he belongs, a
quarter of a mile away. He had passed my man and he did
his best. I have memorized all the possible places into which
he may have gone. But one thing is established, Hepburn—
Dr. Fu Manchu has a Chinatown base. . . ."

9   *THE SEVEN-EYED GODDESS*

JAMES RICHET, known to the organization of which
he was a member as Number 38, stepped through a
doorway—the fifth he had counted—and knew he must be
below sea level. This door immediately closed behind him.

He found himself in a lobby with stone-faced walls. A silk-
shaded lantern hung from an iron bracket. Immediately facing him was another arched doorway, curtained. Above the
curtain-rod glowed a dim semicircle of light. This place

smelled like a joss house. The only other item of furniture was a narrow cushioned divan, and upon this a very old Chinaman was squatting. He wore a garment resembling a blue smock; he crouched forward on the divan, his veinous, clawlike hands resting upon his knees. He was a man of incalculable age: an intricate network of wrinkles mapped the whole of his face. His eyes were mere slits in the yellow skin. He might have been a chryselephantine statue, wrought by the cunning hand of a Chinese master.

A movement ever so slight of the bowed head indicated to Richet that the man on the divan was looking at him. He raised the left lapel of his topcoat. A small badge, apparently made of gold and ivory, not unlike one of the chips used at the Monte Carlo gaming tables, was revealed. It bore the number 38.

"James Richet," he said.

One of the talon hands moved back to the wall—and in some place beyond a bell rang, dimly. A clawish finger indicated the curtained doorway. James Richet crossed the lobby, drew the curtain aside and entered.

The night out of which he had come was wet and icily cold, but the moisture which he wiped now from his forehead was not entirely due to the rain. He had removed his hat and stood looking about him. This was a rectangular apartment, also stone-faced; the floor was of polished stone upon which several rugs were spread. There were seven doors, two in each of the long walls, two in that ahead of him, and the one by which he had entered. Above each of them, on an iron bracket, a lantern was hung, shaded with amber silk. All the openings were draped, and the drapery of each was of a different color. There were cushioned seats all around the walls, set between the seven openings.

There was no other furniture except a huge square block of black granite, set in the center of the stone floor and supporting a grotesque figure which only an ultra-modern sculptor could have produced: a goddess possessing seven green eyes, so that one of her eyes watched each of the openings. There was the same perfume in the place as of stale incense, but nevertheless unlike the more characteristic odor of Chinatown. The place was silent, very silent. In contrast to the bitter weather prevailing up above, it seemed to be tropically hot. There was no one visible.

Ricket looked about him uneasily. Then, as if the proximity even of the mummy-like Chinaman in the lobby afforded some sense of human companionship, he sat down just right

40

of the opening by which he had entered, placing his black hat upon the cushions beside him.

He tried to think. This place was a miracle of cunning—Chinese cunning. As one descended from the secret street door (and this, alone, was difficult to find) a second, masked door gave access to a considerable room. There was no other visible exit from this room. He realized that a police raid would almost certainly end there. Yet there were three more hidden doors—probably steel—and three short flights of stone steps before one reached this temple of the seven-eyed goddess. These doors had been opened from beyond as he had descended.

No sound came from the lobby. Richet slightly changed his position. A green eye seemed to be watching him. But it proved to be impossible to escape the regard of one of those seven eyes; and, viewed from any point, the grotesque idol displayed some feminine line, some strange semblance of distorted womanhood. . . .

James Richet was a qualified attorney, and had practiced for several years in Los Angeles. The yellow streak in his pedigree—his maternal grandmother had been a Kanaka—formed a check to his social ambition. Perhaps it was an operative factor in his selection of an easier and more direct path to wealth than the legitimate practice of his profession had offered him. He had become the legal adviser of one of the big beer barons. Later the underworlds of Chicago and New York held no secrets from him. . . .

The silence of this strange stone cellar was very oppressive; he avoided looking at the evil figure which dominated it. . . .

His former chiefs, one after another, had been piled up on the rocks of the new administration. Then a fresh tide had come in his affairs, at a time when he began seriously to wonder if federal inquiries would become focused upon himself. Some new control had seized upon the broken group of which he was a surviving unit. A highly paid post was found for him as legal adviser and secretary to Abbot Donegal. He was notified that special duties would be allotted from time to time. But in spite of all his cunning—for he was more cunning than clever—he had not up to the present moment succeeded in learning the political aims of the person or persons who, as he had realized for a long time, now controlled the vast underworld network which extended from coast to coast of the United States.

Of his former associates he had seen nothing during the time that he was attached to Abbot Donegal's staff at the Shrine of the Holy Thorn. Copies of the abbot's colossal

41

mailing list he had supplied to an address in New York City; advance drafts of all sermons and lectures; and a précis of a certain class of correspondence.

Personal contact between himself and his real employer was made through the medium of Lola Dumas. His last urgent instructions, which had led to the break-down of Abbot Donegal during a broadcast lecture, had been given to him by Lola . . . that provocative study in slender curves, creamy skin and ebony-black hair; somber almond-shaped eyes (deep, dark lakes in which a man's soul was drowned); petulant, scornful lips . . . Lola.

Lola! She was supremely desirable, but maddeningly elusive. Together, what could they not do? She knew so many things that he burned to learn; but all that he had gathered from her was that they belonged to an organization governed by a board of seven. . . .

Hot though the place was, he shuddered. Seven! This hell-inspired figure which always watched him had *seven* eyes!

From time to time Lola would appear in the near-by town without warning, occupying the best suite in the best hotel, and would summon him to meet her. It was Lola Dumas, on the first day that he had taken up his duties, who had brought him his badge. He had smiled. Later he had ceased to smile. Up to the time that he had fled from the Shrine of the Holy Thorn he had never learned how many other agents of the "seven" were attached to the staff of the abbot. Two only he had met: Mrs. Adair, and a man who acted as night watchman. Now, shepherded from point to point in accordance with typed instructions headed: "In the event of failure" and received by him on the morning before the fateful broadcast, he was in New York; at last in the headquarters of his mysterious chief!

Something in the atmosphere of this place seemed to shake him. He wondered—and became conscious of nervous perspiration—if his slight deviation from the route laid down in his instructions had escaped notice. . . .

One of the colored curtains was swept aside, and he saw Lola Dumas facing him from the end of the temple of the seven-eyed goddess.

10 *JAMES RICHET*

MARK HEPBURN sat at the desk by the telephone,
making notes of many incoming calls, issuing instructions in some cases. Nayland Smith, at the big table by
the window, worked on material which seemed to demand
frequent reference to one of two large maps pinned on the
wall before him. Hepburn lighted numberless cigarettes.
Nayland Smith was partially hidden behind a screen of pipe
smoke.

Despite the lateness of the hour, Fey, the taciturn, might
be heard moving about in the kitchenette.

The doorbell rang.

Smith turned in his chair. Hepburn stood up.

As Fey crossed the sitting room to reach the vestibule:

"Remember orders, Fey!" Smith rapped.

Fey's Sioux-like, leathern features exhibited no expression whatever. He extended a large palm in which a small
automatic rested.

"Very good, sir."

He opened the door. Outside stood a man in Regal-
Athenian uniform and another who wore a peaked cap.

"He's all right," said the man in uniform. "He is a Western
Union messenger. . . ."

When the door was closed again and Fey had returned
to his cramped quarters, Nayland Smith read the letter which
the man had delivered. He studied it carefully, a second and
a third time; then handed it to Hepburn.

"Any comments?"

Mark Hepburn took the letter and read:

> *Weaver's Farm,*
> *Winton, Conn.*

DEAR SIR DENIS:

> *Something so strange has occurred that I feel you should
> know at once. (I regret to say that my telephone is again
> out of order.) A man called upon me early this evening
> who gave the name of Julian Sankey. Before this, he made
> me promise to tell no one but* you *what he had to say. He
> implied that he had information that would enable us to
> locate Orwin. He was a smallish, dark man, with very*

*spruce lank black hair and the slyly ingratiating manners
of an Argentine gigolo. A voice like velvet.*

*I gave my promise, which seemed to satisfy him, and he
then told me that he was a reluctant member of an organization which planned to make Harvey Bragg dictator.
He conveyed the idea that he knew the inside of this organization and that he was prepared, on terms, and with
guaranteed government protection, to place all his knowl-
ege at our disposal. He assured me that Orwin was a prisoner in New York, and that, his (Sankey's) safety being
assured by you, he would indicate the exact spot.*

*I have an address to which to write, and it is evidently
urgent. I shall be in New York tomorrow and will call
upon you, if I may, at four o'clock.*

What do you think we should do?

Very sincerely yours,
SARAH LAKIN.

Mark Hepburn laid the letter down upon the table.

"The description," he said dryly, "would fit James Richet
as well as any man I know."

Nayland Smith, watching him, smiled triumphantly.

"I am glad to hear you say so," he declared. "You order
this man's arrest; he disappears. He is out to save his
skin——"

"It may be."

"If it is Richet, then Richet would be a valuable card to
hold. It's infuriating, Hepburn, to think that I missed grabbing
the fellow tonight! My next regret is that our fair correspond-
ent omits the address at which we can communicate with this
'Julian Sankey.' Does any other point in the letter strike
you?"

"Yes," said Hepburn slowly. "It's undated. But my own
sister, who is an honor graduate, rarely dates her letters.
The other thing is the telephone."

"The telephone is the all-important thing."

Mark Hepburn turned and met the fixed gaze of Nayland
Smith's eyes. He nodded.

"I don't like the disconnected telephone, Hepburn. I know
the master schemer who is up against us ... ! I am wondering
if this information will ever come to hand. ..."

2

A man who wore a plain yellow robe, in the loose sleeves
of which his hands were concealed, sat at a large lacquered

table in a small room. Some quality in the sound which penetrated through three windows, all of them slightly opened, suggested that this room was situated at a great height above a sleepless city.

Two of the walls were almost entirely occupied by bookcases; the lacquer table was set in the angle formed by these books, and upon it, in addition to neatly arranged documents, were a number of queer-looking instruments and appliances.

Also, there was a porcelain bowl in which a carved pipe with a tiny bowl rested.

The room was very hot and the air laden with a peculiar aromatic smell. The man in the yellow robe lay back in a carved, padded chair; a black cap resembling a biretta crowned his massive skull. His immobile face resembled one of those ancient masterpieces of ivory mellowed in years of incense; a carving of Gautama Buddha—by one who disbelieved his doctrine. The eyes in this remarkable face had been closed; now, suddenly, they opened. They were green as burnished jade under moonlight.

The man in the yellow robe put on a pair of tinted spectacles and studied a square, illuminated screen which was one of the several unusual appointments of the table. . . . Upon this screen, in miniature, appeared a moving picture of the subterranean room where the seven-eyed goddess sat eternally watching. James Richet was talking to Lola Dumas.

The profound student of humanity seated at the lacquer table was cruelly just. He wished to study this man who, after doing good work, had seen fit to leave his ordered route and to visit the cousin of Orwin Prescott. Steps had been taken to check any possible consequences. But the fate of the one who had made these measures necessary hung now in the balance.

They stood close together, and although their figures appeared distant, but not so perhaps through the lenses of the glasses worn by the Chinaman, their voices sounded quite normal, as though they were speaking in the room in which he sat.

"Lola, I have the game in my hand." Richet threw his left arm around the woman's shoulders and drew her to him. "Don't pretend. We're in this thing together."

Lola Dumas' lithe body bent backward as he strove to reach her lips.

"You are quite mad," she said breathlessly. "Because I was amused once, why should you think I am a fool?" She twisted, bent, and broke free, turning and facing him, her dark eyes blazing. "I can play, but when I work, I quit play.

You are dreaming, my dear, if you think you can ever get control."

"But I tell you I have the game in my hand!" The man, fists clenched, spoke tensely, passionately. "It is for you to say the word. Why should a newcomer, a stranger, take charge when you and I——"

"You poor fool! Do you want to die so young?"

"I tell you, Lola, *I'm* not the fool. I know Kern Adler, the big New York lawyer, is in this. And what I say goes with Kern. I know 'Blondie' Hahn is. And Blondie stands for all the useful boys still at large. I know how to handle Blondie. We're old friends. I have all the Donegal material. No one knows the inside of the Brotherhood of National Equality as I know it. What's more—I know where to go for backing, and I don't need Bragg! Lola . . ."

A slender ivory hand, the fingernails long, pointed and highly burnished, moved across the lacquered table in that distant high room.

Six of the seven lights over curtained openings went out.

"What's this?" muttered Richet. "What do we do now?"

He was inspired by his own vehemence; he felt capable of facing Satan in person.

"Go into the lighted alcove," said the woman coldly. "The President is ready to interview you."

Richet paused, fists still half clenched, stepped towards the light, then glanced back. Lola Dumas had gone. She was lost in the incense-haunted darkness . . . but one green eye of the goddess watched him out of the shadows. He moved forward, swept the curtain aside and found himself in a small, square stone cell, possessing no furniture whatever. The curtain fell back into place with a faint swishing sound. He looked about him, his recent confidence beginning to wane. Then a voice spoke—a high-pitched, guttural voice.

"James Richet, I am displeased with you."

Richet looked right, left, above and below. Then:

"Who is speaking?" he demanded angrily. "These stage illusions are not impressive. Was *I* to blame for what happened? I wish to see you, speak to you face to face."

"An unwise wish, James Richet. Only Numbers one to twelve have that privilege."

Richet's brow was covered with nervous perspiration.

"I want a square deal," he said, striving to be masterful.

"You shall have a square deal," the implacable, guttural voice replied. "You will be given sealed orders by the Number in charge of Base 3. See that you carry out his instructions *to the letter*. . . ."

46

Mark Hepburn sprang up in bed.

"All right, Hepburn!"—it was Nayland Smith's voice. "Sorry to awake you, but there's a job for us."

The light had been switched on, and Hepburn stared somewhat dazedly at the speaker, then glanced down at his watch. The hour was 3.15 A.M. But Nyland Smith was fully dressed. Now wide awake:

"What is it?" Hepburn asked, impressed by his companion's grim expression and beginning also to dress hastily.

"I don't know—yet. I was called five minutes ago—I had not turned in—by the night messenger. A taxi—perhaps a coincidence, but it happens to be a Lotus taxi—pulled up at the main entrance. The passenger asked the man to step into the lobby and inquire for me——"

"In what name?"

"The title was curiously accurate, Hepburn. It was typed on a slip of paper. The man was told to ask for Federal Agent Ex-Assistant Commissioner Sir Denis Nayland Smith, O.B.E.!"

Hepburn was now roughly dressed. He turned, staring:

"But to everybody except myself and Fey you are plain Mr. Smith!"

"Exactly. That is why I see the hand of Dr. Fu Manchu, who has a ghastly sense of humor, in this. The man proceeded to obey his orders, I gather, but he had not gone three paces when something happened. Let's hurry down. The man is there . . . so is his passenger."

The night manager and a house detective were talking to Fey by the open door of the apartment.

"Queerest thing that ever happened in my experience, gentlemen," said the manager. "I only hope it isn't a false alarm. The string of titles means nothing to me. But you are Mr. Smith and I know you are a federal agent. This way. The elevator is waiting. If you will follow me I will take you by a shorter route."

Down they went to the street level. Led by the manager they hurried along a service passage, crossed a wide corridor, two empty offices, and came out at the far end of the vast pillared and carpeted main foyer. Except for robot-like workers vacuum cleaning, it was deserted and in semidarkness. A lofty, shadow-haunted place. Light shone from the open door of the night manager's room. . . .

A man who wore a topcoat over pajamas was examining

a still figure stretched on a sofa. There were three other men in the room, one of them the taxi driver.

Nayland Smith shot a searching glance at the latter's pale, horrified face as, cap on the back of his head, he stared over the doctor's shoulder, and then, pushing his way forward, he too looked once, and:

"Good God!" he muttered. "Hepburn——" Mark Hepburn was beside him—"what is it? Have you ever met with anything like it?"

There was a momentary silence, grotesquely disturbed by the hum of a distant vacuum cleaner.

The prostrate man, whose torso had been stripped by the resident physician probably in a vain attempt to restore cardiac action, exhibited on his face and neck a number of vivid scarlet spots. They were about an eighth of an inch in diameter and on the dull white skin resembled drops of blood. . . .

"Never."

Mark Hepburn's voice was husky. The doctor looked up. He was a heavily built, Teutonic type, his shrewd eyes magnified by powerful spectacles.

"If you are a brother practitioner," he said, "you are welcome. This case is outside my experience."

"When did he actually die?" rapped Nayland Smith.

"He was already dead when I arrived—although I worked over him for ten minutes or more——"

"The scarlet spots!" blurted the taxi driver in a frightened voice—"That's what he called out, 'The scarlet spots'—and then he was down on the sidewalk rolling about and screaming!"

Mark Hepburn glanced at Nayland Smith.

"You were right," he said; "we shall never get that information."

The dead man was James Richet, ex-secretary to Abbot Donegal!

11 *RED SPOTS*

"WHAT IS IT, mister," the taximan whispered, "some new kind of a fever?"

"No," said Nayland Smith. "It's a new kind of a *murder!*"

"Why do you say so?" the hotel doctor asked, glancing in a puzzled way at the ghastly object on the sofa.

But Nayland Smith did not reply. Turning to the night manager:

"I want no one at present in the foyer," he said, "to leave without my orders. You—" he pointed to the house detective —"will mount guard over the taxicab outside the main entrance. No one must touch it or enter it. No one must pass along the sidewalk between the taxi and the hotel doors. It remains where it stands until further notice. Hepburn—" he turned—"get two patrolmen to take over this duty. Hurry. I need you here."

Mark Hepburn nodded and went out of the night manager's room, followed by the house detective.

"What about anyone living here and coming in late?" asked the night manager, speaking with a rich Tipperary brogue.

"What's your house detective's name?"

"Lawkin."

"Lawkin!" cried Smith, standing in the open door, "any residents are to be directed to some other entrance."

"O.K., sir."

"The use of an office, Mr. Dougherty," Nayland Smith continued, addressing the manager, "on this floor? Can you oblige us?"

"Certainly, Mr. Smith. The office next to this."

"Excellent. Have you notified the police?"

"I considered I had met regulations by notifying yourself and Captain Hepburn."

"So you have. I suppose a man is not qualified to hold your job unless he possesses tact." He turned to the taximan. "Will you follow Mr. Dougherty to the office and wait for me there?"

The driver, a man palpably shaken, obeyed Dougherty's curt nod and followed him out, averting his eyes from the sofa. Two men and the doctor remained, one wearing dinner kit, the other a lounge suit. To the former:

"I presume that you are assistant night manager?" said Nayland Smith.

"That is so. Fish is my name, sir. This—" indicating the square-jowled wearer of the lounge suit—"is James Harris, assistant house detective."

"Good," rapped Nayland Smith. "Harris—give a hand to Lawkin outside." Harris went out. "And now, Mr. Fisk, will you please notify Mr. Dougherty that I wish to remain alone here with Dr.——?"

49

"My name is Scheky," said the physician.

"—with Dr. Scheky."

The assistant night manager went out. Nayland Smith and Dr. Scheky were alone with the dead man.

"I have endeavored to clear this room, Doctor," Smith continued, addressing the burly physician in the topcoat, "without creating unnecessary panic. But do you realize that you and I now face risk of the same death—" he pointed— "that *he* died?"

"I had not realized it, Mr. Smith," the physician admitted, glancing down with a changed expression at the bright-red blotches on the dead man's skin. "Nor do I know why you suspect murder."

"Perhaps you will understand later, Doctor. When Captain Hepburn returns I am sending for certain equipment. If you care to go to your apartment I will have you called when we are ready. . . ."

In an adjoining office, amid cleared desks and closed files, the pale-faced taximan faced Nayland Smith's interrogation.

"I took him up on Times Square. . . . No, I never seen him before. He gave the address 'Regal-Athenian, Park entrance.' . . . Sure he seemed all right; nothing wrong with him. When we get here he says: 'Go in to the desk and ask if this man is in the hotel'—and he slips me the piece of paper through the window. 'Give 'em the paper'—that was what he said. 'It's a hard name——' "

"Sure of that?" rapped Nayland Smith.

"Dead sure. I took the paper and started. . . . There was nobody about. As I moved off, he pulled out of his pocket what looks like a notebook. I guess it's out there now. . . . Next minute I hear his first yell—mister, it was awful! He had the door open in a flash and falls right out onto the sidewalk."

"Where were you? What did you do?"

"I'm halfway up the hotel steps. I started to run back. He's lashing around down there and seems to be tearing his clothes off——"

"Stop. You are quite certain on this point?"

"Sure," the man declared earnestly; "I'm sure certain. He had his topcoat right off and ripped his collar open. . . . He's yelling, 'The scarlet spots!'—like I told you. That's what I heard him yell. And he's fighting and twisting like he was wrestling with somebody . . . Gee!"

The man pulled his cap off and wiped his brow with the back of his hand.

"I run in here. There wasn't a cop in sight. Nobody was

50

in sight. . . . What could I do, mister? I figured he'd gone raving mad. . . . When we got out to him he's lying almost still. Only his hands was twitching. . . ."

The night manager came into the office.

"All heat turned off on this floor," he reported, "and all doors closed. . . ."

Outside the Regal-Athenian the atmosphere was arctic. Two patrolmen watched Mark Hepburn with an electric torch and a big lens examining every square foot of sidewalk and the carpeted steps leading up to the main entrance. Residents who arrived late were directed to a door around the corner. In reply to questions the invariable answer of the police was:

"Somebody lost something valuable."

The death cab had been run into an empty garage. It had been sealed; and at this very moment two men wearing chemist's masks were pumping it full of a powerful germicidal gas.

Later, assisted by Dr. Scheky—both men dressed as if working in an operating theater—Hepburn stripped and thoroughly examined the body and the garments of James Richet. The body was then removed, together with a number of objects found in Richet's possession. The night manager's room was sealed, to be fumigated. The main foyer, Nayland Smith ordered, must be closed to the public pending further orders. Dawn was very near when Dr. Scheky said to Hepburn:

"You are not by chance under the impression that this man died of some virulent form of plague?"

Mark Hepburn stared haggardly at the physician. They were dead beat.

"To be perfectly frank, Doctor," he answered, "I don't know of what he died. . . ."

12 NUMBER EIGHTY-ONE

IN THAT DOMED ROOM, amber lighted through curious Gothic windows, the white-haired sculptor sat smoking Egyptian cigarettes and putting the finishing touches to a sinister clay head which one might have assumed to be his life's work. Pinned upon a wooden panel beside the tripod on which the clay was set, was some kind of small colored picture, part of which had been masked out so that what remained resembled a tiny face surrounded by a margin of white paper.

This the sculptor examined through a powerful magnifying glass, and then lowering the glass, scrutinized the clay. Evidently his work was to attempt to produce a life-size model of the tiny head pinned to the board.

Seeming to be not wholly satisfied, the sculptor laid down the lens with a sigh and wheeled the clay along to the end of the table. At which moment the amber light went out, the dim bell rang. A high-pitched, imperious, guttural voice spoke.

"The latest report from the Regal-Athenian."

"Received at 5.10 A.M. from Number in charge. Foyer closed to the public by federal orders. Night manager's office sealed. Taxi in garage on Lexington. The body of the dead man identified as that of James Richet, late secretary to Abbot Donegal, removed at 5 A.M. to police mortuary. Cause of death unknown. Federal Agents Smith and Hepburn in their quarters in the tower. End of report."

Followed some moments of silence, broken only by an occasional faint ticking from an electric clock. Then:

"Fix the recording attachment, Number 81," came an order. "You are free for four hours."

Amber light poured again into the room. Number 81 stood up. Opening a cupboard in the telephone table, he attached three plugs to a switchboard contained in the cupboard. One of these connected with the curious electric clock which stood upon the desk; another with a small motor which operated in connection with the telephone; and a third with a kind of dictaphone capable of automatically recording six thousand words or more without change of cylinder.

As he was about to close the cupboard, a dim buzz indicated an incoming message. The faint hum of well-oiled machinery followed; a receiver-rest was lifted as if by invisible fingers, and a gleaming black cylinder began to revolve, the needle-point churning wax from its polished surface as the message was recorded. A tiny aluminum disk dropped into a tray below the electric clock, having stamped upon it the exact time at which the telephone bell had rung.

Number 81, as if his endless duties had become second nature, waited until the cylinder ceased to revolve. The telephone rest sprang up into its place; from the electric clock came the sound of a faint tick. Number 81 pressed a button on the desk. The cylinder began to revolve again, and a voice spoke—that of the man whose report had just been recorded.

"Speaking from Base 3. The Abbot Donegal reported missing. There is reason to believe that he slipped away during the night and may be proceeding to New York to be present at the debate at Carnegie Hall. All Numbers along possible routes have been notified, but no report to hand. Number 44 speaking."

Presumably satisfied that the mechanism was running smoothly, Number 81 closed the cupboard and stood up. Thus seen, he was an even bigger man than he had appeared seated; an untidy but an imposing figure. He took up the clay model, lifting it with great care. He slipped a tin of Egyptian cigarettes into a pocket of his dressing gown and walked towards one of the panels which surrounded the seemingly doorless room.

This he opened by pressing a concealed switch. A descending staircase was revealed. Carrying the clay model as carefully and lovingly as a mother carries her newly born infant, he descended, closing the door behind him. He went down one flight and entered a small, self-contained apartment. A table littered with books, plans, and all sorts of manuscripts stood by an open window. There was a bed in an alcove, and beyond, through an open door, a glimpse might be obtained of a small bathroom. Clearing a space on the littered table, Number 81 set down the clay model. He crossed the room and opened a cupboard. It showed perfectly empty. He raised a telephone from its hook. In German:

"The same as last night," he said harshly; "but the liver sausage was no good. Also, I must have the real German lager. This which you send me is spurious. Hurry, please, I have much to do."

These orders given, he crossed to the table and stared down dully at a large open book which lay there, its margins penciled with numerous notes in tiny, neat handwriting. The book was *Inter-stellar Cycles* by Professor Albert Morgenstahl, Europe's greatest physicist, and master mathematician, expelled a year earlier from Germany for anti-Nazi tendencies and later reported to be dead.

At this work Number 81 stared for some time, turning the pages over idly and resting a long tobacco-stained finger upon certain of the notes. There was a creaking in the cupboard and a laden wagon occupied its previously vacant space. Upon this wagon a substantial repast was set. Taking out a long-necked bottle of wine and uncorking it, Number 81 filled a glass. This he tasted and then set it down.

53

He threw open the French windows upon one side of the room, revealing a narrow balcony with a high railing of scrolled ironwork. A weather-beaten table stood there, and for a moment Number 81 leaned upon it, gazing down upon a night panorama of the great city below; snow-covered roofs, dwarf buildings and giant towers; a distant gleam of water; a leaden sky. It was bitterly cold at that great elevation; an icy breeze stirred the mane of white hair.

But, as if immune to climatic conditions, Number 81 bore out the clay head of the majestic Chinaman and set it upon the table. Below him a dome, its veins gilded, every crack and cranny coated with snow, swept down gracefully to a lower parapet. Muffled noises from streets set in deep gulleys reached his ears. He returned for his glass of wine, raised his head to the leaden sky, and:

"To the day of freedom!" he cried. "To the day when we meet face to face." And now his eyes, glaring insanely, were lowered to the clay head—"To the day when we meet face to face; when those wheels in which I am trapped, which seem to move, inexorable as the planets in their courses, are still forever."

He drank deeply, then tossed the remainder of the wine contemptuously into the face of the modeled head. He dashed the glass on the paving at his feet and, picking up the work to which he had devoted so many hours of care, raised it in both hands high above his head.

His expression maniacal, his teeth bared in a wolfish grin, far out over the dome he hurled it. It fell with a dull thud on the leaden covering. It broke, the parts showering down to the parapet, to fall, meaningless fragments, into some street far below. . . .

13 TANGLED CLUES

IN THE LIGHT of a gray wintry dawn creeping wanly through the windows, Nayland Smith and Mark Hepburn stood looking down at some curious objects set out upon the big corner table. These had been found in Richet's possession.

One was a gold and ivory badge. Hepburn took it up and stared at it curiously. It bore the number 38.

"According to the taximan," said Nayland Smith, "to whom I showed it, these badges simply mean that the wearer is an official of Harvey Bragg's League of Good Americans. It appears that no man is eligible for employment by the Lotus Cab Corporation who is not a member of this league."

"There's more in it than that," Hepburn murmured thoughtfully.

"I agree. But I don't think the man knew it. He admitted that they sometimes had orders from wearers of such badges requiring them to pick up certain passengers at indicated points and to report where they set them down."

"But he denied that he had any such orders last night?"

"He stuck to it grimly. According to his account, the choice of his cab by Richet was a coincidence."

Hepburn laid the badge down.

"There are only two other points of interest," said Nayland Smith, "although we may learn more if we can trace Richet's baggage. These are his notes of Weaver's Farm and of this address, and . . . that."

The object to which he pointed, found upon the floor of the taxi, was certainly an odd thing for a man to carry about. It was a cardboard case made to hold a pack of playing cards . . . but there were no cards!

Several sheets of blank paper had also been found, folded in a manner which seemed to indicate that they had been in the cardboard case. This case, in Smith's opinion, was the object which the driver had mistaken for a notebook.

"Richet was actually holding it in his hand, Hepburn," he rapped energetically, "at the moment of the attack. This fact is of first-rate importance."

Hepburn, eyes half closed, nodded slowly. The nervous energy of this man surpassed anything in his experience. And as if recognition of his companion's weariness had come to him suddenly, Nayland Smith grasped Hepburn's arm.

"You are asleep already!" he declared, and smiled sympathetically. "Suppose we arrange to meet for ham and eggs at noon. Don't forget, Miss Lakin is due at four o'clock. If you meet her—not a word about Richet."

2

The bell rang, and Fey, his leathery face characteristically expressionless, crossed the vestibule and opened the door. A woman stood there, tall and composed, her iron-gray hair meticulously groomed as it peeped from beneath the brim of a smart but suitable hat. She was wrapped in furs. Beside her stood a man who wore the uniform of the Regal-Athenian Hotel. He exchanged a glance with Fey, nodded, turned and went away.

"Sir Denis is expecting you, madam," said Fey, standing aside.

And as the visitor entered the vestibule, Nayland Smith hurried from the adjoining sitting room, hand outstretched. His lean brown features exhibited repressed excitement.

"Miss Lakin," he exclaimed, "you are very welcome. I received the letter which you sent by special messenger, but your phone message has intrigued me more than the letter. Please come in and sit down and give me all the details."

The sitting room in which Miss Lakin found herself possessed several curious features. The windows which occupied nearly the whole of one wall afforded a view of a wide area of New York City. Storm clouds had passed; a wintry sun lighted a prospect which had a sort of uncanny beauty. Upon countless flat roofs far below, upon the heads of gargoyles and other grotesque ornamentations breaking the lines of the more towering buildings, snow rested. The effect was that of a city of ice gnomes magically magnified. Through clear, frosty air the harbor was visible, and one might obtain a glimpse of the distant sea. Above a littered writing table set near one of the windows a huge map of the city was fixed upon the wall; the remainder of this wall was occupied by a map, on a much smaller scale, of the whole of the United States. These maps had one character in common: they were studded with hundreds of colored pins which appeared to have been stuck in at random.

"The room is rather warm, madam," said Fey. "Allow me to take your coat."

The heavy fur coat draped carefully across his arm:

"A cup of tea, madam?" he suggested.

"English tea," snapped Nayland Smith; "Fortnum and Mason's."

"Thank you," said Miss Lakin, smiling faintly; "you tempt me. Yes, I think I should enjoy a cup of tea."

Nayland Smith stood before the mantelpiece, hands behind him. He had that sort of crisp, wavy hair, silvery now at the sides, which always looks in order; he was cleanly shaven, and his dark-skinned face offered no evidence of the fact that he had had only six hours sleep in the past forty-eight. He wore a very old tweed suit, and what looked like a striped shirt with an attached collar, but which closer scrutiny would have revealed to be a pajama jacket. As Fey went out:

"Miss Lakin," he continued, and his manner was that of a man feverishly anxious, "you have brought the letter to which you referred?"

Sarah Lakin took an envelope out of her handbag and handed it to Nayland Smith, watching him with her steady, grave eyes. He took it, glanced at the handwritten address, then crossed to the writing table.

"I have also," she said, "a note of the place at which we were to communicate with the very unpleasant person who called upon me yesterday."

Nayland Smith turned; his expression was grim.

"I fear," he said rapidly, "That we cannot hope for much help from that quarter." He turned again to the littered table. "Here are three letters written by Orwin Prescott at Weaver's Farm immediately prior to his disappearance. You know why I detained them and what I have discovered?"

Miss Lakin nodded.

"Copies have been sent to the persons to whom the letters were addressed, but I should judge, although I am not a specialist in the subject, that this is in Dr. Prescott's handwriting?"

"I can assure you that it is, Sir Denis. Intellectually my cousin and I are too closely akin for any deception to be possible. That letter was written by Orwin. Please read it."

A subdued clatter of teacups became audible from the kitchenette to which Fey had retired, as Nayland Smith extracted the letter from the envelope. Sarah Lakin watched Sir Denis intently. He fascinated her. Brief though her acquaintance with him had been, her own fine nature had recognized and welcomed the keen, indomitable spirit of this man who, in an emergency personal and national, had thrown the weight of his trained powers into the scale.

He studied the letter silently, reading it once, twice. He then read it aloud:

"DEAR SARAH,

This is to relieve your anxiety. By this time you will know that I am the victim of a plot; but I have compromised with the enemy, pax in bello, and I congratulate you and those associated with you upon the manner in which you have succeeded in restraining the newspapers from reference to the subject of my temporary disappearance. I have instructed Norbert, who will communicate with you. The experience has been unpleasant and even now I am not wholly my own master. Please conduct yourself as though you were ignorant of this misadventure,

57

but have no fears respecting my appearance at Carnegie Hall. I shall be there. I dislike seeming to mystify, but it would be to my best interests if you make no attempt to communicate with me until the night of the debate. It is unnecessary that I should tell you to have courage.

Always affectionately yours,
ORWIN."

"No date," Nayland Smith commented. "No address. A sheet torn from a common type of writing-block. The envelope, also, is of a very ordinary kind, bearing a New York postmark. H'm . . . !"

He dropped letter and envelope upon the desk and, taking up a tobacco pouch, began to load his pipe. Fey entered with a tea tray which he placed upon a small table before Miss Lakin.

"Cream or milk, madam?"

"Milk, and one piece of sugar, thank you."

Except for a certain haggardness visible on the face of Nayland Smith and the strangeness of his attire in one obviously trained to conform to social custom, there was little in the atmosphere of this room high above the turmoil of New York to suggest that remorseless warfare raged about the pair who faced one another across a tea table.

"I am entirely at a loss what to do, Sir Denis."

As Fey withdrew, the deep voice of Miss Lakin broke the silence; her steady eyes were fixed upon Nayland Smith. He lighted his pipe, paused, looked down at her, and:

"A very foul briar is unusual at teatime," he snapped, and dropped his pipe in an ash tray. "Please forgive me. I am up against the greatest and perhaps the last problem of my life."

"Sir Denis . . ." Miss Lakin bent forward, took up the charred pipe from the tray and extended it towards him. "Surely you know that I understand. I have lived in a wider world than Connecticut, and I want your advice badly. Please concentrate upon the problem in your own way. What should I do? What do you advise me to do?"

Nayland Smith stared hard at those grave eyes of the speaker, then, pipe in hand, began to walk up and down the room, tugging at the lobe of his left ear. They were forty floors above the streets of New York, and yet the ceaseless bombilation of those amazing thoroughfares reached them through such windows as were open: the hooting of tractor horns, the roar of ten thousand engines, the boom of a distant train rumbling along the rails, the warning siren of a towboat on East River. The city was around them, throbbing, living, an entity, a demi-god, claiming them—and as it seemed in this hour, demanding their destruction.

"Is the phrasing characteristic of your cousin's style?" Nayland Smith demanded.

"Yes, broadly."

"I understand. It struck me as somewhat pedantic."

"He has a very scholarly manner, Sir Denis, but as a rule it is not so marked in his intimate letters."

"Ah . . . Who is Norbert?"

"Maurice Norbert is Orwin's private secretary."

"I see. May I take it, Miss Lakin, that in this fight for domination of the United States your cousin did not actually aim at the Presidency?"

"He did not even desire it, Sir Denis. He is what our newspapers term a hundred-per-cent American, but in the best sense of the phrase. He hoped to break the back of Harvey Bragg's campaign. His aims were identical with those of the Abbot Donegal. His disappearance from the scene at this time would be fatal."

"I agree! But it seems that he is not going to disappear."

"Then do you believe that what he says is true?"

"I am disposed to believe it, Miss Lakin. My advice is to conform strictly to the letter and spirit of his request."

Miss Lakin was watching him intently, then:

"I am afraid I don't agree with you, Sir Denis," she said.

"Why?" he turned and faced her.

"That Orwin was kidnaped we know. Thank God he is alive! Surely he was forced to write this letter by the kidnapers. They are playing for time. Surely you can see that they are playing for time!"

14 *THE SCARLET BRIDES*

IN A SMALL, book-lined room, high above New York City, dimly lighted and pervaded by a faint smell of incense, Dr. Fu Manchu, wearing a yellow robe but with no cap crowning his massive skull, sat behind a large lacquered table, his eyes closed. From a little incense burner on one corner of this table a faint spiral of smoke arose—some might have ascribed this to a streak of effeminacy in an otherwise great man, but one who knew the potency of burning perfumes as understood in the ancient Orient would have placed a different construction upon the circumstances. The Delphic Oracle was so inspired; incense cunningly prepared, such as the *khyfi* of the ancient Egyptians, can exalt the subconscious mind. A voice was speaking as though someone stood in the room, although except for the presence of the majestic Chinaman it was empty.

Dr. Fu Manchu pressed a button, the voice ceased, and there was silence in the incense-laden place. For two, three, five minutes the Chinaman sat motionless, his lean, long-fingered hands resting upon the table before him, his eyes closed.

"I am here, Master," said a feeble voice, speaking in Chinese.

"Listen carefully," Dr. Fu Manchu replied in the same language. "It is urgent. How many of our Scarlet Brides from New Zealand have you in reserve?"

"Fifteen, Master. I sacrificed five in the case of the man James Richet, fearing that some might not survive the cold."

"It is reported that Danger Number One—I hear you hiss, my friend—invariably sleeps with his windows open. Sacrifice ten more of our little friends. See that he does not sleep alone tonight."

"My lord, I have no one who could undertake the work. If I had Ali Khân or Quong Wah, or any one of our old servants. But I have none. What can I do in this uncivilized land to which my lord has exiled me?"

Several moments of silence followed. The long ivory hands with their incredible nails, beautiful even in their cruelty, rested motionless upon the table, then:

"Await orders," said the imperious, guttural voice.

Another button was depressed and there was silence. The pencil of smoke rising from the incense burner was growing more and more faint. Dr. Fu Manchu opened his eyes, staring straight before him; his eyes were green as emeralds, glittering gems reflecting an inexorable will. His right hand moved to a small switchboard. He inserted a plug, and presently a spot of red light indicated that he was connected.

"Is that 'A' New York?"

"Kern Adler here."

"You know to whom you are speaking?"

"Yes. What can I do for you, President?"

The voice was unctuous but nervous.

"We have not yet met," the imperious tone continued, "but I assume, otherwise I should not have appointed you,

60

that you can command the services of the New York under-world?"

There was a perceptible pause before Kern Adler replied.

"If you would tell me, President, exactly what you want, I should be better able to answer."

"I want the man called Peter Carlo. Find him for me. I will then give you further instructions."

Another pause . . .

"I can find him, President," the nervous voice replied, "but only through Blondie Hahn."

"I distrust this man Hahn. You have recommended him, but I have not yet accepted him. I have my reasons. However, speak to him now. You know my wishes. Report to me when they can be carried out."

The red light continued to glow; one yellow finger pressed a small switch with the result that the office of Kern Adler, Attorney, and one of the biggest survivors of the underworld clean-up, seemed to become acoustically translated to the study of Dr. Fu Manchu. Adler could be heard urgently calling a number; and presently he got it.

"Hello, Kern," came a coarse voice; "want the boss, I guess. Hold on; I'll get him." There was an interval during which dim sounds of dance music penetrated to the incense-laden room, then:

"Hello, Kern," came in a deep bass; "what's new with you?"

"Listen Blondie. I'm telling you something. If you want a quiet life you have to fall into line. I mean it. It'll be good for your health to go to work again. Either you come in right now or you stay right out. I want something done tonight—you have got to do it."

"Listen to me, Kern. You've spilled a mouthful. But what you don't seem to know is this: you've been washed up—and you figure you're still afloat. You're stone dead but you won't lay down. Come clean and I'll talk to you. I'm standing all ready on my two big feet. I don't need your protection."

"I want 'Fly' Carlo, and I'm prepared to pay for him. He has to get busy tonight. President's orders——"

"President nothing! But listen—you can have Carlo, when *I* hold the pay roll. That's my terms now and always. What's the figure? Carlo will cost the President (like hell he's President!) all of two thousand dollars. He can only get him through me. I'm his sole agent and my rake-off is my own pidgin."

"Your terms are ridiculous, Blondie. Talk sense."

"I'm talking sense all right. And I've got something very

particular to say to *you*." The deep, gruff voice was menacing. "Somebody got busy among my records last night while I was at a party. If I thought it was *you*, I'd steal you away from your girl friends, little man. Next time you wrote a love letter it'd be with a quill from an angel's wing."

At which moment Kern Adler's line became suddenly disconnected.

"Hello there!" Hahn bawled. "You cut me off! What in hell——"

His protests were silenced. A guttural voice came across the wires:

"You have been put through to *me*—the President. . . . Paul Erckmann Hahn—I believe this is your name?—you possess a certain brute force which attracts me. You are crude; but you might possibly be used."

"Used?" Hahn's voice sounded stifled. "Listen——"

"When I speak, it is *you* who must listen. The person 'who got busy among your records,' as you term it, was one of my own agents—in no way connected with Kern Adler. I learned much that I had wished to know about you, Mr. Hahn . . ."

"Is that so?" came a bull-like bellow. "Then listen, pet! —You're a Chink if I ever heard one. That tells me plenty. I've been checking up on *you*. The G men are right on your tail, yellow baby. Centre Street has got your fingerprints, and Hoover knows your toenails by sight. You're using an old hide-out in Chinatown, and there's a blue-eyed boy from Britain on the trail. You're in up to the ears, President. You'll need me badly to save your scalp. Adler can't do it. He's out of print. Come up to date and talk terms."

Long ivory fingers remained quite motionless upon the table. Dr. Fu Manchu's eyes were closed.

"Your remarks impress me," he said softly, sibilantly. "I feel that you are indispensable to my plans. By all means let us talk terms. The matter is urgent. . . ."

2

Mark Hepburn tried, and tried in vain, to sleep. The image of a woman haunted him. He had checked her up as far as possible. He thought that he had her record fairly complete.

She was the widow of a United States naval officer. Her husband had been killed in the Philippines three years before. There was one child of the marriage—a boy. In fact, the credentials with which she had come to Abbot Donegal were authentic in every way. A thousand times, day and night, he had found himself in an imaginary world sweeter than reality—looking into those deep blue eyes. He found it impossible to believe that this woman would stoop to anything criminal. He would not entertain the idea despite damning facts against her.

He wanted to hear evidence for the defense, and he was fully prepared to take it seriously. In all his investigations he hoped yet feared to come across her. He wondered if at last he had fallen in love—and with a worthless woman. Her flight on that night from the Tower of the Holy Thorn, the fact that she had been endeavoring to smuggle away the incriminating manuscript which explained the collapse of Abbot Donegal: these things required explanation. Yet the official record of Moya Eileen Adair, as far as he had traced it, indicated that she was a young gentlewoman of unblemished character.

She came from County Wicklow in Ireland; her father, Commander Breon, was still serving with the British navy. She had met her late husband during the visit of an American fleet to Bermuda, where she had been staying with relatives. He was of Irish descent; he, too, was a man of the sea, and they had been married before the American fleet sailed. All this Mark Hepburn had learned in the space of a few days, employing those wonderful resources at his disposal. Now, tossing wearily on his bed, he challenged himself: Had he been justified in instructing more than twenty agents, in expending nearly a thousand dollars in radio and cable messages, to secure this information?

The fate of the country was kept spinning in the air by those who juggled with lives. Sane men prayed that the Constitution should stand foursquare; others believed that its remodeling as preached by Dr. Prescott would form the foundations of a new Utopia. Others, more mad, saw in the dictatorship of Harvey Bragg a Golden Age for all. . . . And the Abbot of Holy Thorn held a choir of seven million voices in check awaiting the baton of his rhetoric.

Bribery and corruption gnawed ratlike into the very foundations of the State; murder, insolent, stalked the city streets. . . . And he, Mark Hepburn, expended his energies tracing the history of one woman. As he lay tossing upon his pillow the whole-hearted enthusiasm of Sir Denis Nayland Smith became a reproach.

Then, suddenly, he sprang upright in bed, repeater in hand.

The door of his room had been opened very quietly. . . .

"Hands up!" he rasped. "Quick!"

"Not so loud, Hepburn, not so loud."

It was Nayland Smith.

"Sir Denis!"

Smith was crossing the room in his direction.

"I don't want to arouse Fey," the incisive but guarded tones continued. "He has had a trying day. But it's *our* job, Hepburn. Don't make any noise; just slip along with me to my room. . . . Bring the gun."

In silence, pajama-clad, barefooted, Hepburn went along the corridor, turning right just before reaching the vestibule. In the room occupied by Nayland Smith the atmosphere was perceptibly cooler. The windows were wide open; heavy curtains were drawn widely apart; a prospect of a million lights gleamed far below; the muted roar of New York's ceaseless traffic rose like rumbling of distant thunder.

"Close the door."

Mark Hepburn closed the door behind him as he entered.

"You will notice," Nayland Smith continued, "that I have not been smoking for some time, although I have been wide awake. I was afraid of the glow from my pipe."

"Why?"

"For this reason, Hepburn. Our brilliant enemy has become a slave of routine. It is now almost a habit with him to test his death-agents upon someone else, and if the result is satisfactory to try them on me . . ."

"I'm not too clear about what you mean——"

"I mean that unless I am greatly mistaken, I am about to be subjected to an attempt upon my life by Dr. Fu Manchu!"

"What! But you are forty stories up from the street!"

"We shall see. You may remember that I deduced the arrival of certain weapons in the Doctor's armory from circumstances connected with the death of Richet . . ."

"I remember. But a long night's work was wasted."

"Part of our trade," rapped Nayland Smith dryly. "You will notice, Hepburn—there is ample reflected light—two suitcases upon the top of a chest of drawers set against the wall on your left. Climb up and hide yourself behind the suitcases—I have placed a chair for the purpose. Your job is to watch the windows but not to be seen——"

"Good God!" Hepburn whispered, and clutched Smith's arm.

"What is it?"

"There's someone in your bed!"

"There's no one in my bed, Hepburn, nor is there any time to waste. This job is life or death. Get to your post."

Mark Hepburn rallied his resources: that shock of discovering the apparent presence of someone in the bed had shaken him. But now he was icily cool again, cool as Nayland Smith. He climbed onto the chest of drawers, curled up there behind the suitcases, although space was limited, in such a manner that he had a view of the windows while remaining invisible from anyone in the room. This achieved:

"Where are you, Sir Denis?" he asked, speaking in a low voice.

"Also entrenched, Hepburn. Do nothing until I give the word. And now, listen. . . ."

Mark Hepburn began to listen. Clearly he sensed that the menace came from the windows, although its nature was a mystery to him. He heard the hooting of taxis, the eerie wail which denotes that the Fire Department is out, the concerted whine of motor engines innumerable. Then, more intimately, these sounds becoming a background, he heard something else. . . .

It was a very faint noise but a very curious one; almost it might have been translated as the impact of some night bird, or of a bat, against the stone face of the building. . . .

He listened intently, aware of the fact that his heartbeats had accelerated. He allowed his glance to wander for a moment in quest of Nayland Smith. Presently, accustomed now to the peculiar light of the room, he detected him. He was crouching on a glass-topped bureau, set just right of the window, holding what Hepburn took to be a sawn-off shotgun in his hand.

Then again Hepburn directed the whole of his attention to the windows.

Clearly outlined against a sullen sky he could see one of New York's tallest buildings. Only three of its many windows showed any light: one at the very top, just beneath the cupola, and two more in the dome itself which crowned the tall, slender structure. Tensed as he was, listening, waiting, for what was to come, the thought flashed through his mind: Who lived in those high, lonely rooms—who was awake there at this hour?

Another curious light was visible from where he lay—a red glow somewhere away to the left towards the river; a constantly changing light of which he could see only the outer halo. Then a moving blur appeared far below, and a rumbling sound told him that a train was passing . . .

Suddenly, unexpectedly, a sharp silhouette obscured much of this dim nocturne. . . .

Something out of that exotic background belonging to the man who, alone, shared this vigil tonight, had crept up between the distant twinkling lights and Mark Hepburn's view.

Vaguely he realized that the phenomenon was due to the fact that someone, miraculously, had climbed the face of the building, or part of it, and now, as he saw, was supporting himself upon the ledge. There was a moment of tense silence. It was followed by activity on the part of the invader perched perilously outside. A light, yellow-muffled, shone into the room, its searching ray questing around, to rest finally for a moment upon the bed.

Mark Hepburn held his breath; almost, he betrayed his presence.

The appearance of the disordered bed suggested that a sleeper, sheets drawn up right over his head, lay there!

"Dr. Fu Manchu has become a slave of routine"—Nayland Smith's words echoed in Hepburn's mind. "It is almost a habit with him to test his death-agents upon someone else, and if the result is satisfactory to try them on me."

The shadowy silhouette perched upon the window ledge projected some kind of slender telescopic rod into the room. It stretched out towards the bed. . . . Upon it depended what looked like a square box. The rod was withdrawn. The visitor accomplished this with a minimum of noise. Hepburn, his ears attuned for the welcome word of command, watched. An invisible line was wound in, tautened, and jerked.

Suddenly came a loud and insistent hissing, and:

"Shoot!" snapped the voice of Nayland Smith. "Shoot that man, Hepburn!"

3

The shadowy shape at the window had not moved from that constrained, crouching attitude—two enormous hands, which appeared to be black, rested on the window ledge— when Mark Hepburn fired—once, twice. . . . The sinister silhouette disappeared; that strange hissing continued; the muted roar of New York carried on.

Yet, automatic dropped beside him, fists clenched, he listened so intently, so breathlessly, that he heard it. . . .

A dull thud in some courtyard far below.

"Don't move, Hepburn," came Nayland Smith's crisp command. "Don't stir until I give the word!"

An indeterminable odor became perceptible—chemical, nauseating. . . .

"Sir Denis!"

It was the voice of Fey.

"Don't come in, Fey!" cried Nayland Smith. "Don't open the door!"

"Very good, sir."

Only a very keen observer would have recognized the note of emotion in Fey's almost toneless voice.

The hissing noise continued.

"This is terrible!" Hepburn exclaimed. "Sir Denis! what has happened?"

The hissing ceased: Hepburn had identified it now.

"There's a switch on your right," came swiftly. "See if you can reach it, but stay where you are."

Hepburn, altering his position, reached out, found the switch, and depressed it. Lights sprang up. He turned—and saw Nayland Smith poised on top of the bureau. The strange weapon which vaguely he had seen in the darkness proved to be a large syringe fitted with a long nozzle.

The air was heavy with a sickly sweet smell suggesting at once iodine and ether.

He looked towards the bed . . . and would have sworn that a figure lay under the coverlet—a sheet drawn up over its face! On the pillow and beside the place where the sleeper's head seemed to lie rested a small wooden box no more than half the size of those made to contain cigars. One of the narrow sides—that which faced him—was open.

There seemed to be a number of large black spots upon the pillow. . . .

"It's possible," said Nayland Smith, staring across the room, "that I missed the more active. I doubt it. But we must be careful."

Above the muted midnight boom of New York, sounds of disturbance, far below, became audible.

"I'm glad you didn't miss our man, Hepburn!" rapped Nayland Smith, dropping onto the carpeted floor.

"I have been trained to shoot straight," Mark Hepburn replied monotonously.

Nayland Smith nodded.

"He deserved all that came to him. I faked the bed when I heard his approach. . . . Jump into a suit and rejoin me in the sitting room. We shall be wanted down there at any moment. . . ."

Three minutes later they both stood staring at a row of black insects laid upon a sheet of white paper. The reek of iodine and ether was creeping in from the adjoining bedroom. Fey, at a side table, prepared whiskies imperturbably. He was correctly dressed except for two trifling irregularities: his collar was that of a pajama jacket, and he wore bedroom slippers.

"This is your province, Hepburn," said Nayland Smith. "These things are outside my experience. But you will note that they are quite dead, with their legs curled up. The preparation I used in the syringe is a simple formula by my old friend Petrie: he found it useful in Egypt. . . . Thank you, Fey."

Mark Hepburn studied the dead insects through a hand-lens. Shrunken up as they were by the merciless spray which had destroyed them, upon their dense black bodies he clearly saw vivid scarlet spots—"Scarlet spots"—the last words spoken by James Richet!

"What are they, Hepburn?"

"I'm not sure. They belong to the genus *Latrodectus*. The malmignatte of Italy is a species, and the American Black Widow spider. But these are larger. Their bite is probably deadly."

"Their bite is certainly deadly!" rapped Nayland Smith. "An attack by two or more evidently results in death within three minutes—also a characteristic vivid scarlet rash. You know, now, what was in the cardboard box which James Richet opened in the taxicab! No doubt he had orders to open it at the moment that he reached the hotel. One of the Doctor's jests. I take it they are tropical?"

"Beyond doubt."

"Once exposed to the frosty air, and their deadly work done, they would die. You know, now, why I provided myself with that—" he pointed to the syringe. "I have met other servants of Fu Manchu to whom a stone-faced building was a grand staircase."

"Good God!" Mark Hepburn said hoarsely. "This man is a fiend—a sadistic madman——"

"Or a genius, Hepburn! If you will glance at the receptacle which our late visitor deposited on my pillow, you will notice that it is made from a common cigar box. One side lifts shutterwise: there is a small spring. It was controlled, you see, by this length of fine twine, one end of which still rests on the window ledge. This hook on top was intended to enable the Doctor's servant to lift it into the room on the end of the telescopic rod. The box is lightly lined with hay. You may safely examine it. I have satisfied myself that there is nothing alive inside. . . ."

"This man is the most awful creature who has ever appeared in American history," said Hepburn. "The situation was tough enough, anyway. Where does he get these horrors? He must have agents all over the world."

Nayland Smith began to walk up and down, twitching at the lobe of his ear.

"Undoubtedly he has. In my experience I have never felt called upon to step more warily. Also, I begin to think that my powers are failing me."

"What do you mean?"

"For years, Hepburn, for many years, a palpable fact has escaped me. There is a certain very old Chinaman whose records I have come across in all parts of the world; in London, in Liverpool, in Shanghai, in Port Said, Rangoon and Calcutta. Only now, when he is in New York (and God knows how he got here!), have I realized that this dirty old barkeeper is Dr. Fu Manchu's chief of staff!"

Mark Hepburn stared hard at the speaker, and then:

"This accounts for all the men at work in Chinatown," he said slowly. "The man you mean is Sam Pak?"

"Sam Pak—none other," snapped Nayland Smith. "And the truth respecting this ancient reprobate—" he indicated the writing table—"reached me in its entirety only a few hours ago. If you could see him you would understand my amazement. He is incredibly old, and—so much for my knowledge of the East—I had always set him down as one step above the mendicant class. Yet, in the days of the empress, he was governor of a great province; in fact, he was Dr. Fu Manchu's political senior! He was one of the first Chinamen to graduate at Cambridge, and he holds a science degree of Heidelberg."

"Yet in your knowledge of him he has worked in slums in Chinatown—been a barkeeper?"

"It might occur in Russia tomorrow, Hepburn. There are princes, grand dukes—I am not speaking of gigolos or soi-disant noblemen—spread about the world who, the right man giving the word, would work as scavengers, if called upon, to restore the Czars."

"That's true enough."

"And so, you see, we have got to find this aged Chinaman. I suspect that he has brought with him an arsenal of these unpleasant weapons which the Doctor employs so successfully——Hullo! there's the phone. We are wanted to identify the climber. . . ."

15 THE SCARLET BRIDES (concluded)

OLD SAM PAK was performing his nightly rounds of Base 3. Two Chinese boys were in attendance. Up above, political warfare raged; the newspapers gave prominence to the Washington situation in preference to love, murder, or divorce. Dr. Orwin Prescott was reported to be "resting up before the battle." Harvey Bragg was well in the news. Other aspirants to political eminence might be found elsewhere: "Bluebeard of the Backwoods" was front-page stuff. America was beginning to take its Harvey Bragg seriously.

But in the mysterious silence of Base 3, old Sam Pak held absolute sway. Chinatown can keep its secrets. Only by exercise of a special sense, which comes to life after years of experience in the ways of the Orient, may a Westerner know when something strange is afoot. Sidelong glances; sudden silences; furtive departures as the intruder enters. Police officers in Mott Street area had been reporting such trivial occurrences recently. Those responsible for diagnosing Asiatic symptoms had deduced the arrival in New York of a Chinese big shot.

Their diagnosis was correct. By this time every Chinaman from coast to coast knew that one of the Council of Seven controlling the Si-Fan, most dreaded secret society in the East, had entered America.

Sam Pak pursued his rounds. The place was a cunning maze of passages and stairs; a Chinese rabbit warren. One narrow passage, below the level of the room of the seven-eyed goddess, had a row of six highly painted coffins ranged along its wall. They lay on their sides. Lids had been removed and plate glass substituted. This ghastly tunnel was vile with a smell of ancient rottenness.

One of Sam Pak's attendant Chinamen switched on a light. The old mandarin, who had known nearly a century of vicissitudes, carried a great bunch of keys. In his progress he had tried door after door. He now tested the small traps set in the sides of the six coffins. In the sudden glare, insidious nocturnal things moved behind the glass. . . .

There was a big iron door in the wall; it possessed three

locks, all of which proved to be fastened. Here at once was part of that strange arsenal which Nayland Smith suspected to have been imported, and a secret sally-port the existence of which police headquarters would have given much to know about it. It communicated with an old subterranean passage which led to the East River. . . .

On a floor above, Sam Pak opened a grille and looked into a neatly appointed bedroom. Dr. Orwin Prescott lay there sleeping. His face was very white.

A dim whirring sound broke the underground silence. Sam Pak handed the bunch of keys to one of the boys and shuffled slowly upstairs to the temple of the green-eyed goddess. It was in semidarkness; the only light came through the colored silk curtain draped before one of the stone cubicles.

Sam Pak crossed, drew the curtain aside, and spoke in Chinese:

"I am here, Master."

"You grow old, my friend," the cold, imperious tones of Dr. Fu Manchu replied. "You keep me waiting. I regret that you have refused to accept my offer to arrest your descent to the tomb."

"I prefer to join my ancestors, marquis, when the call reaches me. I fear your wisdom. While I live I am with you body and soul in our great aims. When my hour comes I shall be glad to die."

Silence fell. Old Sam Pak, withered hands tucked in wide sleeves, stooping, waited. . . .

"I will hear your own report on the matter which I entrusted to you."

"You know already, Master, that the man, Peter Carlo, failed. I cannot say what evidence he left behind. But your orders regarding the other, Blondie Hahn, were carried out. He brought the man Carlo to Wu King's Bar, and I interviewed them in the private room. I instructed Carlo, and he set out. I then paid Hahn his price. It was waste of good money, but always I obey. Ah Fu and Chung Chow did the rest . . . there are now only three Scarlet Brides left to us. . . ."

2

It was an hour after dawn when Nayland Smith and Mark Hepburn stood looking down at two stone slabs upon which two bodies lay.

One of the departed in life had been a small but very muscular Italian with uncommonly large, powerful hands.

He presented a spectacle, owing to his many injuries, which must have revolted all but the toughest. There was a sound of dripping water.

"You have prepared your report, Doctor?" said Nayland Smith, addressing a plump, red-faced person who was smiling amiably at the exhibits as though he loved them.

"Certainly, Mr. Smith," the police doctor returned cheerily. "It is quite clear that Number One, here (I call him Number One because he was brought in an hour ahead of the other), died as the result of a fall from a great height——"

"Very great height," rapped Nayland Smith. "Fortieth floor of the Regal Tower."

"So I understand. Remarkable. He has two bullet wounds: one in his right hand and one in his shoulder. These would not have caused death, of course. It was the fall which killed him—quite naturally. I believe he was wearing black silk gloves. An electric torch and a telescopic rod of very light metal were found near the body."

Nayland Smith turned to a police officer who stood at his elbow.

"I am told, Inspector, that you have now checked up on this man's history: there is no doubt about his identity?"

"None at all," drawled the inspector, who was chewing gum. "He's Peter Carlo, known as 'The Fly'—one of the most expert upper-story men in New York. He could have climbed the outside of the Statue of Liberty if there'd been anything worth stealing at the top. He always wore a black silk mask and silk gloves. The rod was to reach into rooms he couldn't actually enter. He was so clever he could lift a lady's ring from a dressing table fifteen feet away!"

"I don't doubt it," muttered Mark Hepburn. "So much for Peter Carlo. And, now . . ."

He turned to the second slab.

Upon it lay the body of a huge blond man of Teutonic type. His hands were so swollen that two glittering diamonds which adorned them had become deeply embedded in the puffy fingers. Soddened garments clung to his great frame. Scarlet spots were discernible on both of the hairy hands, and there was a scarlet discoloration on his throat. The glare of his china-blue eyes set in that bloated caricature of what had been a truculently strong face afforded a sight even more dreadful than that of the shattered body of Peter Carlo.

"Brought in from the river just north of Manhattan Bridge ten minutes before you arrived," explained Inspector Mc-Grew, chewing industriously. "May be no connection, but I thought you'd like to see him."

He glanced around, meeting a curiously piercing glance from Federal Agent Smith as he did so. Federal Agent Smith had steely eyes set in a sun-browned face framed, now, in the fur collar of his topcoat; a disconcerting person, in Inspector McGrew's opinion.

"Now, here," explained the smiling police surgeon, "we have a really mysterious case! Although his body was hauled out of East River, he was not drowned——"

"Why do you say so?" Smith demanded.

"It's obvious." The surgeon became enthusiastic and, stepping forward, laid a finger on the bloated, discolored skin. "Note the vivid scarlet urticarial rash which characterizes the edema. This man died from some toxic agency: he was *thrown* into the river. A post-mortem examination will tell us more, but of this much I am sure. And I understand, Inspector——" glancing over his shoulder—"that he, also, is well known to the police?"

"Well known to the police!" echoed Inspector McGrew. "He's well known all over New York. This is Blondie Hahn, one of the big shots of the old days. He was booking agent for 'most all the gunmen that remain in town. These times, I guess he had a monopoly. He ran a downtown restaurant, and although we knew his game, he had strong political protection."

"You are prepared to make your report, Doctor?" said Smith rapidly. "Carlo I examined shortly after he was found. I presume we can now search the person and garments of Hahn."

"That's been done already," Inspector McGrew replied. "The stuff is on the table inside."

The gray-blue eyes of Federal Agent Smith glared out from the haggard brown mask of his face. Inspector McGrew was a hard man, but he found himself transfixed by that icy stare.

"Those were not my orders!"

"It had been done before federal instructions came through."

"I want to know by whose authority!" The speaker's piercing glance never left McGrew's face. "I won't be interfered with in this way. You are dealing, Inspector, not with the operations of a common, successful crook, but with something bigger, vastly bigger than you even imagine. Any orders you receive from me must be carried out to the letter."

"I'm sorry," said the inspector, an expression he had not used for many years, unless possibly to his wife. "But we didn't know you were interested in Hahn, and the boys just went through with the routine."

"Show me these things."

Inspector McGrew opened a door, and Nayland Smith walked through to an inner room, followed by Hepburn and the inspector. In the doorway he turned, and addressing a grim-looking man in oilskins:

"I understand," he said, "that you were in charge of the boat which recovered the body. I shall want to see you later."

On a large, plain, pine table two sets of exhibits were displayed. The first consisted of a nearly empty packet of Lucky Strike cigarettes, a lighter, a black silk mask, black silk gloves, a quill toothpick, three one-dollar bills, and an eight-inch metal baton—which contained fifteen feet of telescopic rods. Smith examined these, the sole possessions found upon Fly Carlo, quickly but carefully. He had seen them already.

"You understand," McGrew explained, "Hahn had only just been brought in—our ordinary routine was interrupted."

"Forget your ordinary routine," came rapidly. "From now on *your* routine is *my* routine."

Federal Officer Smith transferred his attention to the second set of exhibits. These were more numerous than interesting. There was a very formidable magazine pistol of German manufacture; a small pearshaped object easily identified as a hand grenade; a gold cigar case decorated with a crest; a body belt, the pockets of which had been emptied of their contents: ten twenty-dollar gold pieces; an aluminum lighter; two silk handkerchiefs; a diamond pin; a bunch of keys; a packet of chewing gum; and a large shagreen wallet, the contents of which had been removed. These were: a number of letters, and a photograph soddened by immersion. There was, lastly, a limp carton which had once contained playing cards, and two thousand dollars in hundred-dollar bills.

"Where was the diamond pin?" snapped Nayland Smith.

"He always wore it in his coat like it was a badge," Inspector McGrew replied.

"Where were the dollar bills?"

"Right in the card-holder."

"Can you think of any reason," Smith asked, "why a man should carry money in a card-holder?"

"No," the inspector admitted, "I can't."

"Assuming that this money had just been sent to him, can

74

you think of any reason why it should be sent in such a way?"

"No."

Inspector McGrew shook his head blankly, staring in a fascinated way at the speaker.

"Yet the card-holder," Nayland Smith continued, "is the solution of the mystery of Blondie Hahn's death." He turned abruptly—he seemed to move on springs—the man's nervous tension was electrical. "I want all these exhibits to go with me in the car."

He rested his hand on Mark Hepburn's shoulder. Hepburn looked very pale in the gray light.

"Note the two thousand dollars in the card case," he said in a low voice. "There was something else in there as well. Dr. Fu Manchu always settles his debts . . . sometimes with interest. . . ."

16 *"BLUEBEARD"*

Moya Adair closed her eyes as those green eyes opened. The man behind the table spoke, in that imperious, high-pitched voice.

"I accept your explanation," he said. "None of us is infallible."

Mrs. Adair raised her lashes and tried to sustain the speaker's regard, but failed, turning her glance aside.

The face of Dr. Fu Manchu sometimes reminded her of a devil mask which hung upon the wall of her father's study in Ireland.

"You serve me admirably. I regret that your service is one of fear. I prefer enthusiasm. You are a beautiful woman; for this reason I have employed you. Men are creatures of wax which white fingers can mold to their will—to my will. For always, Moya Adair, *your* will must be *my* will—or, we shall part. . . ."

The blue eyes were turned swiftly in his direction, and then swiftly away again. Mrs. Adair was perfectly dressed, perfectly groomed and apparently perfectly composed. But her composure was a brave pretense. This awful Chinaman who had taken command of her life held in his grasp all that made life dear to her. Her gloved hand rested motionless upon the chair-arm, but she turned her head aside and bit her lip.

The air of the small, quiet room was heavy with a smell of stale incense.

"I am an old man," the compelling voice continued; "older than your imagination would permit you to believe." Those jade-green eyes were closed again—the speaker seemed to be thinking aloud. "I have been worshiped, I have been scorned; I have been flattered, mocked, betrayed, treated as a charlatan—as a criminal. There are warrants for my arrest in three European countries. Yet always I have been selfless." He paused. He was so still, so seemingly impassive, that he might have been a carven image. . . .

"My crimes, so termed, have been merely the removal from my path of those who obstructed me. Always I have dreamed of a sane world, yet men have called me mad; of a world in which war should be impossible, disease eliminated, over-population checked, labor found for all willing hands—a world of peace. Save only three, I have found no human soul, of my own race or another, to work wholly for that goal. And now my most implacable enemy is upon me. . . ."

Suddenly the green eyes opened. Long, slender yellow hands with incredibly pointed nails were torn from the sleeves of the yellow robe. Dr. Fu Manchu stood upright, raising those evilly beautiful hands above him. A note of exaltation came into his voice. Mrs. Adair clutched the arms of the chair in which she sat. Never before had her eventful life brought her in touch with inspired fanaticism.

"Gods of my fathers—" pitched so high that strange voice laid a queer stress on sibilants—"masters of the world! Are all my dreams to end in a prison cell, in the death of a common felon?"

For a while he stood upright, arms upraised, then dropped back again into his chair and concealed his hands in the sleeves of his robe.

Moya Adair strove for composure. This man terrified her as no man in her experience ever had had power to do. Instinctively she had realized the dreadful crimes that marked his life. He was coldly remorseless. Now, shaken emotionally by this glimpse of the hidden Fu Manchu, she wondered if she had become subjected to an inspired madman. Or had this eerie master of her destiny achieved a philosophy beyond the reach of her intellectual powers?

When the Chinaman spoke again his harsh voice was perfectly cool.

"In the United States I have found a crude, but efficient, organization ready to my hand. Prohibition attracted to this country the trained lawbreakers of the world. They had no

76

purpose but that of personal gain. The sanity of President Roosevelt has terminated some of these promising careers. Many spiders are missing, but the webs can be mended. You see, Moya Adair—" the green eyes were fixed upon her, glitteringly, hypnotically—"although women can never understand, were not meant to understand—it is to women that men always look for understanding."

Now she was unable to withdraw her gaze. He had taken control of her—she knew herself helpless. There was magic in those long green eyes; their power was terrible. But something there was also—something she had not looked for— which reconciled her to this control.

"I do not trust you—no woman is to be trusted in a world of men. Yet because I am a man too, and very lonely in this my last battle to crush what the West calls civilization . . . I will admit you one step further into my plans—I have means of watching those who profess to serve me. I know where I can place my trust. . . ."

Mrs. Adair experienced a sensation as though the speaker's eyes had usurped the whole of the small room. She was submerged in a green lake, magnetic, thrilling, absorbing. The strange voice reached her from far away: she was resigned to the thralldom.

"There is no crime except the crime of disobedience to my will. My conception of life transcends the laws of all men living today. When I achieve my ambition, those who stand beside me will share my mastery of the world. Of the demagogues battling for power in this troubled country I have selected one as my own. . . ."

Moya Adair emerged from the green lake. Dr. Fu Manchu had closed his eyes. He sat like a carven image of a dead god behind the lacquered table.

"I am sending you," the guttural, imperious voice continued, "to Harvey Bragg. You will act in accordance with instructions."

2

In the large Park Avenue apartment of Emmanuel Dumas, Harvey Bragg was holding one of those receptions which at once scandalized and fascinated his millions of followers when they read about them in the daily newspapers. These orgiastic entertainments, which sometimes resembled a burlesque of a Neronian banquet and sometimes a parody of a Hollywood cabaret scene, had marked his triumphal progress from the state which he represented right up to New York.

"Bluebeard of the Backwoods"—as some political writer

77

had dubbed him—Bragg had interested, amused, scandalized and horrified the inhabitants of the South and of the Middle West, and now was preparing to show himself a second Cyrus, master of the modern Babylon. New York was the bright orange upon which his greedy eyes were set. New York he would squeeze dry.

Lola Dumas' somewhat equivocal place in his affairs merely served to add glamour to the man's strange reputation. Now, entertaining in her father's home, he demonstrated himself to be that which he believed himself to be—an up-to-date emperor whose wishes transcended all laws.

Lola had been twice married and twice divorced. After each of these divorces she had reverted to her family name, of which she was inordinately proud. Emmanuel Dumas, who had made a colossal fortune in the boom and lost most of it in the slump, claimed, without warranty which any man could recognize, to be descended from the brilliant quadroon who created the Three Musketeers. If a picturesque personality and a shock of frizzy white hair had been acceptable as evidence, then any jury must have granted his claim.

A moral laxity notable even during the regime of Prohibition had characterized his scandalous life. In later years, when most of his Wall Street contemporaries had been washed up, the continued prosperity of Emmanuel Dumas became a mystery insoluble. The prurient ascribed it to the association between his beautiful daughter and the flamboyant but electric politician who threatened to become the Mussolini of the United States.

The room in which the reception was being held was decorated with a valuable collection of original drawings by Maurice Leloir, representing episodes in the novels of Alexandre Dumas. Rapiers, pistols, muskets adorned the walls. Here was a suit of armor which had once belonged to Louis XIII; there a red hat in a glass case, which, according to an inscription, had been worn by that king's subtle minister, the Cardinal de Richelieu. There were powder boxes, mirrors and jewels, once the property of Anne of Austria. These historical objects, and many others, arrested the glance in every direction.

Lola Dumas wore an emerald-green robe, or rest gown, its gauzy texture scarcely more than veiling her slender body. She was surrounded by a group of enthusiastic journalists. Her father was attired in a sort of velvet smock tied with a loose black bow at his neck. He, also, held court.

As a prominent supporter, and frequently the host, of Harvey Bragg, he had entered upon a new term of notoriety.

These two, father and daughter, by virtue of their beauty alone, for Emmanuel Dumas was a strikingly handsome man, must have focused interest in almost any gathering.

The room was packed from end to end. Prominent society people, who once would have shunned the Dumas apartment, might be seen in groups admiring the strange ornaments, studying the paintings; eager to attract the attention of this singular man once taboo, but now bathed in a blaze of limelight.

Politicians of all shades of opinion were represented.

The air was heavy with tobacco smoke; the buzz of chatter simian; champagne flowed almost as freely as water from the fountains of Versailles. Many notable people came and went unnoticed from this omnium-gatherum, for the dazzling personalities of the hostess and her father outshone them all. One would have thought that no man and few women could have diverted attention from the glittering pair; yet when, unheralded, Harvey Bragg came striding into the room, instantly the Dumas were forgotten.

All eyes were turned in Bragg's direction. Sascha lamps appeared from leather cases in which they had lain ready; a platoon of cameras came into action; notebooks were hastily opened.

Bluebeard Bragg was certainly an arresting figure. His nickname was double-edged. Bragg's marital record alone would have explained it; the man's intense swarthiness equally might have accounted for the "bluebeard." Slightly above medium height, he was built like an acrobat. The span of his shoulders was enormous: his waist measurement would have pleased many women. Withal, he had that enormous development of thigh and the muscular shapely calves seen in male members of the Russian Ballet. He had, too, the light, springy walk of a boxer; and his truculent, black-browed face, lighted by clear hazel eyes that danced with humor, was crowned by a profusion of straight, gleaming, black hair. Closely though he was shaved, for Harvey Bragg was meticulous in his person, his jaw and chin showed blue through the powder.

"Folks!" he cried (his voice resembled that of a ship's officer bellowing orders through a gale). "I'm real sorry to be late, but Mr. and Miss Dumas will have been taking good care of you, I guess. To tell you the truth, folks, I had a bad hangover . . ."

This admission was greeted by laughter from his followers.

"I've just got up, that's the truth. Knew I was expected to see people; jumped in the bath, shaved, and here I am!"

79

There came a dazzling flash of light. The cameras had secured a record, in characteristic pose and costume, of this ex-lord of the backwoods who aimed at the White House.

He wore a sky-blue bathrobe, and apart from a pair of red slippers, apparently nothing else. But he was Harvey Bragg—Bluebeard; the man who threatened the Constitution, the coming Hitler of the United States. His ugliness—for despite his power and the athletic lines of his figure the man was ugly—dominated that gathering. His circus showman's voice shouted down all opposition. No normal personality could live near him. He was Harvey Bragg. He was "It." He was the omnipresent potential Dictator of America.

Among the group of reporters hanging on Bragg's words was one strange to the others; a newcomer representing New York's smartest weekly. He was tall, taciturn, and slightly built. He had thick, untidy hair, graying over the temples, a stubbly black beard and mustache, and wore spectacles. His wide-brimmed black hat and caped coat spoke of Greenwich Village.

His deep-set eyes had missed nothing, and nobody, of importance in the room. He had made few notes. Now he was watching Bluebeard intently.

"Boys and girls!"—arms raised, Harvey Bragg gave his benediction to everyone present. "I know what you all want to hear. You want to hear what I'm going to say to Orwin Prescott at Carnegie Hall."

He lowered his arms in acknowledgment of the excited buzz followed by silence which greeted this remark.

"I'm going to say just one thing. And this goes, boys—" he included with a sweeping gesture of his left hand the whole of the newspaper men present—"with you as well as with everybody else. I'm going to say just this: Our country, which we all love, is unhappy. We have seen hard times— but we've battled through. We've got sand. We're not dead yet by a long shot. No sir! But we're alive to the dangers ahead. And I want to ask you, Dr. Orwin Prescott, just this: Are you peddling junk for the Abbot of Holy Thorn or are you selling goods of your own?"

Loud applause followed this, led by Dumas père et fille.

"I'm not saying, folks, that Abbot Donegal's stuff is all backfire. I'm saying that second-hand promises are bad debts. I want to hear of anything that Orwin Prescott has promised which Orwin Prescott has done. *I* don't promise things. I *do* things. No decent citizen ever reported for work to a depot of the League of Good Americans who didn't get a job!"

Again he was interrupted by loud applause. . . .

"The man we're all looking for is the man who does things. Very well. Seconds out! The fight starts! On my right, Donegal—Prescott. On my left: Harvey Bragg! America for every man and every man for America!"

Cheers and a deafening clapping of hands rewarded the speaker. Harvey Bragg stood, arms upraised forensically, dominating that gathering excited by his crude oratory. At which moment, even as Sascha lights flashed and cameras clicked:

"A lady to see you, Mr. Bragg," came a discreet whisper.

Harvey Bragg lowered his arms, reluctantly relinquishing that heroic pose, and glanced aside. His confidential secretary, Salvaletti, stood at his elbow. There was an interchange of glances. Reporters surged around them.

"Urgent?" Harvey Bragg whispered.

"Number 12."

Bragg started, but recovered himself.

"Easy-looking?"

"A beauty."

"Excuse me, folks!" Bragg cried, his tremendous voice audible above the excitement. "I'll be right back in two minutes."

Of those who actually overheard this whispered conversation, Lola Dumas was one. She bit her lip, turned, and crossed to a senator from the South who was no friend of Harvey Bragg's. The other was the new reporter. He followed Lola Dumas and presently engaged her in conversation.

More wine was uncorked. Newspaper men always welcomed an assignment to the Dumas apartment. . . .

Rather more than five minutes had elapsed when Harvey Bragg came back. He was holding the hand of a very pretty woman whose smart frock did justice to a perfect figure, and whose little French hat displayed mahogany curls to their best advantage.

"Folks!" he roared. "I want you all to know my new secretary." His roving glance sought and found Lola Dumas: he smiled wickedly. "What this little girl doesn't know about the political situation not even Harvey Bragg can tell her. . . ."

3

Although one calling might not have suspected the fact, the whole of the Regal Tower, most expensive and fashionable part of the Regal-Athenian Hotel, was held by police officers and federal agents. Those visitors who applied for accommodation in this section of the hotel were informed that it was full; those who had been in occupation had very courteously been moved elsewhere on the plea of urgent alterations.

From the porters at the door in the courtyard to the clerks in the reception desk, the liftman and the bellboys, there was no man whose uniform did not disguise a detective.

Elaborate precautions had been taken to ensure the privacy of incoming and outgoing telephone calls. No general headquarters ever had been more closely guarded. Armageddon was being waged, but few appreciated the fact. In the past Wellington had crushed Buonaparte's ambition to control Europe, but the great Corsican fought at Waterloo with a blunted sword. Foch and his powerful allies had thrown back Marshal von Hindenburg and the finest military machine in history since the retreat from Moscow broke the Grand Army of Napoleon. But now, Nayland Smith, backed by the government of the United States, fought, not for the salvage of the Constitution, not for the peace of the country, but for the future of the world. And the opposing forces were commanded by a mad genius. . . .

Dressed in an old tweed suit, pipe clenched between his teeth, he paced up and down the sitting room. His powers were all that a field marshal could have demanded. His chief of staff, Mark Hepburn, was one such as he would have selected. But . . .

Someone had unlocked the door of the apartment.

Fey appeared in the vestibule as if by magic, his right hand in his coat pocket. Nayland Smith stepped smartly to the left, taking up a position from which he could see the entrance. A tall, pale, bearded man came in, wearing a caped coat and a wide-brimmed black hat. . . .

"Hepburn!" cried Smith, and hurried forward to meet him. "Thank heavens you're back safe. What news?"

Captain Mark Hepburn, U.S.M.C., a parody of his normal self, smiled wryly. His pallor, his graying temples, were artificial, but the beard and mustache were carefully tended natural products, although at the moment chemically improved. The character he was assuming was one which he might be called upon to maintain for a considerable time, in accordance with plan.

"Just left the Bragg reception at the Dumas apartment," he said, removing his glasses and staring rather haggardly at Nayland Smith. "There isn't much to report except that Bragg's confidential secretary, Salvaletti, is pretty obviously the link with Fu Manchu."

"Then Bragg is doubly covered," said Nayland Smith

grimly. "Lola Dumas is almost certainly one of Dr. Fu Manchu's agents."

"Yes." Mark Hepburn dropped wearily into an armchair. "But there's some friction in that quarter. A woman was announced just before I left, and Bragg went out to interview her. I managed to pick up scraps of the conversation between Salvaletti and Bragg, but from the way Lola Dumas watched Bragg, I gathered that their relations were becoming strained."

"Describe Salvaletti," said Nayland Smith succinctly.

Mark Hepburn half closed his eyes. Smith watched him. There was something odd in Hepburn's manner.

"Above medium height, pale, stooping. Light-blue eyes, dark, lank hair, a soft voice and a sickly smile."

"Seen him before?"

"Never! He's a new one on me."

"Probably indigenous to the American underworld," Smith murmured; "therefore I should not know him. You are sure it was a woman who was announced?"

"Positive. Harvey Bragg brought her into the room and displayed her to the company as his new secretary. It's about this woman I want to talk to you. I want your advice. I don't know what to do. It was Mrs. Adair . . . who escaped, thanks to my negligence, from the Tower of the Holy Thorn . . ."

17 *THE ABBOT'S MOVE*

IN THE GOTHIC DOME where most of the life of the Memory Man was passed, lights were extinguished. A red spark marking the tip of a burning Egyptian cigarette glowed in the darkness.

There was a short silence, and then:

"Report," directed the familiar, hated voice, "from Numbers covering Nayland Smith."

"Three have been received since I relayed. Shall I repeat them in detail or summarize their contents?"

"Summarize."

"There is no certain evidence that he has left his base during the last twelve hours. A report from Number 44 suggests that he may have visited the police mortuary.

83

This report unconfirmed. Two Numbers and eight operatives, with two Z-cars, covering Centre Street. Federal Agent Hepburn not reported to have moved out from the Regal Tower. This is a summary of the three reports."

Darkness still prevailed. . . .

"The latest report regarding Abbot Donegal."

"Received thirty minutes after that last relayed. A man answering to the abbot's description reported as hiring a car at Elmira. Believed to have arrived there from the West by American Airlines. Posing as Englishman. Wears single eyeglass and carries golfing kit. . . ."

In the tower study so oddly corresponding in point of elevation with Nayland Smith's headquarters, but which bore an atmosphere of stale incense whereas the apartment high above the Regal-Athenian Hotel was laden with fumes of broad-cut smoking mixture, Dr. Fu Manchu sat behind the lacquer table. There was no one else in the room.

The life of one who aspires to empire—though thousands may await his commands—is a wan and lonely life. Solitude is the mother of inspiration. The Chinaman, these reports from the Memory Man received, sat in his high, carven chair, eyes closed. He was speaking as though to one standing near him. On the little polished switchboard two spots of light glowed; green, and amber.

"Dispatch a party in a Z-car," he directed, his voice unemotional but the gutturals very marked. "Explore all farms, roadhouses and hotels along the route which I have indicated. Abbot Donegal is reported as traveling incognito. He may be posing as an English tourist. If found, he is not to be molested, but he must be detained. Instruct the Number in charge to send in reports from point to point. This is a personal order from the President."

A slender yellow hand with long, pointed nails reached out. The two lights disappeared. Dr. Fu Manchu opened his eyes: their greenness was dimmed. He raised the lid of a silver box which stood upon the table and from it took a small, exquisitely made opium-smoking outfit. He lighted the tiny lamp and inserted a gold bodkin into a container holding the black gum which is born of the white poppy. He had not slept for forty-eight hours. . . .

Almost at the same moment, in a room at the top of the Regal Tower, Mark Hepburn spoke on the telephone. He had had all calls put through to his own room in order that Nayland Smith might not be disturbed; for, at last, Smith was sleeping.

"This Englishman who left Airlines at Elmira," he said in

his dry, monotonous voice, "sounds to me like the man we're looking for. The fact that he wears plus fours and a monocle doesn't count, nor the fact that he is traveling with a golf bag. I have learned that Abbot Donegal used a single eyeglass before he took to spectacles. He could probably get along with it quite well except for reading. Also, he's a golfer. The English accent means nothing. Abbot Donegal is a trained orator. Check up on all roadhouses and hotels along possible routes which he might follow if, as you suspect, he left by road from Elmira. Take a radio car so we keep track of you. Report from point to point. If he is definitely identified take no action until you have my instructions. We have contrived to silence the newspapers about his disappearance. But he is probably coming to New York to take Prescott's place at Carnegie Hall—if Prescott fails to arrive. This would ruin our plans. . . . All right—good-bye."

He hung up the receiver.

2

In the vestibule of a small country hotel two men sat over their coffee before a crackling log fire. Outside, a storm raged. The howling of the wind could be heard in the chimney, and whenever the main door was opened a veil of sleet might be seen in the light shining out from inside. It was a wild night.

The men seated before the fire were an odd couple. One, of slight but wiry build, clean-shaven and fresh colored, lean faced, his hair graying, wore a tweed suit with plus fours, thick woolen stockings and brown brogues. A monocle glittered in the firelight as he bent to refill his pipe. His companion, a clergyman equally lean of feature, watched him, blinking his eyes in the way of one shortsighted. A close observer might have noted a physical but not a spiritual resemblance.

"I mean to say," said the man with the monocle, stuffing tobacco into the bowl of his briar, "it's a bad time to see America. I agree. But I couldn't help myself, if you see what I mean. It had to be the now or never sort of thing. People have been awfully nice—" he paused to strike a match— "*I* am the silly ass; nobody else to blame. Thanks to you, I know it would be stupid to push on tonight."

"I am told," said the priest, his gentle voice a contrast to that of the other speaker, "That Colonel Challoner lives some twenty miles from here. For my own part I have no choice."

"What!" The man with the monocle, in the act of lighting his pipe, paused, looked up. "You're pushing on?"

"Duty demands."

"Oh, I see, sir. A sick call, I take it?"

The clergyman watched him silently for a few moments. "A sick call—yes. . . ."

The outer door opened, admitting a blast of icy air. Three men came in, the last to enter closing the door behind him. They were useful-looking men, thickset and hard.

"In luck at last!" one of them exclaimed.

All three were watching the man with the monocle. One, who was evidently the leader of the party, square-jawed and truculent, raised his hand as if to silence the others, and stepped forward. As he did so the proprietor of the hotel appeared through an inner doorway. The man paused, glanced at him.

"Find some Scotch," he ordered—"real Scotch. Not here —inside, someplace. Me and these boys have business to talk over."

The proprietor, a taciturn New Englander, nodded and disappeared. The speaker, not removing his hat, stood staring down at the man with the eyeglass. His companions were looking in the same direction. The focus of attention, pipe between his teeth, gazed at the three in blank astonishment.

"Don't want to intrude—" the leader gave a cursory nod to the clergyman—"real sorry to interrupt; but I must ask *you*—" he placed a compelling hand on the shoulder of the wearer of the monocle—"to step inside for just a minute. Got a couple o' questions to put to you."

"What the deuce d'you mean?"

"I'm a government agent, and I'm on urgent business. I take it you'll help?" He indicated the inner doorway. "Just a couple o' questions."

"I never heard such balderdash in my life," the other declared. He turned to the clergyman. "Did you?"

"It will probably save trouble in the long run if you assist the officer."

"Right-oh. I'm obliged for the tip. Very funny and odd, but still . . ."

Pipe firmly clenched between his teeth, he walked out followed by the leader of the party, the other two members of which brought up the rear. They found themselves in a small back hallway from which arose a stair communicating with upper floors. On a table stood a bottle of whisky, glasses and a pitcher of ice water.

"No need to go further," said the agent; "we're all set here." He stared hard at the man in plus fours. "Listen, Abbot: why the fancy dress?"

"What d'you mean, Abbot?" was the angry reply. "My name's not Abbot, and if it were you'd have a damned cheek to address me in that way!"

"Cut the funny lines. They ain't funny. I'm here on business. You don't have to try to make me laugh. What's the name that goes with the eye-window?"

"I'm tempted," said the man addressed, speaking with a cold anger which his amiably vacant manner would not have led one to anticipate, "to tell you to go to hell." He focused an icy stare in turn upon each of the three grim faces. "You've stepped off with the wrong foot, my friends."

He plunged to an inside pocket. Instantly three steel barrels covered him. He ignored them handing a British passport to the leader of the party. There was a minute of ominous silence, during which the man scrutinized the passport and the photograph, comparing the latter with its subject. At last:

"Boys!"—he turned to his satellites—"we're up the wrong gum tree. We've got hold of Captain the Honorable George Forsdyke-Forsdyke of the Grenadier Guards! Schultz, jump to the phone. Notify Base and ask for President's instructions. . . ."

Some ten minutes later the Honorable George Forsdyke-Forsdyke found himself in sole possession of the little vestibule. The three federal officers had gone. He had had a glimpse through the driving sleet of a powerful car drawn up before the door. The amiable clergyman had gone. He was alone, mystified, irritated.

"Well, I'm damned!" he said.

At which moment, and while through the howling of the storm the purr of the departing car might still be heard, came the roar of a second and even more powerful engine. Again the door was thrown open, and two men came in. Forsdyke-Forsdyke turned and faced them.

"O.K. this time, Chief!" said one, exhibiting a row of glittering white teeth.

The other nodded and stepped forward.

"Good evening, Dom Patrick Donegal," he said, and pulled aside a dripping leather overcoat to exhibit a gold badge. "A nice run you've given us!"

"Here! I say!' exclaimed Forsdyke-Forsdyke. "This damn joke is getting stale!"

And in a dilapidated but roadworthy Ford the amiable priest was drilling furiously through the storm in the direction of New York: the Abbot of Holy Thorn was one stage further on his self-imposed journey.

18 *MRS. ADAIR REAPPEARS*

MOYA ADAIR stepped out of the elevator, crossed the marble lobby of the luxurious apartment house and came out onto Park Avenue. She was muffled up in her mink coat, the little Basque beret which she wore in rough weather crushed tightly upon mahogany-red curls. A high, fiercely cold wind had temporarily driven the clouds away, and a frosty moon looked down from a glittering sky. Moya inhaled delightedly the ice-cold air from the Avenue. It was clean and wholesome in contrast to the smoke-laden atmosphere of the Dumas' apartment.

Her new assignment terrified her. For some reason known only to the President, that awful Chinaman who dominated her life, she had been chosen to supplant Lola Dumas. And she feared the enmity of Lola Dumas second only to that of the President. It was the yellow streak, more marked in her than in her father, which made her terrible; Moya, who had met her several times, had often thought of Lola as a beautiful, evil priestess of Voodoo—a dabbler in strange rites.

She began to walk briskly in the direction of a near-by hotel where, as Miss Eileen Breon, accommodation had been provided for her by the organization to which unwillingly she belonged. She felt as though she had escaped from an ever-present danger.

Harvey Bragg, potential Dictator of America, had accepted her appearance in the spirit in which sultans had formerly welcomed the present of a Circassian slave girl. And she had nowhere to turn for help—unless to the President. Oddly enough, she trusted that majestic but evil man.

The newspapers, in which politics occupied so much space, were nevertheless giving prominence to the mysterious death of James Richet. In her heart of hearts Moya Adair believed that James Richet had been executed by the President's orders. The power of the sinister Chinaman was terrifying; yet although he held a life dearer than her own in his hands, Moya's service was not wholly one of fear. He had never called upon her to do anything which her philosophy told her to be despicable. Sometimes in her dreams she thought that he was Satan, fallen son of the morning, but in her very soul she knew that his word was inviolable; that execrable though his deeds appeared to Western eyes, paradoxically he might be trusted to give measure for measure.

Her first instructions in regard to Bragg had related to the forthcoming debate at Carnegie Hall. She had given him certain typed notes, with many of which he had quarreled furiously. The odd fact had dawned upon her during this first interview that Bragg had never met the President!

"I'll play this bunch of underground stiffs just as long as their funds last out," he had declared. "But you can tell your 'President' that what I need is his money, not his orders!"

Moya pointed out that directions received in the past had invariably led to success. Bragg, becoming more and more deeply intrigued, had tried to cross-examine. Failing, he had changed his tactics and made coarsely violent love to her. . . .

She raised her face, as she hurried along, to the healing purity of the moonlight. Salvaletti tactfully had terminated that first hateful interview; but she shrank from Salvaletti as she instinctively shrank from snakes. Since then, the scene had been re-enacted—many times.

She had reached her hotel and was just turning into the doorway when a hand touched her shoulder. . . .

It had come—and, almost, it was welcome!

Since that snowy night outside the Tower of the Holy Thorn, hourly she had expected arrest. She glanced swiftly aside.

A tall, bearded man who wore glasses, a black hat and a caped topcoat stood at her elbow.

"Live here, Mrs. Adair?" he asked dryly.

A stream of traffic released at that moment by a changing light almost drowned her reply, in so low a voice did she speak.

"Yes. Who are you, and what do you want?"

Yet even as she spoke she knew that she had heard that monotonous voice before. Under the shadow of his hat brim the man's eyes glistened through the spectacles.

"I want to step inside and have a word with you."

"But I don't know you."

The man pulled the caped coat aside, and she saw the glitter of a gold badge. Yes, she had been right—a federal officer! It was finished: she was in the hands of the law; free of the awful President, but . . .

The lobby of the expensively discreet apartment hotel was deserted, for the hour was late. But as they sat down facing each other across a small table, Moya Adair had entirely recovered her composure. She had learned in these last years that she could not afford to be a woman; she blessed the heritage of courage and common sense which was hers. It had saved her from madness, from suicide; from even worse than suicide.

And now the federal agent removed his black hat. She knew him and, in the moment of recognition, wondered why she was glad.

She smiled into the bearded face—and Moya was not ignorant of the fact that her smile was enchanting.

"Am I to consider myself under arrest?" she asked. "Because, if so, I don't expect to have the same luck as last time."

Mark Hepburn removed his black-rimmed spectacles and stared at her steadily. She remembered his deep-set eyes—remembered them as dreamy eyes, the eyes of a poet. Now, they were cold. Her brave flippancy had awakened the Quaker ancestors, those restless Puritan spirits who watched eternally over Mark Hepburn's soul. This was the traditional attitude of a hardened adventuress. When he replied, his voice sounded very harsh.

"Technically, it's my duty to arrest you, Mrs. Adair; but we're not so trammeled by red tape as the police." He was watching her firm, beautifully modeled lips and trying to solve the mystery of how she could give her kisses to Harvey Bragg. "I have been waiting ever since that night at the Tower for a chat with you."

She made no reply.

"An associate of yours on Abbot Donegal's staff was murdered recently, right outside the Regal Hotel. You may have heard of it?"

Moya Adair nodded.

"Yes. But why do you say he was murdered?"

"Because I know who murdered him and so do you: *Dr. Fu Manchu.*"

He laid stress on the name, staring into Moya's eyes. But with those words he had enabled her to speak the truth, unafraid. That he referred to the President she divined; but to all connected with the organization the President's name was unknown, except that on two occasions she had heard him referred to as "the Marquis."

"To the best of my knowledge," she replied quietly, "I have never met anyone called Dr. Fu Manchu."

Mark Hepburn, who had obtained Nayland Smith's consent to handle this matter in his own way, realized that he had undertaken a task beyond his powers. This woman knew that she was fighting for her freedom—and he could not torture her. He was silent for a while, watching her, then:

"I should hate to think of you," he said, "undergoing a police interrogation, Mrs. Adair. But you must know as well as I know that there's a plot afoot to obtain control of this country. You are in on it: it's *my* business to be. I can guarantee your safety; you can quit the country if you like. I know where you come from in County Wicklow; I know where your father is at the present time. . . ."

Moya Adair's eyes opened fully for a moment, and then quite closed. This man was honest, straight as a die: he offered her freedom, the chance to live her own life again . . . and she could not, dared not, accept what he offered!

"You have no place in murder gangs. You belong in another sphere. I want you to go back to it. I want you to be on the right side, not on the wrong. Trust me, and you won't regret it, but try any tricks and you will leave me no alternative."

He ceased speaking, watching Moya's face. She was looking away from him with an unseeing gaze. But he knew because of his sensitively sympathetic character that she had understood and was battling with some problem outside his knowledge. The half-lighted lobby was very quiet, so that when a man who had been seated in a chair at the further end, unsuspected, crossed to the elevator, Mark Hepburn turned sharply, glancing in his direction. Mrs. Adair remained abstracted. At the end of a long silence:

"I am going to trust you," she said, and looked at him steadily, "because I know I can. I am glad we have met—for after all there may be a way. Will you believe me if I swear to carry out what I am going to suggest? . . ."

Two minutes later, the man who had gone up in the elevator was speaking on the telephone in his apartment.

"Miss Eileen Breon talking in the lobby with a bearded man wearing spectacles and a black caped topcoat. Time 2.55 A.M. Report from Number 49."

19 *THE CHINESE CATACOMBS*

ORWIN PRESCOTT opened his eyes and stared about the small bedroom—at two glass-topped tables, white enameled walls, at a green-shaded lamp set near an armchair in which a nurse was seated; a very beautiful nurse whose dark eyes were fixed upon him intently.

He did not speak immediately, but lay there watching her and thinking.

Something had happened—at Carnegie Hall. The memory was not clear-cut; but something had happened in the course of his debate with Harvey Bragg. Had overstudy, overanxiety, resulted in a nervous breakdown? This was clearly a clinic in which he found himself.

In this idea he thought he saw a solution of the mental confusion in his mind. He was fascinated by the darkly beautiful face framed in the white nurse's cap. Vaguely, he knew that he had seen the nurse before. He moved slowly, and found to his delight that there seemed to be nothing physically wrong with him. Then he spoke:

"Nurse—" his voice was full, authoritative; he recognized that in brain and body he was unimpaired by whatever had happened—"this is very bewildering. Please tell me where I am."

The nurse stood up and walked to the bed: she was very slender, her movements were graceful.

"You are in the Park House Clinic, Dr. Prescott, and I am happy to say entirely your old self again."

He watched her full lips, sensitive with sympathy.

"I collapsed during the debate?"

She shook her head smilingly.

"What a strange idea, Doctor. But I can understand that that would be upon your mind. Surely you remember walking out from Weaver's Farm, your cousin's home? There was snow on the ground, and you slipped and fell; you were unconscious for a long time. They brought you here. You are under the care of Dr. Sigmund. But all's well, you see."

"I feel as well as I ever felt in my life."

"You *are* as well."

She sat down beside the bed and rested a cool hand on his

forehead. Her dark eyes when she bent towards him he thought extraordinarily beautiful.

And now Orwin Prescott sat up. There was vigor in his movements.

"Still I don't understand. I assure you I recall whole passages in the debate at Carnegie Hall! I can remember Bragg's triumph, my own ineptitude, my inability to counter his crude thrusts . . ."

"You were dreaming, Doctor; naturally the debate has been on your mind. Don't overtire yourself."

Gently she compelled him to lie down again.

"Then what really occurred?" he challenged.

The nurse smiled again soothingly.

"Nothing has occurred yet; except that we have got you in splendid form for the debate tonight."

"What!"

"The debate at Carnegie Hall takes place tonight, and after a talk with your secretary, Mr. Norbert, who is waiting outside, I am quite sure you will be ready for it."

Orwin Prescott stared at the speaker fixedly. A new, a dreadful idea, had presented itself to him, and:

"Do you assure me," he said—"I beg you will be frank— that the debate has not taken place?"

"I give you my word," she answered, meeting his glance with absolute candor. "There is no mystery about it all except that you have had a vivid dream of the thing upon which your brain has been centered for so long."

"Then I have been here——?"

"Ever since the accident, Doctor." She stood up, crossed, and pressed a bell. "I am sending for Mr. Norbert," she explained. "He is naturally anxious to see you."

But whole phases of the debate seemed to ring in Prescott's ears! He saw himself, he saw Bragg, he saw the vast audience as though a talking picture were being performed inside his brain!

The door opened, and Norbert came in; dark, perfectly groomed. The neat black mustache suggested a British army officer. He came forward with outstretched hand.

"Dr. Prescott!" he exclaimed, "this is fine." He turned to the nurse. "Nurse Arlen, I must congratulate you. Dr. Sigmund I know is delighted."

"Perhaps, Norbert," said Prescott, "now that you are here we can get this thing straight. There are many points which are quite dark to me. It is all but incredible that I could have lain here——"

"Forget all that, Doctor," Norbert urged, "for the moment. I am told that you are fit to talk shop, and so there is one thing upon which to concentrate—tonight's debate."

"It really is tonight?"

"I understand your bewilderment—but it really is tonight. Imagine our anxiety! It means the biggest check in Bragg's headlong career to the White House. I am going to refresh your memory with all our notes up to the date of the accident at Weaver's Farm. I had left you, you recall, to go to Washington. I have added some later points. Do you feel up to business?"

He turned to the nurse. "Nurse Arlen, you are sure it will not tire him?"

"Dr. Sigmund is confident that it will complete his cure."

Orwin Prescott's glance lingered on the beautiful dark face. Then, again sitting up, he turned to Maurice Norbert. He was conscious of growing enthusiasm, of an intense ardor for his great task.

"Perhaps one day I shall understand," he said, "but at the moment——"

Norbert opened his portfolio.

2

In a small, square stone-faced room deep in the Chinese Catacombs, old Sam Pak crouched upon a settee placed against a wall. One would have thought, watching the bent, motionless figure, that it was that of an embalmed Chinaman. There was little furniture in the room: a long narrow table, with a chair set behind it; upon the table appointments suggesting a medical consultant; upon the floor two rugs. The arched doorway was closed by scarlet tapestry drapings.

Now these were drawn aside. A tall figure entered, a man who wore a black overcoat with a heavy astrakhan collar, and an astrakhan cap upon his head; also, he wore spectacles. As he entered, and he entered quite silently, Sam Pak stood up as if electrified, bowing very low in the Chinese manner. The tall man walked to the chair behind the table and seated himself.

He removed his spectacles. The wonderful lined face which had reminded so many observers of that of Seti I was revealed in its yellow mastery. Dr. Fu Manchu spoke.

"Be seated," he said.

Sam Pak resumed his seat.

"You guarantee," the harsh, guttural voice continued—those brilliant green eyes were fixed inflexibly upon the ancient Chinaman, "the appearance of Dr. Orwin Prescott to-night?"

"You have my word, Marquis."

"Three drops of the tincture must be administered ten minutes before he leaves."

"It shall be administered."

"Already, my friend, we are suffering at the hands of the bunglers we are compelled to employ. The pestilential priest Patrick Donegal has slipped through all our nets. Nor is it certain that he is not in the hands of Enemy Number One."

The ancient head of Sam Pak was slowly nodded.

"The appearance of the Abbot at Carnegie Hall," Dr. Fu Manchu continued, "might be fatal to my plans. Yet—" removing heavy gloves he laid two long bony hands upon the table before him—"I remain in uncertainty."

"In war, Master, there is always an element of uncertainty."

"Uncertainty is part of the imperfect plan," Fu Manchu replied sibilantly. "Only the fool is uncertain. But the odds are heavy, my friend. Produce to me the man Herman Grosset, whom you have chosen for tonight's great task."

Sam Pak moved slightly, pressing a bell. The curtain was drawn aside, and a Chinese boy appeared. A few words of rapid instructions and he went out, dropping the curtain behind him.

There was silence in the queer room. Dr. Fu Manchu, eyes half closed, leaned back in his chair. Sam Pak resembled a mummy set upright in ghastly raillery by some lightminded excavator. Then came vigorous footsteps, the curtains were switched aside, and a man strode in.

Above medium height, of tremendously powerful build, dark faced and formidable, Herman Grosset was a man with whom no one would willingly pick a quarrel. He looked about him challengingly, meeting the gaze of those half-closed green eyes with apparent indifference and merely glancing at old Sam Pak. He stepped to the table, staring down at Dr. Fu Manchu.

His movements, his complete sang-froid, something, too, in the dark-browed face, might have reminded a close observer of Harvey Bragg; and indeed, Grosset was a half brother of the potential dictator of the United States.

"So you are the President?" he said—and his gruff voice held a note of amused self-assurance. "I'm sure glad to meet you, President. There's some saying about 'fools step in . . .' I don't know if it applies to me, but it's kind of funny that you've stayed in the background with Harvey, but asked me to step right into the office."

"The circumstances under which you stepped into the office," came coldly, sibilantly, "are such that if you displease me, you will find it difficult to step out again."

"Oh! I'm supposed to be impressed by the closed auto and the secret journey?" Grosset laughed and banged his fist on the table. "Look!"

With a lightning movement he snatched an automatic from his pocket and covered Dr. Fu Manchu.

"I take big risks because I know how to protect myself. While you're for Harvey, I'm for you. If I thought you'd dare to cross him, you'd start out for your Chinese paradise this very minute. Harvey is going to be President. Harvey is going to be Dictator. Nothing else can set the country to rights. I wouldn't hesitate—" he tapped the gun barrel on the table, watching out of the corner of his eye the old Chinaman on the settee—"I wouldn't hesitate to shoot down any man living that got in his way. When he made me boss of his bodyguard he did the right thing."

Dr. Fu Manchu's long, yellow hands with their cruelly pointed nails remained quite motionless. He did not stir a muscle; his eyes were mere green slits in the yellow mask. Then:

"No one doubts your loyalty to Harvey Bragg," he said softly; "that point is not in dispute. It is known that you love him."

"I'd die for him."

The automatic disappeared into the pocket from which it had been taken. Two men stripped to the waist entered so silently that even the movement of the curtain was not audible. They sprang from behind like twin panthers upon Grosset.

"Hell!" he roared, "what's this game!"

He bent his powerful body forward, striving to throw one of his assailants across his shoulder, but realized that he was gripped in a stranglehold.

"You damned yellow double-crosser," he groaned, as his right arm was twisted back to breaking point.

From behind, an expanding gag was slipped into his gaping mouth. He gurgled, groaned, tried to kick, then collapsed as the pressure of fingers made itself felt, agonizingly, upon his eyeballs. . . .

He had not even seen his assailants when straps were buckled about his legs, and his arms lashed behind him.

Throughout, Dr. Fu Manchu never stirred. But when the

man, his eyes fixed in frenzied hate upon the Chinese doctor, was carried, uttering inarticulate sounds, from the room, and the curtain fell behind his bearers:

"It is good, my friend," Fu Manchu said gutturally, addressing the mummy-like figure on the settee, "that you succeeded in bringing me a few expert servants."

"It was well done," old Sam Pak muttered.

"Tonight," the precise tones continued, "we put our fortunes to the test. The woman Adair, to whom I have entrusted the tuition of Harvey Bragg, is one I can rely upon; I hold her in my hand. But the man himself, in his bloated arrogance, may fail us. I fear for little else." His eyes became closed; he was thinking aloud. "If Enemy Number One has Abbot Donegal, all approaches to Carnegie Hall must be held against them. This I can arrange. We have little else to fear."

From the material upon the table he delicately charged a hypodermic syringe with a pale-green fluid. Sam Pak watched him with misty eyes, and Dr. Fu Manchu stood up.

"It is unfortunate," he said, but there was a note of scientific enthusiasm in the guttural voice, "that my first important experiment in the use of this interesting drug should involve in success or failure such high issues. Come, my friend; I desire you to be present. . . ."

Across the silent temple of the seven-eyed goddess they went: Fu Manchu with his catlike walk; old Sam Pak shuffling behind. The place was silent and empty. They descended a stone stair, traversed the corridor lined with the six painted coffins, and passed the steel door beyond which a secret passage led to East River.

In a small, cell-like room, brightly lighted by a pendent lamp, Herman Grosset lay strapped to a fixed teak bench. The two immobile Chinamen had just completed their task as Dr. Fu Manchu entered, and:

"Go!" he commanded in Chinese.

The men bowed and went out; their muscular bodies were dewy with perspiration. Grosset's skin also gleamed wetly. He had been stripped to the waist; his eyes were starting from his head.

"Remove the gag, my friend," Dr. Fu Manchu directed.

Old Sam Pak stepped forward, bent over Grosset, and with a sudden, amazingly agile movement, wrenched the man's mouth open and plucked out the expanding gag. Grosset turned his head aside and spat disgustedly; then:

"Dirty yellow thugs!" he whispered: he was panting. "You've been bought over! Maybe you think—" his powerful chest expanded hugely—"that if you get Harvey, Orwin Prescott has a chance! I'm telling you this: If any harm comes to Harvey, there'll never be a Dictator in the United States."

"We do not doubt," said Dr. Fu Manchu, "your love for Harvey Bragg."

"No need to doubt it! Looks like I'm dying for him right here and now. I want to tell you this: He's the biggest man this country has known for a whole generation and more. Think that over. I say it."

"You would not consider changing your opinion?"

"I knew it!" Grosset was recovering vigor. "Saw it coming. Listen, you saffron-faced horror! You couldn't buy me for all the gold in Washington. I've lived for Harvey right along . . . I'll die for Harvey."

"Admirable sentiments," Dr. Fu Manchu muttered, and bent over the strapped figure, hypodermic syringe in hand.

"What are you going to do to me?" Grosset shrieked, a sudden note of horror in his voice. "What are you going to do to me? Oh, you filthy yellow swine! If only my hands were free!"

"I am going to kill you, my friend. I have no future place for you in my plans."

"Well, do it with a gun," the man groaned, "or even a knife if you like. But that thing——"

He uttered a wild, despairing shriek as the needle point was plunged into his flesh. Veins like blue whipcords sprang up on his forehead, on his powerful arms, as he fought to evade the needle point. All was in vain: he groaned and, in the excess of his mental agony, became still.

Dr. Fu Manchu handed the syringe to the old mandarin, who unemotionally had watched the operation. He stooped and applied his ear to the diaphragm of the unconscious man. Then, standing upright, he nodded.

"The second injection two hours before we want him." He looked down at the powerful body strapped to the bench. "You have killed many men in defense of your idol, Grosset," he murmured, apostrophizing the insensible figure. "Seven I have checked, and there are others. You shall end your career in a killing that is really worth while. . . ."

3

Carnegie Hall was packed to saturation point. It was an even bigger audience than Fritz Kreisler could have commanded; an audience equally keen with anticipation, equally tense. The head'ong advance made by Harvey Bragg, once regarded as a petty local potentate by serious politicians, now recognized as a national force, had awakened the country to the fact that dictatorship, until latterly a subject for laughter, might, incredible though it seemed, be imminent.

The League of Good Americans reputedly numbered fifteen million members upon its roll. That many thousands of the homeless and hopeless had been given employment by Harvey Bragg was an undisputed fact. The counter measures of the old administration, dramatically drastic, had apparently done little to check a growing feverish enthusiasm awakened throughout the country by "Bluebeard."

An ever-expanding section of the public regarded him as a savior; another and saner element recognized that he was a menace to the Constitution. Dr. Orwin Prescott, scholarly, sincere, had succeeded in driving a wedge between two conflicting bodies—and the gap was widening.

That Orwin Prescott advocated a sane administration, every sensible citizen appreciated. His avowed object was to split the Bragg camp; but there were those who maintained, although he had definitely denied the charge, that secretly he aimed at nomination to the Presidency.

There was a rumor abroad that he would declare himself tonight.

Among the more thoughtful elements he undoubtedly had a large following, and if the weight of the Abbot of Holy Thorn at the eleventh hour should be thrown into the scales, it was obvious to students of the situation that the forces of Orwin Prescott would become nearly as formidable as those of Harvey Bragg.

In the course of the last few hectic months other contestants had been wiped off the political map. Republican voters, recanting their vows of 1932, had rallied to Orwin Prescott. Agriculture stood solid for the old administration, although Ohio had a big Bragg faction. The ghost of a conservative third party had been exorcised by Abbot Donegal, a close friend of Prescott.

There was a certain studious mystery about Dr. Orwin Prescott which appealed to a large intellectual class. His periodical retirements from public life, a certain aura of secret studies which surrounded him, and the recent silence of Abbot Donegal, had been interpreted as a piece of strategy, the importance of which might at any moment become manifest. One would have had to search far back in American history for a parallel of the almost hysterical excitement which dominated this packed assembly.

The huge building was entirely in the hands of police and federal agents. Hidden patrols covered the route from the

Dumas apartment on Park Avenue right to the door of the hall by which Harvey Bragg would enter. Up to an hour before the meeting was timed to open, no one knew where Prescott was, or even if he were in the city. The audience, which numbered over three thousand, had been admitted to their seats, every man and woman closely scrutinized by hawk-eyed police officers. The buzz of that human beehive was something all but incredible.

A military band played patriotic music, many numbers being sung in unison by three thousand voices. Suspense was intense; excitement electrical.

Nayland Smith, in an office cut off from the emotional vibrations of that vast gathering, was in constant touch with police headquarters, and with Fey, who sat at the telephone at the top of the Regal Tower. Mark Hepburn, bearded and bespectacled, ranged the building from floor to floor, reporting at intervals in the office which Nayland Smith had made his temporary base.

Outside, limelight turned night into day, and a team of cameramen awaited the arrival of distinguished members of the audience. Thousands who had been disappointed in obtaining admittance thronged the sidewalks; the corner of 57th Street was impassable. Patrolmen, mounted and on foot, kept a way open for arriving cars.

Hepburn walked into the office just as Nayland Smith replaced the telephone. Smith turned, sprang up.

Sarah Lakin, seated in a rest-chair on the other side of the big desk, flashed an earnest query into the bespectacled eyes. Mark Hepburn shook his head and removed his spectacles.

"Almost certainly," he said in his dry, unemotional way, "Abbot Donegal is not in the hall, so far."

Nayland Smith began to walk up and down the room tugging at the lobe of his ear, then:

"And there is no news from the Mott Street area. I am beginning to wonder—I am beginning to doubt."

"I have deferred to your views, Sir Denis," came the grave voice of Miss Lakin, "but I have never disguised my own opinion. In assuming on the strength of a letter, admittedly in his own hand, that Orwin will be here tonight, I think you have taken a false step."

"Maurice Norbert's telephone message this morning seemed to me to justify the steps we have taken," said Hepburn dryly.

"I must agree with you there, Captain Hepburn," Miss Lakin admitted, "but I cannot understand why Mr. Norbert failed to visit me or to visit you. It is true that Orwin has a custom of hiding from the eye of the Press whenever an important public engagement is near, but hitherto I have been in his confidence." She stood up. "I know, Sir Denis, that you have done everything which any man could do to trace his whereabouts. But I am afraid." She locked her long, sensitive fingers together. "Somehow, I am very afraid."

A sound of muffled cheering penetrated to the office.

"See who that is, Hepburn," snapped Nayland Smith.

Hepburn ran out. Miss Lakin stared into the grim, brown face of the man pacing up and down the floor. Suddenly he stopped in front of her and rested his hand upon her shoulder.

"You may be right and I may be wrong," he said rapidly. "Nevertheless, I believe that Orwin Prescott will be here tonight."

Mark Hepburn returned.

"The Mayor of New York," he reported laconically. "The big names are beginning to arrive." He glanced at his wrist watch. "Plenty of time yet."

"In any event," said Nayland Smith, "we have neglected no possible measure. There is only one thing to do—wait."

20 THE CHINESE CATACOMBS (concluded)

ORWIN PRESCOTT dressed himself with more than his usual care. Maurice Norbert had brought his evening clothes and his dressing case, and in a perfectly appointed bathroom which adjoined the white bedroom, Prescott had bathed, shaved, and then arrayed himself for the great occasion.

The absence of windows in these apartments had been explained by Nurse Arlen. This was a special rest room, usually employed in cases of overtired nerves and regarded as suitable by Dr. Sigmund, in view of the ordeal which so soon his patient must face. The doctor he had not seen in person; quite satisfied with his progress, the physician—called to a distant patient—had left him in the care of Nurse Arlen. Orwin Prescott would have been quite prepared to remain in her care for a long time. Although he more than suspected the existence of a yellow streak in Nurse Arlen's blood, she was the most fascinating creature with whom he had personally come in contact.

101

He knew that he was forming an infatuation for this graceful nurse, whose soothing voice had run through all the troubled dreams which had preceded his complete recovery. And now, as he stood looking at himself in the glass, he thought that he had never appeared more keenly capable in the whole of his public life. He studied his fine, almost ascetic features. He was pale, but his pallor added character to the curt, gray, military mustache and emphasized the strength of the dark eyebrows. His gray hair was brushed immaculately.

The situation he had well in hand. Certainly there were remarkable properties in the prescriptions of Dr. Sigmund. His mental clarity he recognized to be super-normal. He had memorized every fact and every figure prepared for him by Norbert! He seemed to have a sort of pre-vision of all that would happen; his consciousness marched a step ahead of the clock. He knew that tonight no debater in the United States could conquer him. He had nothing to fear from the crude rhetoric of Harvey Bragg.

Satisfied with his appearance, delighted with the issue of this misadventure which might well have wrecked his career, he rang the bell as arranged, and Maurice Norbert came in. He, too, was in evening dress and presented a very smart figure.

"I have arranged, Doctor," he said, "for the car to be ready in twenty minutes. I will set out now to prepare our friends for your arrival, and to see that you are not disturbed in any way until the debate is over. I have never seen you look more fit for the fray."

"Thanks to your selection of a remarkable physician, Norbert, I have never felt more fit."

"It's good to hear you say so. I'll go ahead now; you start in twenty minutes. I will collect the brushes and odds and ends tomorrow. I thought it best to arrange for a car with drawn shades. The last thing we want is an ovation on the street which might hold you up. You'll be driven right to the entrance, where I shall be waiting for you."

Less than two minutes after Norbert's departure, Nurse Arlen came in.

"I was almost afraid," said Orwin Prescott, "that I was not to see you again before I left."

She stood just by the door, one hand resting on a slender hip, watching him with those long, narrow, dark eyes.

"How could you think I would let so interesting a patient leave without wishing him every good fortune for tonight?"

102

"Your wishes mean a lot to me. I shall never forget the kindness I have experienced here."

The woman's dark eyes closed for a moment, and when they reopened, their expression had subtly changed.

"That is kind of you," she said. "For my own part I have only obeyed orders."

She seated herself beside him on the settee and accepted a cigarette he offered from the full case which Norbert had thoughtfully brought along. Vaguely he was conscious of tension.

"I hope to see you again," he said, lighting her cigarette. "Is that too much to hope?"

"No," she replied laughingly, "there is no reason why I shouldn't see you again, Doctor. But—" she hesitated, glanced at him quickly, and then looked aside—"I have practically given up social life. You would find me very dull company."

"Why should you have given up social life?" Orwin Prescott spoke earnestly. "You are young, you are beautiful. Surely all the world is before you."

"Yes," said Nurse Arlen, "in one sense it is. Perhaps someday I may have a chance to try to explain to you. But now . . ." She stood up. "I have one more duty before you leave for Carnegie Hall—physician's orders."

She crossed to a glass-topped table and, from a little phial which stood there, carefully measured out some drops of a colorless liquid into a graduated glass. She filled it with water from a pitcher and handed it to Orwin Prescott.

"I now perform my last duty," she said. "You are discharged as cured."

She smiled. It was the smile which had haunted his dreams: a full-lipped, caressing smile which he knew he could never forget. He took the glass from her hand and drained its contents. The liquid was quite tasteless.

Almost immediately, magically, he became aware of a great exhilaration. His mental powers, already keen, were stimulated to a point where it seemed that his heel was set upon the world as on a footstool; that all common clay formed but stepping-stones to a goal undreamed of by any man before him. It was a kind of intoxication never hitherto experienced in his well-ordered life. How long it lasted he was unable to judge, or what of it was real, and what chimerical.

He thought that, carried out of himself, he seized the siren woman in his arms; that almost she surrendered but finally resisted. . . .

Then, sharply, as lightning splits the atmosphere, came sudden and absolute sobriety.

Orwin Prescott stared at Nurse Arlen. She stood a pace away watching him intently.

"That was a heady draught," he said, and his tones were apologetic.

"Perhaps my hand shook," Nurse Arlen replied; her caressing voice was not quite steady. "I think it is time for you to go, Dr. Prescott. Let me show you the way."

He presently found himself in a small elevator, which Nurse Arlen operated. Stepping out at the end of a narrow corridor, and a door being opened, he entered a covered courtyard where a Cadillac was waiting. The chauffeur, who wore driving-glasses, was yellow skinned—he might have been an Asiatic. He held the door open.

"Good night," said Orwin Prescott, one foot on the step.

He held Nurse Arlen's hand, looking, half afraid, into her dark eyes.

"Good night," she replied—"good luck!"

The windows were shaded. A moment after the door was closed the big car moved off.

2

Dr. Fu Manchu sat in the stone-faced room behind that narrow table whose appointments suggested those of a medical consultant. His long yellow fingers with their pointed nails rested motionless upon the tabletop. His eyes were closed. The curtain which draped the opening was drawn aside, and Sam Pak entered: "Sam Pak"—a name which concealed another once honored in China.

Dr. Fu Manchu did not open his eyes.

"Orwin Prescott is on his way to Carnegie Hall, Master," the old man reported, speaking in Chinese, but not in the Chinese which those of the London police who knew him and who knew something of Eastern languages were accustomed to hear. The woman did her work, but not too well. I fear there were four and not three drops in the final draught."

"She is a broken reed." The sibilant voice was clearly audible, although the thin-lipped mouth appeared scarcely to move. "She was recommended in high quarters, but her sex vibrations render her dangerous. She is amorous, and she has compassion: it is the negroid strain. Her amours do not concern me. If men are her toys, she may play; but the fiber and reality of her womanhood must belong to *me*.

If she betrays me, she shall taste the lingering kiss of death. . . . For this reason I removed her from Harvey Bragg in the crisis, and substituted the woman Adair. You are uncertain respecting the drops?"

The jade-green eyes opened, and a compelling stare fixed itself upon the withered face of Sam Pak.

"I was watching—her hand was not steady; he became intoxicated. By this I judged."

"If she has failed me, she shall suffer." The guttural voice was very harsh. "The latest report regarding this pestilential priest?"

"Number 25, in charge of Z-cars covering Carnegie Hall, reports that the Abbot Donegal has not entered the building."

There was a silence of several moments.

"This can mean only one of two things," came sibilantly. "He is there, disguised, or he is in federal hands and Enemy Number One may triumph at the last moment."

Old Sam Pak emitted a sound resembling the hiss of a snake.

"Even I begin to doubt if our gods are with us," the high, precise voice of Fu Manchu continued. "What of my boasted powers, of those agents which I alone know how to employ? What of the thousands of servants at my command throughout the world? That Nayland Smith has snapped at my heels—may now at any moment bark outside my door. This brings down my pride like a house of cards. Gods of my fathers—" his voice sank lower and lower—"is it written that I am to fail in the end?"

"Quote not from Moslem fallacies," old Sam Pak wheezed. "Your long contact with the Arabs, Marquis, is responsible for such words."

Few living men could have sustained the baleful glare of those jade-green eyes now fully opened. But Sam Pak, unmoved by their hypnotism, continued:

"I, too, have some of the wisdom, although only a part of yours. The story of your life is traced by your own hand. This you know: fatalism is folly. I, the nameless, speak because I am near to you, and loving you am fearless in your service."

Dr. Fu Manchu stood up; his bony but delicate fingers selected certain objects on the table.

"Without you, my friend," he said softly, "I should indeed be alone in this my last battle, which threatens to become my Waterloo. Let us proceed—" he moved catlike around the end of the long table—"to the supreme experiment. Failure means entire reconstruction of our plans."

"A wise man can build a high tower upon a foundation of failures," crooned old Sam Pak.

Dr. Fu Manchu, silent-footed, went out into the room haunted by the seven-eyed goddess; crossed it, descended stairs, old Sam Pak following. They passed along the corridor of the six coffins and came to the dungeon where Herman Grosset lay upon a teak bench. The straps had been removed—he seemed to be sleeping peacefully.

One of Sam Pak's Chinamen was on guard. He bowed and withdrew as Dr. Fu Manchu entered. Old Sam Pak crouched beside the recumbent body, his ear pressed to the hairy chest. Awhile he stayed so, and then looked up, nodding.

Dr. Fu Manchu bent over the sleeping man, gazing down intently at the inert muscular body. He signaled to Sam Pak, and the old Chinaman, exhibiting an apelike strength, dragged Grosset's tousled head aside. With a small needle syringe Dr. Fu Manchu made an injection. He laid the syringe aside and watched the motionless patient. Nearly two minutes elapsed. . . . Then, with an atomizer, Dr. Fu Manchu projected a spray first up the right and then up the left nostril of the unconscious man.

Ten seconds later Grosset suddenly sat upright, gazing wildly ahead. His gaze was caught and held by green compelling eyes, only inches removed from his own. His muscular hands clutched the sides of the bench; he stayed rigid in that pose.

"You understand—" the strange voice was pitched very low: "The word of command is 'Asia.'"

"I understand," Grosset replied. "No man shall stop me."

"The word," Fu Manchu intoned monotonously, "is Asia."

"Asia," Grosset echoed.

"Until you hear that word—" the voice seemed to come from the depths of a green lake—"forget, forget all that you have to do."

"I have forgotten."

"But remember . . . remember, when you hear the word 'Asia' . . ."

"Asia."

"Sleep and forget. But remember that the word is *Asia*."

Herman Grosset sank back and immediately became plunged in deep sleep.

Dr. Fu Manchu turned to Sam Pak.

"The rest is with you, my friend," he said.

21 *CARNEGIE HALL*

HARVEY BRAGG turned around in the chair set before the carved writing table in the study of the Dumas apartment. He was dressed for the meeting, destined to take its place in American history. Above the table, in a niche and dominating the room, was a reproduction of the celebrated statue of Bussy d'Ambois. The table itself was an antique piece of great value, once the property of Cardinal Mazarin.

"Listen, baby. I want to get this right." Harvey Bragg stood up. "I'm all set, but I'm playing a part, and I'm not used to playing any part but the part of Harvey Bragg. Bring me into the party, Eileen. Nobody knows better than you. Lola is a hard case, but I guess you're a regular kid."

Moya Adair, seated at the end of the table, raised her eyes to the speaker.

"What do you want to know?" she asked.

"I want to know—" Bragg came a step nearer, rested his hands on the table, and bent down—"I want to know if I'm being played for a sucker; because if I am, God help the man who figures to put that stuff over on me! I've had dough to burn for long enough—some I could check up and some from this invisible guy, the President. Looks to me like the President's investment is a total loss . . . and I never met a rich guy who went around looking for bum stock. This crazy shareholder is starting to try to run my business for me. Listen, Eileen: I'll step where I'm told, if I know where I'm stepping."

There was a momentary silence broken only by the dim hum of traffic in Park Avenue below.

"You would be a fool," said Moya calmly, "to quarrel with a man who believed in you so implicitly that he is prepared to finance you to the extent of many million dollars. His object is to make you President of the United States. He has selected me to be your secretary because he believes that I have the necessary capacity for the work. I can tell you no more. He is a man of enormous influence, and he wishes to remain anonymous. I can't see that you have any cause for quarrel with him."

Harvey Bragg bent lower, peering into the alluring face.

"I've learned up a lot of cues," he said; "cues you have given me. Seems I have to become an actor. And—" he banged his open hand upon the table—"I don't know even at this minute that Orwin Prescott is going to be there!"

"Orwin Prescott will be there."

"It's big fun, isn't it—" now his face was but inches removed from Moya's—"to know that my secretary is wised up on the latest moves and that I'm a pawn in the game? There's another thing, Eileen. Maybe you know what's become of Herman Grosset? He checked in on nowhere more than an hour back, and I never move out without Herman."

He grasped Moya's shoulders. She turned her head aside.

"You're maybe wiser than you look, pretty. You know where I stand. No President can balk me now. We've started wrong. Let's forget it. Look at me. I want to tell you something——"

Came a discreet rap on the study door.

"Hell!" growled Harvey Bragg. He released Moya, stood upright and turned:

"Come in."

The door opened, and Salvaletti entered, smiling but apologetic.

"Well!" Bragg challenged.

"It's time we left for Carnegie Hall."

Salvaletti spoke in a light, silvery voice.

"Where's Herman? I want to see him."

Salvaletti slightly inclined his head.

"You have naturally been anxious; so have I. But he is here."

"What!"

"He arrived only a few minutes ago. His explanation of his absence is somewhat . . ." He shrugged.

"What! on the booze, on a night like this?"

"I don't suggest it. But anyway he is perfectly all right now."

"Ask him to step right in here," roared Harvey Bragg, his voice booming around the study. "I want a few words with Herman."

"Cutting it rather fine. But if you insist . . ."

"I do insist."

He cursed under his breath as Salvaletti went out, turned, and stared angrily at Moya Adair; her calm aloofness maddened him.

"Something blasted funny going on," he growled. "And I guess, Miss Breon, you know all about it."

"I know no more than you know, Mr. Bragg. I can only ask you in your own interests to remember——"

"The coaching! Sure I'll remember it. I'm in up to the eyebrows. But after tonight, I climb out!"

The door was thrown open, and Herman Grosset burst in. His eyes were wild as he looked from face to face.

"Harvey," he said hoarsely, "I'm real sorry. You won't believe me, but I've been dead sober all day. I guess it must be blood pressure, or maybe incipient insanity. It's in the family, isn't it, Harvey? Listen—" he met the angry glare: "Don't talk yet—give *me* a word. I got a funny phone message more than an hour back. I thought it needed investigation. But hell burn me! that's all I can remember about it!"

"What do you mean?" growled Harvey Bragg.

"I mean I don't know what happened from the time I got that message which I can't remember—up to five minutes ago, when I found myself sitting on a chair down in the vestibule feeling darn sleepy and wondering where in hell I'd been."

"You're a drunken sot!" Harvey Bragg bawled. "That's what you are—a drunken sot. You've been soused all afternoon. And this is the damn-fool story you think you can pull on me. Get out to the cars; we're late already."

"I don't like your words," said Herman Grosset truculently. "They ain't just, and they ain't right."

"Right or wrong—get out!" yelled Harvey Bragg. "Get on with your job. I have to get on with mine. . . ."

Two minutes later a trio of powerful cars roared down Park Avenue bound for Carnegie Hall. In the first were four armed bodyguards; in the second Harvey Bragg and Salvaletti; in the third, three more guards and Herman Grosset.

"Bluebeard" was well protected.

2

In Nayland Smith's temporary office in Carnegie Hall silence, vibrant with unspoken thoughts, had fallen.

Maurice Norbert had just ceased speaking. He stood looking smilingly from face to face. Nayland Smith, seated on the edge of the desk, lean brown hands clutching one upraised knee, watched him unflinchingly. Sarah Lakin's steady grave eyes were fixed upon him also.

Senator Lockly, one of Orwin Prescott's most fervent supporters, had joined the party, and his red, good-humored face now registered bewilderment and doubt. Nayland Smith broke the silence.

"Your explanation, Mr. Norbert," he rapped, "presents certain curious features into which at the moment we have no opportunity to inquire. We are to understand that Dr. Prescott communicated with you roughly at the same time that he communicated with Miss Lakin, and gave you certain instructions which you carried out. These necessitated your meeting a car at an agreed point and being driven to an unknown destination, where you found Dr. Prescott receiving medical attention under the care of a physician whom you did not meet?"

"Exactly."

Maurice Norbert continued to smile.

"You had been instructed to take a suitcase and other items, and we are to understand that Dr. Prescott has come to some arrangement with those responsible for his disappearance whereby he will be present here, tonight?"

"Exactly," Maurice Norbert repeated.

Sarah Lakin continued fixedly to watch Norbert, but she did not speak. Senator Lockly cleared his throat, and:

"I don't understand," he declared, "why, having found him, you left him. It seems to me there's no guarantee even now that he will arrive."

"One of the curious features," rapped Nayland Smith, standing up and beginning to pace the floor, "to which I referred. . . ." He turned suddenly, facing Norbert. "I don't entirely understand your place in this matter, Mr. Norbert. And I believe—" glancing aside—"that Miss Lakin shares my doubts."

"I do," Sarah Lakin replied in her deep, calm voice.

"Forgive me—" Norbert bowed to the speaker—"but in this hour of crisis we are naturally overwrought, every one of us. It isn't personal, it's national. These facts will wear a different complexion tomorrow. But accept my assurance, everybody, that Dr. Prescott will be here." He glanced at his wrist watch. "In fact, I must go down to meet him. I beg that you will do as I have asked. Senator, will you join me. He has requested that we shall be with him on the platform."

Senator Lockly looked rather helplessly from Sarah Lakin to Nayland Smith, and then followed Norbert out of the office. As the door closed behind them:

"How long employed by Dr. Prescott?" rapped Nayland Smith.

"Maurice Norbert," Sarah Lakin replied, "has been in my cousin's service for rather more than a year."

"Hepburn has been checking up on him. It has proved difficult, but we expect all the details tomorrow."

At which moment the door was thrown open again, and the Abbot of Holy Thorn, wearing the dress of a simple priest, stepped into the office!

The bearded face of Mark Hepburn might have been glimpsed over his left shoulder. Nayland Smith sprang forward.

"Dom Patrick Donegal!" he cried, "thank God I see you here! and safe!"

Mark Hepburn came in and closed the door.

"My experiences, Mr. Smith," the abbot replied calmly, "on my journey to the city, have convinced me that I have incurred certain dangers." He smiled and gripped the outstretched hand. "But I think I warned you that I am a prisoner hard to hold. It is my plain duty in this crisis, since I am denied the use of the air, to be here in person."

"One of our patrol cars," said Hepburn dryly, "picked up the abbot twenty minutes ago and brought him here under escort. I may add . . . that the escort was necessary."

"That is quite true," the priest admitted. "A very tough-looking party in a Cadillac had been following me for several miles. But—" he ceased to smile and assumed by a spiritual gesture the role of his Church—"I have achieved my purpose. If I am to consider myself technically under arrest I must nevertheless insist, Mr. Smith, upon one thing. . . . Failing the appearance of my friend, Orwin Prescott, *I* shall confront Harvey Bragg tonight."

A sound resembling an approaching storm made itself audible. Mark Hepburn nodded to Nayland Smith and went out. Sarah Lakin stood up, her grave calm ruffled at last. Smith stepped to the doorway and stared along the corridor.

The sound grew louder—it was the cheering of thousands of voices. Dimly the strains of a military band were heard. Mark Hepburn came running back.

"Dr. Prescott is on the platform!" he cried, completely lifted out of himself by the excitement of the moment. "Harvey Bragg has just arrived. . . ."

3

The classic debate which the Moving Finger was writing into American history took place in an atmosphere of tension unequaled in the memory of anyone present. After the event there were many who recalled significant features; as, for instance, that Harvey Bragg used notes, his custom being to speak extemporaneously (if in the mood, for many hours). Also, that he frequently glanced in the direction of his

111

secretary, Salvaletti, who seemed at times to be prompting him.

Hidden from the audience, Dom Patrick Donegal looked on at the wordy duel. And, helpless now to intervene, he realized, as everyone in that vast gathering realized, that Dr. Orwin Prescott was a beaten man.

As oratory, his performance was perhaps the finest in his career; his beautiful voice, his scholarship, put to shame the coarse bellowing and lamentable historical ignorance of his opponent. But in almost every sentence he played into the hands of Harvey Bragg; he fell into traps that a child could have avoided. With dignity, assurance, perfect elocution, he made statements which even the kindest critic must have branded as those of a fool.

At times it seemed that he was conscious of this. More than once he raised his hand to his forehead as if to collect his thoughts, and especially it was noticed that points raised in response to the apparent promptings of Salvaletti resulted in disaster for Dr. Orwin Prescott.

His keenest supporters lost heart. It appeared long before the debate was ended that Harvey Bragg offered the country prosperity. Dr. Prescott had nothing to offer but beautifully phrased sentences.

And the greatest orator in the United States, the Abbot of Holy Thorn, dumbly listened—looked on! while his friend Orwin Prescott, with every word that he uttered, broke down the fine reputation which laboriously and honorably he had built up.

It was the triumph of "Bluebeard."

4

In that book-lined room high above New York, where sometimes incense was burned, Dr. Fu Manchu sat behind the lacquered table.

The debate at Carnegie Hall was being broadcast from coast to coast. Robed in yellow, his mandarin's cap upon his head, he sat listening. Reflected light from the green-shaded table lamp enhanced his uncanny resemblance to the Pharaoh Seti I; for the eyes of Dr. Fu Manchu were closed as he listened.

His hands, stretched out upon the table before him, had remained quite motionless as Orwin Prescott became involved more deeply in the net cunningly spread for him by Harvey Bragg. Only at times, when the latter hesitated, fumbled for words, would the long pointed nails tap lightly upon the polished surface.

On three occasions during this memorable debate an amber point came to life on the switchboard.

Without in any way allowing his attention to be distracted, Dr. Fu Manchu listened to reports from the man of miraculous memory. These all related to Numbers detailed to intercept Abbot Donegal. The third and last induced a slight tapping of long nails upon the lacquered surface. It was a report to the effect that a government patrol had rescued the abbot (picked up at last within a few miles of New York) from a Z-car which had been tracking him. . . .

The meeting concluded with wildly unrestrained cheers for Harvey Bragg. In that one hour he had advanced many marches nearer to the White House. Politically he had obliterated the only really formidable opponent who remained in the field. Except for the silent Abbot of Holy Thorn, the future of the United States now lay between the old regime and Harvey Bragg.

Deafening cheers were still ringing throughout Carnegie Hall when Dr. Fu Manchu disconnected. Silence fell in that small book-lined room distant from the scene of conflict. Bony fingers opened the silver box: Fu Manchu sought the inspiration of opium. . . .

Orwin Prescott, bewildered, even now not understanding that he had wiped himself off the political map, that he was committed to fatal statements which he could never recall, dropped down into an armchair in Nayland Smith's office, closed his eyes and buried his face in his hands.

Sarah Lakin crossed and sat beside him. Senator Lockly had disappeared. Nayland Smith glanced at Mark Hepburn, and they went out together. In the corridor:

"Where is Abbot Donegal?" said Nayland Smith.

"In care of Lieutenant Johnson," Hepburn answered dryly. "Johnson won't make a second mistake. Abbot Donegal stays until he has your permission to leave."

"Orwin Prescott was either drugged or hypnotized, or both," rapped Nayland Smith. "It's the most damnably cunning thing Fu Manchu has ever done. With one stroke tonight, he has put the game into Harvey Bragg's hands."

"I know." Mark Hepburn ran his fingers through his disheveled hair. "It was pathetic to listen to, and impossible to watch. Abbot Donegal was just quivering. Sir Denis! this man is a magician! I begin to despair."

Nayland Smith suddenly grabbed his arm as they walked along the corridor.

113

"Don't despair," he snapped, "yet! There's more to come."

They had begun to descend to the floor below when Harvey Bragg, flushed with triumph, already tasting the sweets of dictatorship, the cheers of that vast gathering echoing in his ears, came out into a small lobby packed with privileged visitors and newspapermen.

His bodyguard, as tough a bunch as any man had ever collected in the United States, followed him in. Paul Salvaletti walked beside him.

"Folks!" Bragg cried, "I know just how you feel." He struck his favorite pose, arms raised. "You're all breathing the air of a new and better America. . . . That's just how *I* feel! Another obstacle to national happiness is swept away. Folks! there's no plan but my plan. At last we are getting near to the first ideal form of government America has ever known."

"Which any country has ever known," said Salvaletti, his clear, musical voice audible above the uproar. "America, Africa, Europe—or Asia."

As he spoke the word *Asia*, Herman Grosset, hitherto flushed with excitement, suddenly became deathly pale. His eyes glared, foam appeared at the corners of his mouth. With that lightning movement which no man of the bodyguard could equal, he snatched an automatic from his pocket, sprang forward and shot Harvey Bragg twice through the heart. . . .

There was a moment of dazed silence; a sound resembling a moan. Then the faithful bodyguard, one second too late, almost literally made a sieve with their bullets of Herman Grosset.

He died before the man he had assassinated. Riddled with lead, he crashed to the floor of the lobby as Harvey Bragg collapsed in the arms of Salvaletti.

"Herman! my God! *Herman!*" were Bragg's dying words.

22 *MOYA ADAIR'S SECRET*

"I AM UNCERTAIN, Hepburn," rapped Nayland Smith, pacing up and down the sitting room. "I cannot read sense into the crossword puzzle."

"Nor can I," said Mark Hepburn.

Smith stared out at the never familiar prospect. The day was crystal clear, the distant Statue of Liberty visible in sharp detail. Some strange quality in the crisp atmosphere seemed to have drawn it inland, so that it appeared like a miniature of itself. Towering buildings had crept nearer: a wide section of New York City seemed to be looking in at the window.

"That Orwin Prescott should suffer a nervous collapse and entirely lose his memory was something for which I was not unprepared. His deplorable exhibition at Carnegie Hall was the result of some kind of post-hypnotic suggestion, a form of attack of which Dr. Fu Manchu is a master."

Mark Hepburn lighted a cigarette.

"There was a time," he said slowly, "when I thought that the powers which you attributed to this man must be exaggerated. I think now that all you said was an understatement. Sir Denis! he's more than the greatest physician in the world—he's a magician."

"Cut the 'Sir Denis,'" came crisply; "I was born plain Smith. It's time you remembered it."

Mark Hepburn smiled—a rare event in these days: it was the self-conscious smile of a nervous schoolboy; life had never changed it.

"I am glad to hear you say that," he declared awkwardly—"Smith, because I'm proud to know that we are friends. Maybe that sounds silly, but I mean it."

"I appreciate it."

"I can understand," Hepburn went on, "after what you have told me, that it might be possible—although it's quite outside my own medical experience—to drug a man in some way and impose certain instructions upon him to be carried out later. I mean I can believe that this is what happened to Orwin Prescott. It's a tough story, but your experience can provide parallels. Mine can't. We are dealing with a man who seems to be a century ahead of modern knowledge."

"Dismiss Prescott," said Nayland Smith curtly; "he's out of the political arena. But he's in good hands now, and I hope to heaven he recovers from whatever ordeal he has passed through. I am disappointed about the escape of the man Norbert. That was bad staff work, Hepburn, for which I take my full share of responsibility."

"We'll get him yet," said Hepburn harshly, "if we comb every state for him. His getaway had been cunningly planned. I have checked it all up. Nobody is to blame. This thing goes back a year or more. Dr. Fu Manchu must have been working, through agents, long before he arrived in person."

"I know it," rapped Nayland Smith; "I have known it for some time past. But what I don't know and cannot work out is this: Where does the death of Harvey Bragg fit into the Doctor's plans?"

He fixed a penetrating stare upon Hepburn and almost automatically began to load this pipe. . . .

"The man Herman Grosset was a drunken ruffian; his only redeeming virtue seems to have been his attachment to his half brother. He was a killer, as your records show. Such a man is like an Alsatian dog—his savagery may be turned upon his master. I wonder . . ." He dropped his pouch back into the pocket of his dressing gown and lighted a match. . . . "I wonder? . . ."

"So do I," said Mark Hepburn monotonously; "I have been wondering ever since it happened. That this damnable Chinaman was running Harvey Bragg is a fact beyond doubt. It isn't conceivable that Bragg's death should form any part of his plan. If he wanted to turn a blustering demagogue into a hero, he has succeeded. Why—" he paused . . . "Smith! He lay in state right here in New York City! Now his embalmed body is being taken back to his home town. He's a bigger man dead than alive. Fifty per cent of uninformed American opinion today thinks that the greatest statesman since Lincoln has been snatched away in the hour of need."

"That's true." Nayland Smith blew a puff of smoke into the air. "As I said a while ago, I cannot read sense into the crossword puzzle. I am tempted to believe that the Doctor's plans have been thwarted."

He began to walk up and down again restlessly.

"Salvaletti's broadcast oration," said Hepburn monotonously, "was quite in the classic manner. In fact it was brilliant, although I don't see its purpose. It has made Harvey Bragg a national martyr."

"Salvaletti is going South by special train," jerked Nayland Smith, "with the embalmed body. There will be emotional scenes at every stop. Have we details regarding this man?"

"They should be to hand any moment now. All we know, so far, is that he's of Italian origin, was trained for the priesthood, left Italy at the age of twenty-three, and became a United States citizen five years ago. He's been with Bragg since early 1934."

"I listened to him, Hepburn. Utterly out of sympathy as I am with the subject of his eloquence, I must confess that I never heard a more moving speech."

116

"No—it was wonderful. But now—er—Smith, I am worried about this projected expedition of yours."

Nayland Smith paused in his promenade and stared, pipe gripped between his teeth, at Mark Hepburn.

"No more worried than I am regarding yours, Hepburn. You know what Kipling says about a rag and a bone and a hank of hair . . ."

"That's hardly fair, Smith. I quite frankly admitted to you that I'm interested in Mrs. Adair. There's something very strange about a woman like that being in the camp of Dr. Fu Manchu."

Nayland Smith paused in front of him, reached out and grasped his shoulder.

"Don't think I'm cynical, Hepburn," he said—"we have all been through the fires—but, be very careful!"

"I just want time to size her up. I think she's better than she seems. I admit I'm soft where she's concerned, but maybe she's straight after all. Give her a chance. We don't know everything."

"I leave her to you, Hepburn. All I say is: be careful. I'd gamble half of the little I possess to see into the mind of Dr. Fu Manchu at this moment! Is he as baffled as I am?"

He resumed his promenade.

"However . . . we have a heavy day before us. Learn all you can from the woman. I am devoting the whole of my attention to Fu Manchu's Chinatown base."

"I am beginning to think," said Hepburn, with his almost painful honesty, "that this Chinatown base is a myth."

"Don't be too sure," rapped Nayland Smith. "Certainly I saw the late secretary of Abbot Donegal disappear into a turning not far from Wu King's Bar. Significant, to say the least. I have spent hours, in various disguises, exploring that area and right to the water fronts on either side of it."

"I worry myself silly whenever you delay at——"

"My *own* Chinatown base?" Nayland Smith suggested.

He burst out laughing—and his laughter seemed to lift a load of care from his spirits. . . .

"You should congratulate me, Hepburn. In the character of a hard-drinking deck hand sacked by the Cunard and trying to dodge the immigration authorities until I find a berth, I have made a marked success with my landlady, Mrs. Mulrooney of Orchard Street! I have every vice from hashish to rum, and I begin to suspect she loves me!"

"What about the rag and a bone and a hank of hair?" Hepburn asked impishly.

Nayland Smith stared for a moment, and then laughed even more heartily.

"A hit to you," he admitted. "But frankly I feel that my inquiries are not futile. The Richet clue admittedly has led nowhere; but my East River investigations are beginning to bear fruit."

He ceased laughing. His lean brown face grew suddenly grim.

"Think of the recovery by the river police of the body of the man Blondie Hahn."

"Well?"

"All the facts suggested to me that he did not die on the water front or even very near to it. I may be wrong, Hepburn . . . but I think I have found Dr. Fu Manchu's watergate!"

"What!"

"We shall see. The arrival in New York this morning of the Chinese general, Li Wu Chang, has greatly intrigued me. I have always suspected Li Wu Chang of being one of the Seven."

"Who are the Seven?"

Nayland Smith snapped his fingers.

"Impossible to go into that now. I have much to do today if our plans are to run smoothly tonight. Your post is in Chinatown. We both have plenty to employ us in the interval. Should I miss you, the latest details will be on the desk—" he pointed—"and Fey will be here in constant touch. . . ."

2

Mark Hepburn, from his seat overlooking the pond in Central Park, watched the path from the Scholar's Gate. Presently he saw Moya Adair approaching.

It was a perfect winter's day; the air was like wine, visibility remarkable. Because his heart leapt, his dour training reproached him. He had abandoned the cape, property of an eccentric artist friend, and now his bearded chin stuck out from an upturned fur collar.

On the woman's side this meeting was a move in a fight for freedom. But Mark Hepburn, starkly honest, knew that on his side it was a lover's meeting. It was unfair to Nayland Smith that this important investigation, which might lead to control of a bridge to the enemy's stronghold, should have been left in his hands. Moreover, it was torture to himself. . . .

He loved the ease of her walk, the high carriage of her head. There was pedigree in every graceful line. Her existence in this gang of superthugs, who now apparently controlled the whole of the American underworld, was a mystery which balked his imagination.

She smiled as he stood up to meet her. He allowed the mad idea that they were avowed lovers—that he had a right to take her in his arms and kiss her—to dazzle his brain for one delirious moment. Actually, he said:

"You are very punctual, Mrs. Adair."

She sat down beside him. Her composure, real or assumed, was baffling. There was a short silence, an uneasy one on Mark Hepburn's side; then:

"I suppose," he said, "the death of Harvey Bragg means a change of plan?"

Moya shook her head.

"For me, no," she replied. "I am continuing my work at Park Avenue. The League of Good Americans is to go on, and Paul Salvaletti has taken charge."

She spoke impersonally, a little wearily.

"But you must regret the death of Harvey Bragg?"

"As a Christian, I do, for I cannot think that he was fit to die. As a man—" she paused for a moment, staring up at the cold, blue sky—"if he had lived, I don't know what I should have done. You see—" she turned to Hepburn—"I had no choice: I had to go to him. But my life there was hell."

Mark Hepburn looked away. He was afraid of her eyes. Nayland Smith's injunction, "Be very careful," seemed to ring in his ears.

"Why did you have to go to him?" he asked.

"Well—although I know how hard this must be for you to understand—Harvey Bragg, although he never knew it, was little more than a cog in a wheel. I am another cog in the same wheel." She smiled, but not happily. "He never really controlled the League of Good Americans, nor the many other organizations of which he was the nominal head."

"Then who does control them?" he questioned harshly.

"When I say that I don't know, I am literally speaking the truth. But there's someone far bigger than Harvey Bragg working behind the scenes. Please believe that I dare not tell you any more now."

Hepburn clenched his fists, plunged deep in the pockets of his topcoat.

"Was Harvey Bragg's murder in accordance with the—" he hesitated—"revolutions of this wheel?"

"I don't know. All I know is that it is not to be allowed to interfere with the carrying on of the objects of the league."

"What are these objects?"

Moya Adair paused for a moment.

"I think, but I am not sure, to introduce a new form of government into the United States. Truly——" she stood up ——"it is impossible for me to tell you any more. Mr. Purcell, you made a bargain with me, and our time is very short. When you understand more about my position you will see how hard it is to answer some of your questions."

Mark Hepburn stood up also, and nodded. His middle name (his mother's) was Purcell, and as Purcell he had introduced himself to Mrs. Adair.

"Which way do we go?"

"This way," said Moya, and side by side they walked in the direction of the Sherman equestrian statue. Hepburn was silent, sometimes glancing aside at his equally silent companion. She made no attempt to break this silence until they had passed the end of the bridle path, when:

"Shall we want a taxi?" Hepburn asked.

"Yes, but not a Lotus."

"Why?"

They came out through the Scholar's Gate.

"I have my reasons. Look! this one will do."

As the taxi moved off to a Park Avenue address of which he made a careful mental note:

"I understand," said Hepburn dryly, "that Harvey Bragg was a director of the Lotus Transport Corporation?"

"He was."

The immensity of the scheme was beginning to dawn upon him. Vehicles belonging to the Lotus Corporation, of one kind or another, ranged practically over the whole of the States. All employees belonged to the League of Good Americans: so much he knew. Assuming that they could be used, if necessary, as spies, what a network lay here at command of the master mind! As the countless possibilities presented themselves he turned and stared at Moya Adair. She was watching him earnestly.

"When we arrive at the apartment to which we are going," she said, "I shall have to ask you to play the part of an old friend. Do you mind?"

Mark Hepburn clenched his teeth. Moya's gloved hand rested listlessly upon the seat beside him. He grasped and held it for a moment.

"I sincerely wish I were," he replied.

She smiled; and he thought that her smile, although passionless, was almost affectionate.

"Thank you. I mean, we must address each other by our Christian names. So you have my permission to call me Moya. What am I to call *you?*"

Suddenly that alluring coquetry which had delighted and then repelled him at the Tower of the Holy Thorn made her eyes dance. A little dimple appeared at the left corner of her mouth.

"Mark."

"Thank you," said Moya. "I think very soon you will find yourself christened 'Uncle' Mark."

3

Dr. Fu Manchu pressed a button on his table, and in a domed room where the Memory Man, as a result of many hours of patient toil, had nearly completed another of those majestic clay heads the making of which alone relieved the tedium of his life, the amber light went out.

"Give me the latest report," came a curt, guttural order. "from the Number in charge of Mott Street patrol."

"To hand at 3.10 P.M. Report as follows: Strength of government agents and police in this area doubled since noon. Access to entrances one and two impossible. A government agent, heavily guarded and so far unidentified, in charge. Indications point to a raid pending. This report from Number 41."

Amber light prevailed again in the Gothic room, and the sculptor, Egyptian cigarette in mouth, proceeded delicately to accentuate the gibbous brow of his subject. . . .

Dr. Fu Manchu, who had produced this change of light by the pressure of a button, sat for a while with closed eyes. The first steps in his campaign had been successfully taken. The next step was by far the most difficult. The atmosphere of that strange study must have been unbreathable by an average man. A graying pencil of smoke arose from an incense burner set upon one corner of the table. Dr. Fu Manchu had his own methods of inducing mental stimulation. Presently he touched a switch, and two points of light appeared. A moment he waited, and then:

"Attend carefully to the orders I am about to give," he directed: he spoke in Chinese.

"I am listening, Master," the voice of old Sam Pak replied.

"A plot is brewing to set the dogs upon us, my friend. Listen with great care. No one is to enter or to leave Base 3 until further instructions are received from me. Doors leading to street entrances are to remain locked. Our visitors tonight will enter by the river-gate. Their safety rests with you. All are important; some are distinguished. I shall keep you informed. . . ."

4

"That is the reason . . . Mark (I must get used to calling you Mark while you are here) why I am so helpless."

Through uncurtained French windows Mark Hepburn looked out from the penthouse apartment onto a roof garden. The vegetation of the rock plants was scanty at this season; a little fountain was frozen over. But he could imagine that in spring and summer this was a very pleasant spot. In the frosty sunlight a small, curly-haired boy was romping with a nurse, a capable-looking woman nearing middle age. Her habitual expression Hepburn assumed to be grim, but now she was laughing gaily as she played with her little charge.

Her gaiety was not forced—that of a dutiful employee; it radiated real happiness. With the aid of a pile of cushions set beside the wall the small boy was making strenuous endeavors to stand on his head. His flushed face, every time that he collapsed and looked up at her, reduced the nurse to helpless laughter. He gave it up after a while and sat there grinning.

"God bless us, bairn, you'll bring all the blood to your daft little head if you keep on," she exclaimed, speaking with a marked Scottish accent.

"Is there blood in my head, Goofy?" the boy inquired, wide eyed. "I fought it on'y came up to here"—he indicated his throat.

"Where d'you think it comes from when your nose bleeds?"

"Never fought of that, Goofy."

Mark Hepburn, watching the mop of red-brown curls ruffled by the breeze, the clear blue eyes, the formation of the child's mouth, the roundness of his chin, experienced an unfamiliar sensation of weakness compounded of pity and of swift, intense affection. He turned his head slowly, looking at Moya Adair.

Her lips trembled, but her eyes were happy as she smiled up at him and waited.

"There's no need for me to ask," he said. His harsh voice seemed to have softened slightly. He was recalling the details of Mrs. Adair's record which he had been at such pains to secure. "I should have remembered."

"Yes." She nodded. "My big son. He's just four. . . ."
122

When, presently, Mark Hepburn met Robbie Adair, the boy registered approval save in regard to Hepburn's budding beard. He was a healthily frank young ruffian and took no pains to disguise his distastes. He had a disarmingly cheerful grin.

"I like you, Uncle Mark, all 'cept your whiskers," was his summary.

This dislike of beards, so expressed, produced a shocked protest from Nurse Goff and led to further inquiries by Moya, frowning, although her eyes danced with laughter. Interrogation brought to light the fact that Robbie associated beards and untidy hair with a peculiar form of insanity.

"There's someone I know, up there," he explained, pointing vaguely apparently towards heaven; "his hair blows about in the wind all in a mess like yours. And he's got funny whiskers too. He makes heads. He holds 'em up, and then he smashes 'em. So you see, Uncle Mark, he *is* mad."

Robbie grinned.

"Whatever are you talking about, Robbie?" Moya, kneeling on a cushion, threw her arm around the boy's shoulders and glanced up at Mark Hepburn. "Do *you* know what he means?"

Mark shook his head slowly, looking into the beautiful eyes upraised to his, so like, yet so wonderfully different from, the eyes of the boy. He became aware of the fact that he was utterly happy; a kind of happiness he had never known before. And down upon this unlawful joy (for why should *he* be happy in the midst of stress, conflict, murder, black hypocrisy) he clapped the icy hand of a Puritan conscience. Nurse Goff had gone into the apartment, leaving the three together.

Some change in Hepburn's expression made Moya turn aside. She pressed her cheek against Robbie's curly head.

"We don't know what you mean, dear," she said. "Won't you tell us?"

"I mean," said Robbie stoutly, turning and staring into her face from a distance of not more than an inch away, "there's a man who is mad; he has whiskers; and he lives up there!"

"Where exactly do you mean, Robbie?"

She glanced aside at Mark Hepburn. He was watching her intently.

The boy pointed.

"On the very top of that tall tower."

Mark Hepburn stared in the direction which Robbie indicated. The building in question was the Stratton Tower, one of New York's very high buildings, and the same which formed a feature of the landscape as viewed from the apartment he shared with Nayland Smith. He continued to stare in that direction, endeavoring to capture some memory which the sight of the obelisk-like structure topped by a pointed dome sharply outlined against that cold, blue sky, stirred in his mind.

He stood up, walked to the wall surrounding the roof garden and took his bearings. He realized that he stood at a level much below that of the fortieth floor of the Regal Tower, but in point of distance much nearer to the building the boy indicated.

"He always comes out at night. On'y sometimes I's asleep and don't see him."

It was the word "night," which gave Hepburn the clue, captured a furtive memory—a memory of three lighted windows at the top of the Stratton Tower which he had seen and speculated about on the night when, with Nayland Smith, he had waited for the coming of Fly Carlo.

He turned and stared at Robbie with new interest.

"You say he makes heads, young fellow?"

"Yes. I seen him up there, making 'em."

"At night?"

"Not always."

"And then you say he smashes them?"

"Yes, he always smashes 'em."

"How does he smash them, dear?" Moya asked, glancing up at the earnest face of Mark Hepburn.

According to the boy's graphic description, this notable madman hurled them down onto the dome below, where they were shattered into fragments.

Hepburn, conquered again by the picture of the charming mother kneeling with one arm around Robbie's shoulders, stooped and succumbed to the temptation of once again ruffling the boy's curly head.

"You seem to have quite a lot of fun up here, Robbie!" he said.

Later, in the cozy sitting room delicately feminine in its every appointment, Mark Hepburn sat looking at Moya Adair. She smiled almost timidly.

"I suppose," she said, "it's hard for you to understand, but——"

The door opened, and a curly head was thrust into the room, followed by a grin.

"Don't go, Uncle Mark," Robbie cried, "till I say good-bye."

He disappeared. Mark Hepburn, watching Moya as with mock severity she signaled the boy to run away, wondered if there was anything more beautiful in nature than a young and lovely mother.

"I am glad," he said, and his monotonous voice in some queer way sounded different, "that you have this great interest in your life."

"My only interest," she replied simply. "I go on for him. Otherwise—" she shook her head—"I should not be here now."

"Still I don't understand why you serve this man you call the President."

"Yet the explanation is very simple. Although the guards are not visible, both entrances to this building are watched night and day. Whenever Robbie goes out with his nurse he is covered until they return. He is never allowed to walk on the streets, but is driven to the garden of a house on Long Island. That is his only playground except the one on the roof outside."

"I suppose I am dense," said Mark Hepburn, "but even now I don't understand!"

"This apartment belongs to the President, although he rarely visits it. Mary Goff is my own servant; she has been in my service since the boy was born. Otherwise—I have no one. For two months Robbie disappeared———"

"He was kidnaped?"

"Yes, he was kidnaped. That was before all this began. Then the President sent for me. I was naturally distracted; I think I should very soon have died. He made me an offer which, I think, any mother would have accepted. I accepted without hesitation. I am allowed to come here, even to bring friends, while I carry out the duties allotted to me. If I failed—" she bit her lip—"I should never see Robbie again."

"But after all," Mark Hepburn exclaimed hotly, "there's a law in the land!"

"You don't know the President," Moya replied. "*I* do. No law could save my boy if he determined to spirit him away. You've promised, and you will keep your promise? You won't attempt to do anything about Robbie without my consent?"

Mark Hepburn watched her silently for a while, and then:

"No," he replied. "But it's a very unpleasant situation. I have exposed you to a dreadful danger. . . . You mean—" he hesitated—"that my visit here today will be reported to the President?"

"Certainly. But Robbie is allowed visitors if they are old friends. You seem to know enough of my history to pass for an old friend, I think?"

"Yes," said Mark Hepburn; "you may regard me as an old friend. . . ."

6

In the room where the Memory Man worked patiently upon his strange piece of modeling, a distant bell rang and the amber light went out.

"Give me the latest report," came the hated, dominating voice, "of the Number in charge of party covering Base 3."

"A report to hand," came an immediate reply in those terse, Teutonic tones, "timed 5.15. Police have been further reinforced. Chinese approaching the areas one, two and three have been interrogated. Government agent in charge not yet identified. Several detectives and federal agents have been in Wu King's Bar since noon. Report ends. From Number 41."

Following a silent interval, during which in the darkness the Memory Man lighted a fresh Egyptian cigarette from the stump of the old one:

"The latest report," the voice directed, "from the Number covering Eileen Breon."

"Report to hand timed 4.35. A man, bearded, wearing glasses and a driving coat with a fur collar, age estimated at thirty-five, arrived in her company at the apartment at 3.29. He remained for an hour; covered on leaving. He proceeded on foot to Grand Central. Operatives covering lost his track in the crowd. Report ends. This is from Number 39."

"Most unsatisfactory. Give me the latest report from the Regal-Athenian."

"Only one to hand, timed 5.10 P.M. Owing to long non-appearance of Federal Agents Hepburn and Smith, Number suggests——"

"Suggestions are not reports," the guttural voice said harshly. "What is this man's number?"

"Number 52."

Following a further brief silence:

"Make the connection," the harsh voice directed. "You are free for four hours."

Amber light prevailed again. The sculptor, brushing back his mane of white hair with a tragic gesture, adjusted the dictaphone attachment which during his hours of rest took the place of his phenomenal memory. No message came

126

through during the time that he gathered up lovingly the implements of his art, sole solace of the prisoner's life.

Carrying the half-completed clay model, he crossed to the hidden door, opened it, and descended to that untidy apartment which, with the balcony outside, made up his world. He threw wide the French windows and went out.

A setting sun in a cloudless sky fashioned strange red lights and purple shadows upon unimaginable buildings, streaked the distant waters almost reluctantly with a phantom, carmine brush, and painted New York City in aspects new even to the weary eyes of the man who had looked down upon it so often.

Setting the clay upon the table, he returned and took a photographic printing-frame from its place in the window. Removing the print, he immersed it in a glass tray. As its tones grew deeper, it presented itself as an enlargement of that tiny colored head—the model which eternally he sought to reproduce.

7

Mark Hepburn, fully alive to the fact that he had been covered from the moment when he had left the apartment where Moya Adair's small son lived—a prisoner—experienced an almost savage delight in throwing his pursuers off the track in the great railway station.

He had detected them—they were two—by the time that he descended the steps. He knew that Moya's happiness, perhaps the life of Robbie, depended upon his maintaining the character of a family friend. Whatever happened, he must not be identified as a federal agent.

Furthermore, at any cost he must combat a growing fear, almost superstitious, of the powers of Dr. Fu Manchu; even a minor triumph over the agents of that sinister, invisible being would help to banish an inferiority complex which threatened to claim him. He succeeded in throwing off his pursuers, very ordinary underworld toughs, without great difficulty.

A covered lorry was waiting at a spot appointed. In it, he donned blue overalls and presently entered a service door of the Regal-Athenian, a peaked cap pulled down over his eyes and carrying a crate upon his shoulder.

The death of Blondie Hahn, demigod of the underworld, and of Fly Carlo, notorious cat burglar, had been swamped as news by the assassination of Harvey Bragg. In the railway station, on every newsstand that he had passed, the name

Bragg flashed out at him. The man's death had created a greater sensation than his life. Thousands had lined up along the route of the funeral train to pay homage to Harvey Bragg, dead.

Mark Hepburn abandoned the problem of how this atrocity fitted into the schemes of that perverted genius who aimed to secure control of the country. He was keyed up to ultimate tension, insanely happy because he had read kindness in the eyes of Moya Adair; guiltily conscious of the fact that perhaps he had not performed his duty to the government, indeed, did not know where it lay. But now, as Fey, stoic faced, opened the door of the apartment, he found himself to be doubly eager for the great attempt planned by Nayland Smith to trap some, at least, of these remorseless plotters—it might be even the great chief—in their subterranean lair.

23 *FU MANCHU'S WATER-GATE*

"SHUT OFF," snapped Nayland Smith. "Drift on the current."

The purr of the engine ceased.

A million lights looked down through frosty air upon them, lights which from river level seemed to tower up to the vault of the sky. Upon the shores were patches of red light, blue light and green, reflected upon slowly moving water. Restless lights, like fireflies, darted, mingled, and reappeared again upon the bridges. The lights of a ferry boat crossed smoothly astern: lights of every color, static and febrile, fairy lights high up in the sky, elfin lights, Jack-o'-lanterns, low down upon the sullen tide. Hugging the shore, the motor launch, silent, drifted in an ebony belt protected from a million remorseless eyes. In the shadows below a city of light they crept onward to their destination.

"I understand—" Nayland Smith's voice came through the darkness from the bows—"that a fourth man has been reported?"

"Correct, Chief," Police Captain Corrigan replied. "He was checked in and reported by flash two minutes ago."

Staccato, warning blasts of tugs, sustained notes of big ships, complemented that pattern painted by the lights: the ceaseless voice of the city framed it. The wind had dropped to a mere easterly breeze; nevertheless it was an intensely cold night.

"There's a ladderway," said Corrigan, "with a trap opening on the dock above."

"And the property belongs to the South Coast Trade Line?"

"That's correct."

The late Harvey Bragg, as Nayland Smith had been at pains to learn, had held a controlling interest in the South Coast Trade Line. . . .

"Here we are," a voice announced.

"No engine," Nayland Smith directed. "Ease her in; there's plenty of hold."

The lights of Manhattan were lost in that dusky waterway. Sirens spoke harshly, and a ferry returning from the Brooklyn shore threw amber gleams upon the oily water. A towboat passed very close to them; her passage set the launch dancing. All lights had been doused when that of an electric torch speared the darkness.

A wooden platform became visible. From it a ladder arose and disappeared into shadow above. The tidal water whispered and lapped eerily as they rode the swell created by the backwash of the towboat.

"Quiet now!" Nayland Smith spoke urgently. "Lift the spar up and get it across the rail. How many men, Corrigan?"

"Forty-two, Chief."

"I can't see a soul."

"Good work by me!"

Nayland Smith rested his hand upon the shoulder of the man in the bows and mounted to the wooden platform. Another towboat went by as Corrigan joined him. Her starboard light transformed the launch party below into a crew of demons and gleamed evilly on the barrel of a gun which Corrigan carried.

"It was the same two men who brought the fourth passenger?" Smith asked.

"Can't confirm that until we check up with Eastman, who's in charge above. But the other three were brought down by a pair of Chinks, and one of the Chinks rang a bell—which I guess I can locate: I was watching through binoculars. How many times he rang—except it was more than once—is another story."

"I know how many times he rang, Corrigan. *Seven* times. . . . Find the bell."

"Got my hand on it!"

129

The spar, raised upon the shoulders of the launch party, now rested on the rail of the platform. Slowly, quietly it was moved forward. Corrigan snapped his fingers as a signal when it all but touched the door.

"We don't know which way it opens," he whispered—"always supposing it *does* open."

The spar separated the two men.

"That doesn't matter. Ring seven times."

Police Captain Corrigan raised his hand to a sunken bell-push and pressed it seven times. Almost immediately the door opened. Beyond was cavernous darkness.

"Go to it, boys!" Corrigan shouted.

Lustily the spar was plunged through the opening. Nayland Smith and Corrigan shot rays of light into the black gap. Somewhere above a whistle blew. There came a rush of hurrying footsteps upon planking, a subdued uproar of excitement.

"Come on, Corrigan!" snapped Nayland Smith.

Corrigan leaped over the spar and followed his leader into black darkness now partly dispersed by the light of two torches. It was a brick tunnel in which they found themselves, illimitable so far as the power of the lights was concerned. Corrigan paused, turned, and:

"This way, boys!" he shouted.

The patter of feet echoed eerily in that narrow passage. Vaguely, against reflection from the river, the spar could be seen jammed across the doorway. Nayland Smith's light was already far ahead.

"Wait for me, Chief!" Corrigan yelled urgently.

The officer in charge of the hidden party which secretly had been assembling for many hours appeared, a silhouette against a background of shimmering water, leading his men as Corrigan sprang along the tunnel behind Nayland Smith.

Five paces Corrigan had taken when Nayland Smith turned.

"Wait for the men, Corrigan," he cried, his snappy instructions echoing weirdly.

Corrigan paused, turned, and looked back. A line of figures, antlike, streamed in from the river opening. Then:

"My God! what's this?" Corrigan groaned.

Something, something which created a shattering crash, had blotted out the scene. Corrigan turned his light back. Nayland Smith was running to join him.

An iron door, resembling a sluice-gate, had been dropped between them and the river. . . . They were cut off!

THE TEMPLE of the seven-eyed goddess was illuminated by light which shone out from its surrounding alcoves. Since each of these was draped by a curtain of different color, the effect was very curious. These curtains were slightly drawn aside so that from the point occupied by the seven-eyed idol it would have become apparent that many of the cells were occupied.

There were shadowy movements depicted upon the curtains. At the sound of a gong these movements ceased.

The brazen note was still humming around the vault-like place when Dr. Fu Manchu came in. He wore his yellow robe, and a mandarin's cap was set upon his high skull. He took his seat at a table near the pedestal of the carved figure. He glanced at some notes which lay there.

"Greeting," he said gutturally.

A confused murmur of voices from his hidden audience responded.

"I may speak in English," he continued, his precise voice giving its exact value to every syllable which he uttered, "for I am informed that this language is common to all of us present tonight. Those of the Seven not here in person are represented by their accredited nominees, approved by the council. But in accordance with our custom whereby only one of the Seven shall know the other six, it has been necessary, owing to the presence of such nominees, to hold this meeting in the manner arranged."

A murmur which might have been one of assent greeted his words.

"I have succeeded in placing the chief executive we have selected in a position from which no human agency can throw him down. You may take it for granted that he will enjoy the support of the League of Good Americans. The voice of the priest, Patrick Donegal, I have not yet contrived wholly to control. . . . Because of a protective robe which seems to cover him, I regard this priest as the challenge of Rome to our older and deeper philosophy. . . .

"Suitable measures will be taken when the poppy is in flower. There is much more which I have to say, but it

131

must be temporarily postponed, since I have arranged that we shall all hear our chosen executive speak tonight. He is addressing a critical audience in the assembly hall in which Harvey Bragg formerly ruled as king. This is his second public address since Bragg was removed. It will convince you more completely than any words of mine could do of the wisdom of our selection. I beg for silence: you are now listening to a coast-to-coast broadcast."

So closely had Dr. Fu Manchu timed his words that the announcer had ceased speaking when radio contact was made.

Tremendous uproar rose to an hysterical peak, and then slowly subsided. Paul Salvaletti began to speak—a speech destined both by virtue of beauty, phrasing, and the perfect oratory of the man to find a permanent place in American forensic literature.

Salvaletti, to be known from that hour as "Silver Tongue," was, as befitted a selection of Dr. Fu Manchu, probably one of the four greatest orators in the world. Trained by the oratorian fathers and then perfected in a famous dramatic academy of Europe, he spoke seven languages with facility, and he had learned the subtle art of mass control as understood by the Eastern adepts in the Tibetan monastery of Rachê Churân. For two years, efficiently but unobtrusively, he had labored in silence as confidential secretary to Harvey Bragg. He had the absolute confidence of the Bragg following. He had a more intimate knowledge of the inner workings of the League of Good Americans, of the Lotus Transport Corporation, and of the other enterprises which had formed the substantial background of the demagogue, than any man living. He understood human nature, but had the enormous advantage over Bragg of a profound culture. He could speak to the South in the language of the South; he could speak to the world in the language of Cicero.

He began, with perfect art, to deliver this modern version of Mark Antony's oration over the body of Caesar. . . .

2

"What in hell's this?" growled Police Captain Corrigan. "We're jammed!"

The light of his own torch and that of Nayland Smith's became concentrated upon the iron door which had fallen behind them. Dimly, very dimly, they could hear the voices of the party outside.

"Hadn't counted on this," muttered Nayland Smith. "But we mustn't get bothered—we must think."

"Looks to me, Chief," said the police officer, "as if the seven rings work automatically, and that after an interval this second door comes down—like as not to make sure that a big party isn't bulling in."

"Something in that, Corrigan," Nayland Smith rapped. "Outstanding point is—we are cut off."

"I know it."

They stood still, listening. Shouted orders from somebody who had taken charge became dimly audible. Words reached their ears as mere murmurs. The iron door was not only heavy but fitted perfectly in its grooves.

"Can you hear a sound like water, Chief?" Corrigan said in a low voice.

"Yes."

The ray from Nayland Smith's torch searched the floor, the walls, as far ahead as it could reach, revealing nothing but an apparently endless brick tunnel.

"I kind of fancy," Corrigan went on, "that I've heard there used to be a brook or a stream hereabouts in the old days, and that it was switched into a sewer. You can hear running water?"

"I can," said Nayland Smith.

"I guess we're beside it or over it. Used to run from some place near Columbus Park where there was a pond. . . ."

"We have to suppose," said Nayland Smith quietly, "that so far everything is in order——"

"Except that we're trapped!"

"I mean, if, as you suggest, the river door opens mechanically and this outer door falls at an agreed interval, we shall be quite safe in pushing ahead."

"I should feel safer with forty men behind me."

"So should I. The proper routine would be in all probability to reclose the river door, ring the bell seven times, and continue in this way until the whole party was inside."

"Sounds reasonable—but how do we do it? . . . Hullo! look at this!"

Corrigan directed the light of his torch downwards; his hand shook with excitement. Discord of shouting voices grew louder. A crack appeared at the bottom of the iron door. Slowly, it was being raised!

"The opening of the outer door drops it automatically in half a minute or less," said Nayland Smith. "Normally it is raised when the door is closed. They must have moved the spar. Contact has been established which raised it again."

"I'm waiting," Corrigan replied grimly, his gaze fixed upon the slowly moving door. "I'm not built like an eel. When I can get out I'll be the first to cheer. . . ."

In the streets of Chinatown a cordon had been drawn around the suspected area. During the course of the day a census had been taken of the inhabitants in the section indicated by Nayland Smith; outgoings and incomings, all had been accounted for. Most of those interrogated were Chinese, and the Chinaman is a law-respecting citizen. Almost any other would have openly resented the siege conditions to which the inhabitants of this section of New York City found themselves subjected on this occasion.

Mark Hepburn with a guard of three men directed operations. He was feverishly anxious, as his deep-set eyes indicated to everyone he approached. His duty was to make sure that none of the invisible members of Dr. Fu Manchu's organization should escape by the street exits which the vigilance of government men and police engaged upon the inquiry had failed to detect. The importance of his duty was great enough to enable him to force into the background the problem of Moya Adair. Apart from his personal interest, she formed an invaluable link, if only he could succeed in reconciling his conscience with his duty, his own interests with those of the State.

The night had grown bitterly cold; high winds had blown themselves away across the Atlantic; the air had that champagne quality which redoubles a man's vigor.

Many streets were barricaded; a sort of curfew had been imposed upon part of Chinatown. Every householder had been made responsible for the members of his household. Restaurants and cafés were scrutinized from cellar to roof, particularly Wu King's Bar. Residents returning to the barricaded area were required to establish their identity before being admitted. Visitors who did not reside there were escorted to their destination and carefully checked up.

Mark Hepburn had tackled the situation with his usual efficiency. Pretense had been cast aside. All Chinatown knew that the section was being combed for one of the big shots of the underworld.

And all Chinatown remained in suspense; for now the news had spread through those mysterious channels which defy Occidental detection that other members of the Council of the Seven of the Si-Fan were in the city. The dreaded Black Dragon Society of Japan was no more than an offshoot of the Si-Fan, which embraced in its invisible tentacles practically the whole of the colored races of the world. No dweller east of Suez or west of it to Istanbul would have gambled a dollar on the life of a man marked down by the Si-Fan.

3

In the cave of the seven-eyed goddess Dr. Fu Manchu sat, eyes closed, long, ivory hands extended upon the table before him, listening to the silver tones of that distant speaker, to the rising excitement of the audience which he addressed; an audience representing but a fraction of that which from coast to coast hung upon his words—words destined to play a strange part in the history of the country. The other listeners, invisible in the queer cells which surrounded the central apartment, were equally silent, motionless.

In the seventh of these, that which communicated with a series of iron doors protecting the place from the street above, old Sam Pak crouched mummy-like upon a settee listening with the others to that wonderful, inspiring voice speaking in a southern state.

A very faint buzz directly above his head resulted in slit-like eyes being opened in the death mask. Sam Pak turned, glanced up. A tiny disk of blue light showed. Slowly he nodded his shriveled head and watched this blue light. Two, three, four minutes elapsed—and the blue light still prevailed. Whereupon that man of vast knowledge and experience acted. There was something strange here.

The appearance of the blue light was in order, for a seventh representative even now was expected by way of the river-gate. The blue light indicated that the river-gate had been opened by one of the two men on duty who knew its secret. Its persistence indicated that the river-gate had not been reclosed; and this was phenomenal.

But even as Sam Pak stood up and began silently to shuffle in the direction of the door, the blue light flickered, dimmed, flickered again and finally went out.

Something definitely was wrong!

A lesser man would have alarmed the council, but Sam Pak was a great man. Quietly he opened the iron door and ascended the stairs beyond. He opened a second door and mounted higher, switching on lights. Halfway along a stone-faced corridor, stone-paved, he paused beneath a pendent lamp. Reaching up he pulled this pendent.

It dropped, lever fashion, and a section of the seemingly solid wall some five feet high and three feet wide dropped backward like a drawbridge. So perfectly was it fitted, so solid its construction, that he would have been a clever detective indeed who could have found it when it was closed.

Sam Pak, stooping, went into the dark opening. An eerie lapping of moving water had become audible at the moment that the secret door had dropped back. There was a dank, unwholesome smell. He reached for, and found, an iron rail; then from beneath his blue robe he produced a torch and shone its ray ahead.

He stood on a gallery above a deep sewer, an inspection-gallery accessible to, and sometimes used by, the sanitary authorities of the city. Into this a way had been struck from the secret warren below Chinatown and another way out at the further end by the river-bank.

He moved slowly along, a crouched, eerie figure in a whispering, evil place.

At a point where the oily waters disappeared beneath an arch, the gallery seemingly ended, and before a stone wall he paused.

His ancient, clawlike hands manipulated some piece of mechanism, and a small box came to light, a box in which a kind of telephone stood. Sam Pak raised the instrument; he listened.

"Chee, chee, chee!" he hissed.

He hung up the telephone, reclosed the box in which it was hidden and began to return along the iron gallery, moving now with extraordinary rapidity for a man of his years. The unexpected, but not the unforeseen, had happened.

The enemy had forced the water-gate.

4

At the corner of Doyers Street a crowd had gathered beyond the barricade. Those who wished to pass were referred by the police officer on duty to another point, which necessitated a detour. A tall, bearded man, his coat collar turned up and his hat brim pulled down, stood beside a big car, the windows of which were bulletproof, lurking in shadow and studying the group beyond the barricade. A messenger from local police headquarters made his way to his side.

"Captain Hepburn?"

"Yes. What is it?"

"We seem to have lost contact with the party operating under Federal Officer Smith down on East River."

"No news?"

"Not a thing."

Mark Hepburn experienced a sudden, great dread. The perils of the river-gate, although a large party had been assembled, were unknown—unknown as the resources of the formidable group which Nayland Smith sought to break up. His quick imagination presented a moving picture of things which might have happened. Johnson was perfectly capable of taking charge of routine here on the street; indeed, Johnson had done most of the work, Hepburn merely supervising and taking reports. On the other hand, a dash to the waterfront would be technically to desert his post. He turned to the man beside him.

"Go personally," he directed in his monotonous way; "take a launch if you can't make it on shore. Then hurry right back to me to report just what you have seen."

"All right, Captain."

The man set out.

Mark Hepburn entered the bulletproof car and gave brief directions to the driver.

Outside Wu King's Bar the car stopped. Mark Hepburn went in, followed by the three men who had accompanied him. The place was almost wholly patronized by Asiatics, except when squads of sightseers were brought there, Wu King's being one of the show places in Chinatown tours.

A buzz of conversation subsided curiously as the party entered. Following Hepburn's lead they walked through the restaurant to the bar at the further end, glancing keenly at the groups of men and women occupying the tables set in cubicles. Behind the bar Wu King, oily and genial, presided in person, his sly eyes twinkling in a fat, pock-marked face.

"Ah, gen'l'men," he said, rubbing his hands and speaking with an accent which weirdly combined that of the Bowery and Shanghai, "you want some good beer, eh?"

Everyone in the place except Wu King spoke now in a lowered voice; this serpentine hissing created a sinister atmosphere.

"Yes," said Hepburn, "some beer and some news."

"Anything Wu King know, Wu King glad to tell." He pumped up four glasses of creamy lager. "Just say what biting you and Wu King put right, if know enough, which plobably not."

Mark Hepburn paid for the beer and nodded to his companions. Leaning against the bar they all directed their attention towards the groups in the little cubicles. There was another room upstairs, and according to the local police, still another above that where fan-tan and other illegal amusements sometimes took place.

"You seem to be pretty busy?" Hepburn said.

"Yes." The Chinaman revealed a row of perfect but discolored teeth. "Pletty busy. Customers complain funny business outside. You gen'l'men know all about it I guess?"

"My friends here may know. What I want is copy."

"Oh, sure! You a newspaperman?"

"You've got it, Wu. I guess you know most of your customers?"

"Know 'em all, mister. All velly old friend. Some plenty money, some go tick, but all velly good friend. Chinaman good friend to each other, or else—" he shrugged his shoulders—"what become of Chinaman?"

"That's true enough. But I'm out for a story." He turned, fixing deep-set eyes upon the fat face of the proprietor. "I'm told that one of *the Seven* is in town. Is that right, Wu?"

Less experienced than Nayland Smith in the ways of the Orient, he looked for some change of expression in the pockpitted face—and looked in vain. Wu King's immobile features registered nothing whatever.

"The Seven?" he said innocently. "What seven's that, mister?"

5

"I'll say I'm glad to get out," said Corrigan as, assisted by willing helpers, he crawled under the partly raised iron door. "I don't like the looks of that tunnel."

From out of the echoing hollow under the dock came a shouted order:

"Silence!"

A buzz of excited words ceased. The men crowded into the narrow space between the two doors—the outer one partly jammed open by the spar—became silent.

"That's Eastman," said Corrigan. "Let's see what's new."

Outside in a Dantesque scene peopled by moving shadows:

"Launch just been signaled from the bridge," the invisible Eastman explained. "Are you held up there?"

"We were," Corrigan replied shortly. He turned to Nayland Smith. "What now?"

Nayland Smith, a parody of his normal self, wearing a shabby suit and a linen cap which had once been white pulled down over one eye, stood silent behind the speaker. He was tugging at the lobe of his left ear.

"A change of plan," he rapped. "This is something I had not foreseen. Get all the men under cover again, Corrigan, and run the launch out of sight downstream. Pick two good men to remain with us. Jump to it."

"D'you hear that, Eastman?" Corrigan shouted. "Everybody under cover, just like when we first came up. The launch to clear the dock, lay up and wait for signals. Get busy." He turned to two men who stood near to the spot where the spar projected into the partly open doorway. "You two," he said, "stand by. Everybody else up the ladder."

An ordered scuffling followed; three men tumbled into the launch and the others, some of whom had been crowded into the narrow space between the two doors, hurried up the ladder to the deck of the dock above. The launch went out astern, a phantom craft against the myriad lights reflected in the water, and disappeared from view.

"I want a small wedge fixed in that door; a clasp-knife would do, or anything that will bear the pressure."

Smith ran inside, flashing the light of his torch ahead, and springing over the spar which crossed the tunnel. The iron door beyond was about two-thirds raised.

"All ready, Chief," came a voice. "I've got the door jammed."

"Good. Now, Corrigan, join us. You two men get inside but hang on to the door."

There came a further scuffling. The men, two black silhouettes, crossed the narrow opening.

"Are you ready?" rapped Nayland Smith.

"All ready, Chief."

"Pull. Now, Corrigan, we have to get the spar inside."

Pulling simultaneously, the thing was done and the spar laid down against one wall of the tunnel.

"Now," Nayland Smith directed breathlessly, "ease the door to. Don't let it bang if you can help it."

Slowly the door, propelled by a powerful spring, closed, almost dragging the two men with it; and as it closed, that second door which resembled a sluice-gate rose, inch by inch. At last:

"Can't hang on any longer, Captain," one of the men reported; "we shall get our hands jammed."

"Let go," Smith ordered.

The door snapped to; there was a slight grinding sound as its edge came in contact with the obstacle which had been placed there to hold it. Nayland Smith flashed his light upward. . . .

Less than two inches of the drop-gate showed in the slot in the ceiling of the tunnel.

139

The exact working of this cunning mechanism was not clear, and the place in which they stood afforded no cover whatever.

"I get your idea," said Corrigan, "but short of shooting 'em down, we haven't a chance."

"No shooting without orders."

"I guess they'll see the door's phony, anyway," said one of the men.

"Once they're under the dock, Eastman will drop on 'em," Corrigan replied. "Get your guns out, boys. The moment that door comes open, the order is 'stick 'em up.'"

There was a moment of silence broken only by river sounds audible through the narrow opening made by the wedge.

"Just check up," said Corrigan. "I'm thinking, Chief, maybe the machinery won't work unless the door is tight closed. There's just time to see if we can haul it open. Go to it, boys!"

"I can just get a hold," came hoarsely.

"Pull—not far—just to see if she moves."

Another interval and then:

"Sure, we could haul it open right enough."

"Then stand by," rapped Nayland Smith; "haul if there's any hitch."

Up above, Eastman, peering through a gap in a row of barrels, saw the little motor craft stealing downstream, sometimes bathed in light, sometimes lost in darkness. One of the two Chinamen on board squatted in the bows, looking out sharply ahead, as the other drove the engine. A dim figure was seated astern; mist hovered over the water.

"This is some damned conjuring trick," Eastman muttered.

The man in the stern, as moving lights from a passing steamboat momentarily had revealed, wore black oilskins and a gleaming sou'wester beneath the brim of which his features were entirely hidden. His dress was identical with that of the four who had preceded him as passengers in the launch!

The concealed party on the dock watched breathlessly as the little craft, rolling on an oily swell, was turned into the narrow opening all but invisible from midriver and brought to the ladderway. The maneuver was performed smoothly; the man in the bows grasping the rail, extending one hand to the passenger in the stern. The engine had been shut off as they took the bend, and all lights doused.

Stepping cautiously, the passenger came forward and was assisted onto the ladder. There was an exchange of whispered words, indistinguishable to the men above. But Eastman, who had watched a previous arrival through binoculars from a police boat, guessed that the Chinaman who had been in the bows was leading the way. . . .

Inside, in utter darkness, four men waited tensely. Faintly to their ears came the sound of footsteps on the ladder.

"Stand by," said Corrigan in a low voice; "cover 'em."

The door opened—whether automatically or because it was pulled by the two men on duty was not at the moment apparent.

"Hands up!" rapped Nayland Smith.

He shot the ray of a torch fully into the face of the man who entered; a meaningless Mongolian face, which even under these circumstances exhibited no change of expression whatever. The man raised his hands above his head. The figure immediately behind him clad in gleaming black made a similar movement.

From outside came a muffled shout, a clatter of footsteps —the sound of a splash in the river, and:

"Get that man!" Eastman was heard shouting. "He went in off the stern of the boat!"

Answering shouts responded, scurrying movements.

"Search the blackbird, Waygood," Corrigan directed."You —search the Chink."

The man addressed as Waygood roughly snatched the sou'wester from the head of the traveler and peeled back his oilskin at the same moment that the other roughly overhauled the immobile Chinaman.

Nayland Smith stared eagerly into the face revealed. Recognition of an astounding fact had come to him. By one of those divine accidents which so rarely rallied to his aid, he had selected for this attempt on Fu Manchu's underground quarters a night when influential supporters of the movement were meeting in conference!

He had hoped to see the stoical features of General Li Wu Chang—but he was disappointed.

He saw a face Oriental in character, but rather of the Near than of the Far East; a proud, olive-skinned face with flashing dark eyes and supercilious lips. But the man was unknown to him.

The Chinaman was relieved of an automatic and a wicked-looking knife. The other was apparently unarmed, but a curious fact came to light when his oilskins were slipped off. Beneath them he wore a black robe, with a cowl!

Eastman burst in at the door.

"We've lost the second Chink," he reported. "I guess he swims like a shark. He must have swum under water

141

for a long time, unless he knocked himself out! Anyway, there's no trace of him. And there's a sea mist coming up."

"Bad luck," snapped Nayland Smith, "but keep a sharp lookout." Turning to Corrigan: "Have this Chinaman taken outside," he directed. "I have some questions to put to the other."

A few moments later he stood before the dignified Oriental upon whose face Corrigan directed the light of a torch.

"Do you know the Chinaman, Corrigan?"

"No. But Finney, down on Mott Street, will know him when he sees him; he knows every Chink in the town."

Nayland Smith fixed his penetrating regard upon the features of the Egyptian: that the man was an Egyptian he had now determined.

"What is your name?" he demanded.

"By what authority do you ask?"

The man, who retained a remarkable composure, spoke easily, in perfect English and with a cultured voice.

"I am a government agent. What is your name?"

"Judging from the treatment received by my Chinese acquaintance," the Egyptian replied, "I have nothing but a man-handling to gain by silence. My name is Ahmed Fayume. Would you care to see my passport?"

"Hand it to Police Captain Corrigan."

The Egyptian, from beneath the curious robe which he wore, produced a passport which he handed to Corrigan, who glared at him in that intimidating manner cultivated by the police and opened the document savagely as though he hated it.

"When did you arrive in New York?"

"Last night by the *Île de France*."

"And you are staying at . . ."

"The Grosvenor-Grand."

"What is your business in the States?"

"I am on a visit to Washington."

"Are you a diplomat?"

"I am attached to the personal suite of King Fuad of Egypt."

"That's right," growled Corrigan, looking up from the passport. "Something funny about this."

His expression became puzzled.

"Perhaps, Mr. Fayume," said Nayland Smith crisply, "you can explain what you are doing here tonight in the company of two suspected men."

The Egyptian smiled slightly.

"Naturally I was unaware that they are suspected men,"

he replied. "When the Egyptian consulate put me in touch with them, I was under the impression that I was being taken to a unique house of entertainment where hashish and other amusements were provided."

"Indeed. But why the fancy dress?"

The black domino?" The Egyptian continued to smile. "This was provided by my guides, as visitors to the establishment to which I refer do not invariably wish to be recognized."

Nayland Smith continued to stare into the large velvety eyes of the speaker, and then:

"Your story requires investigation, Mr. Fayume," he said dryly. "In the meantime, I must ask you to regard yourself as under arrest. Will you be good enough to empty your pockets?"

Ahmed Fayume shrugged his shoulders resignedly and obeyed the order.

"I fear," he said calmly, "that you are creating an international incident. . . ."

6

A report received out on the street as the party left Wu King's Bar, from the man whom Hepburn had dispatched to East River, was reassuring. The water-gate referred to by Nayland Smith had actually been discovered; two arrests had been made: operations on that front were proceeding in accordance with plan.

The life of Chinatown within the barricaded area carried on much along its usual lines. The stoicism of the Asiatic, like the fatalism of the Arab, makes for acceptance of things as they are. From a dry-goods store, when a customer entered or emerged, came mingled odors of joss stick and bombay duck; attractively lighted restaurants seemed to be well patronized; lobsters, crayfish and other crustacean delicacies dear to the Chinese palate were displayed in green herbal settings. John Chinaman blandly minded his own business, so that there seemed to be something quite grotesque about the guarded barrier at the end of the street.

Mark Hepburn was badly worried. Nayland Smith's unique experience had enabled him to postulate the existence of a Chinatown headquarters and of a river-gate. Right in this, it seemed improbable that he was wrong in his theory that there were exits and entrances somewhere on the streets surrounding this particular block.

He turned to Detective Inspector Finney, who silently walked beside him.

"You tell me there's nothing secret about Chinatown any more," he said slowly; "if that's true, there's a bad muddle here."

Inspector Finney, a short, thickset man with a red, square-jawed face, wearing rainproofs and a hard black hat, turned and stared at Hepburn.

"There's no more iron doors," he declared definitely. "An iron door couldn't get unloaded and set up without I knew about it. There used to be gambling joints and opium dens, but since the new regulations they've all moved over to the other shore, see? It's different over there—not so strict. All my boys can't be deaf and blind. When we get the word, we'll check up the block. If any strangers have arrived they'll have to show their birthmarks."

Mark Hepburn, inside one of the barriers beyond which stood a group of curious onlookers, pulled up sharply, and turning to Finney:

"There's just one part of this area," he said, "which I haven't explored—the roofs." He turned to one of a group behind him, and: "You're in charge, Johnson," he added. "I don't expect to be long."

Ten minutes later, followed by Inspector Finney and two men, Hepburn climbed the fire ladders at the back of a warehouse building which seemed to be deserted. No light showed from any of the windows. When at last they stepped upon the leads:

"Stick to the shadow," said Hepburn sharply. "There's a high point at the end of the block from which we might be seen."

"Sure," Finney replied; "that's the building where Wu King's Bar is located. He goes three floors up—the rest is a Chinese apartment house. I checked up on every apartment six o'clock this evening, and there's a man on the street entrance. Outside of this block we're overlooked plenty any way."

"There are lights in the top story of the Wu King building. Maybe you recall who lives there?"

"Wu King and his wife live up there," came the voice of one of the men, hidden in shadows behind him. "He owns the whole building but rents part of it out. He's one of the wealthiest Chinks around here."

Mark Hepburn was becoming feverishly restless. He experienced an intense urge for action. These vague, rather aimless investigations failed to engross his mind. Even now, with the countless lights of the city around him, the curiously altered values of street noises rising to his ears, the taunting mystery which lay somewhere below, he found his thoughts, and not for the first time that night, leading him into a dream world inhabited by Moya Adair.

He wondered what she was doing at that moment—what duties had been imposed upon her by the sinister President. She had told him next to nothing. For all he knew to the contrary, her slavery might take her to the mysterious Chinatown base, that unimaginable den which in grotesque forms sometimes haunted his sleep. The awful idea presented itself that if Nayland Smith's raid should prove successful, Moya might be one of the prisoners!

A damp gray mist borne upon a fickle breeze was creeping insidiously through the streets of Chinatown.

"Is there any way of obtaining a glimpse of that apartment?" he asked.

"We could step right up and ring the bell," Finney answered. "Otherwise, not so easy. Looks to me as if the ladders from that point join up with the lower roof beyond the dip. And I don't know if we can get from this one down to the other."

"Stay in the shadows as much as possible," Hepburn directed.

He set out towards the upstanding story of Wu King's building, which like a squat tower dominated the flat surface of the leads.

7

"There's something wrong here," said Nayland Smith.

From the iron gallery upon which he stood he shone the light of his torch down upon slowly moving, evil-smelling water.

"We've got into one of the main sewers," said Corrigan: "that's what's wrong. From the time it's taken us to make it I should say we're way up on Second; outside the suspected area, anyway."

He turned, looking back. It was an eerie spectacle. Moving lights dotted the tunnel—the torches of the raiding party. Sometimes out of whispering shadows a face would emerge smudgily as a straying beam impinged upon it. There were muffled voices and the rattle of feet on iron treads.

"Suppose we try back," came a muffled cry. "We might go on this way all night."

"Turn back," snapped Nayland Smith irritably. "This place is suffocating, and we're obviously on the wrong track."

"There's a catch somewhere," Corrigan agreed. "All we can do is sit around the rat hole and wait for the rat to come out."

This was by no means what Nayland Smith had planned. He was savagely disappointed. Indeed, the failure of his ambitious scheme would have left a sense of humiliation had it not been for the arrests made on the East River. Here at least was confirmation of his theory that the door under the dock belonging to the South Coast Trade Line undoubtedly was used by the group surrounding Dr. Fu Manchu.

It was infuriating to realize, as he had realized at the moment of the arrest of the Egyptian, that in all probability a meeting of the Council of Seven was actually taking place tonight!

The cowled robe was particularly significant. There were reasons why those summoned to be present did not wish to divulge their identity to the others: this was obvious. Ahmed Fayume was one of the Seven—a director of the Si-Fan. But it was improbable, owing to the man's diplomatic credentials, that they would ever succeed in convicting him of any offense against the government of the United States.

From experience he knew that all attempts to interrogate the Chinese prisoner must fail. He took it for granted that the captive was a servant of Fu Manchu: that such an admission could ever be forced from his lips was wildly improbable. The other Chinaman had escaped; by now, had probably given the alarm. . . .

Corrigan's words offered the only consolation. He recognized that it would be impracticable to sustain the siege of an area of Chinatown long enough to make it effective. He had been right, but he had failed. There was only one glimmer of hope. And suddenly he felt glad that the other Chinaman had escaped.

If, and he had little doubt upon the point, notable conspirators were present tonight, the raid on the secret watergate might result in a desperate bid for freedom above!

But he was very silent as he brought up the rear of the party with Corrigan, groping back along the noisome tunnel. At points, vague booming noises echoed from above, the sound made by the heavy traffic. Always there was the echoing whisper of water. At a point where a lower inspection gallery crossed beneath that which they were following, he paused.

"Where do you estimate we stand, Corrigan?" he snapped.

"I should say about under Bayard and East Broadway. It's a guess—but I don't think I'm far out."

"Detail men to watch this junction."

8

"Stand on the foot of the ladder, Finney," Hepburn directed.

The detective inspector gingerly took his place.

"Now, you," indicating another man, "stand underneath and hold the rungs; and you," to a third, "hang onto the side so that it doesn't topple over. All set?"

The ladder, a short one, had been discovered in the warehouse yard and brought up onto the roof. Now, held by the three men, it perilously overhung a yawning gap, a gulley at the bottom of which, seen through a curtain of mist, were lights moving and stationary. Human voices distorted by the fog, muted sounds of movement were audible; but the characteristic hooting of taxicabs was missing, for this was one of the barricaded streets: the entrance to Wu King's Bar lay immediately beneath.

"All ready, Captain."

Mark Hepburn cautiously began to climb the ladder.

He moved in the shadow of the top story of Wu King's apartment house. It was a dizzy proceeding: at the cold, starry sky which seemed to beckon to him from the right of the building he could not trust himself to look, nor downward into the misty chasm of the street. Rung by rung he mounted—his objective that lighted window still some six feet above. Upward he climbed.

And, presently, standing two rungs from the top, he could rest his hands upon the ledge and look into the room to which this window belonged.

He saw a sight so strange that at first he could not fathom its significance. . . .

An oddly appointed sitting room was visible, its character and the character of the lamps striking a definite Oriental note. Brightly colored rugs were strewn upon the floor, and he saw that there were divans against two of the walls. The predominant color scheme of illumination seemed to be purple, so that he found great difficulty in making out what was taking place at the further end.

A window there was widely opened, and two Chinamen seemed to be engaged in hauling upon a line. This in itself was singular, but the third and only other figure in the room struck an ultimate note of the bizarre.

147

It was that of a man wearing a black cowled robe. The cowl entirely covered his face, but was provided with two eyeholes, so that save for the color of his dress he resembled one of the Misericordia Brethren!

He was standing quite still just behind the Chinamen, who, as Mark Hepburn watched, hauled in at the open window an equipment resembling a bosun's chair. Even now the significance of what was going on had not fully penetrated to his mind. The cowled man, clutching his robe about his legs and assisted by one of the Chinamen, took his place in the chair. Again they began hauling.

The black figure disappeared through the window. . . .

Now the truth burst upon him. Nayland Smith's raid of the water-gate had succeeded. . . . This was an emergency exit from the surrounded block!

How many had gone before? How many were yet to come? It was clear enough. A ropeway had been thrown across the street to some tall building on the opposite side, and above the very heads of the patrolling police the wanted men were being wound across to safety!

He moved his foot, urgent to descend. It was not too late to locate that other building. . . .

Then he paused.

As the two Chinamen bore upon the line, from a curtained opening left of the room another figure entered.

It was that of a tall man wearing a yellow robe; a man whose majestic features conveyed a sense of such power that Hepburn's movement was arrested. Tightly clutching the ledge, he watched—watched that high-shouldered, imposing figure standing motionless in the curtained entrance. Perhaps his regard became so intense as to communicate a sense of his presence to the majestic newcomer.

Slowly the massive head was turned. Hepburn, through the glass of the window, met the regard of a pair of vivid green eyes which seemed to be looking directly into his own. . . . Never in his life had he seen such eyes. If, under the circumstances, he was actually visible from inside the room he could not be sure; but of one fact, one astounding fact, he was certain:

This was Dr. Fu Manchu!

Mark Hepburn, keyed up by the immensity of the moment, ventured to the very top of the swaying ladder. He clutched a hook on one side of the window, placed there for the convenience of window-cleaners, and crashed his right heel through a pane of glass.

Stooping, he thrust his automatic through the opening, and:

"Hands up, Fu Manchu!" he shouted, his voice rising from syllable to syllable upon notes of excitement.

The sea mist continued its insidious invasion of the streets of Chinatown. One by one it blotted out the lights below. A voice spoke from the leads at the foot of the ladder:

"Go easy, Captain; we can't catch you if you fall!"

Hepburn scarcely heeded the cry: his entire interest was focused upon the uncanny being who stood in the curtained opening. The two men straining on the rope were wonderfully trained servants; for at the glass crash and harsh words of command they had not started, had not turned, but had continued to perform mechanically the duty allotted to them!

Slowly, the perturbing regard of those green eyes never wavering, the tall Chinaman raised his hands. If he could not see the speaker, he could see the barrel of the automatic. From below:

"Bear left!" came urgently. "We can't hold the ladder."

During one irrevocable moment Hepburn tore his attention away. In that moment the room became plunged in darkness!

Clutching at the hook he fired in the direction of the curtained doorway . . . and the flash showed it to be empty. Further shots would be wasted. He craned downward.

"Pass the word there's a ropeway across the street. This damnable fog has helped them. Have the house opposite covered and searched."

Now came shouted orders, sounds of running, muffled cries from the police below. . . .

"Arrest everyone in Wu King's. Search the place from roof to cellar."

He fired again in the direction of the distant window, aiming over the heads of the Chinamen. Craning forward, he heard scurrying footsteps; then came silence. Perilously, but aided by a high exaltation which had come to him in the moment when he knew that he actually stood in the presence of the all but fabulous Dr. Fu Manchu, he found his foothold on the ladder and descended to the roof. Finney, one arm thrown out, hauled him back from the parapet upon which the ladder was poised, and:

"What's up there, Captain?" he demanded hoarsely. "I feel a fool glued down here to the ladder."

"A getaway across the street. Get busy. We must hurry."

But already, delegating to a competent junior the matter of Wu King's and of those inside it, Lieutenant Johnson had entered the building indicated.

It consisted of a dry-goods store which had been closed half an hour before, and of apartments above. (Investigations were to prove that the landlord was none other than Wu King.) Employing those methods peculiar to the police responsible for the good conduct of Chinatown, entrance was forced to every apartment and every room right to the top. Here a hitch occurred.

On the top story was a lodge of the Hip Sing Tong. No key was forthcoming, and the door defied united attack.

As a precautionary measure every man, woman and child found in the building had been arrested. Laden police wagons were taking them to the Tombs when Hepburn came racing up to the landing. The work of the demolition of the door of the Tong temple had commenced. It was proving a tough job when a cry came:

"Make way there!"

A grim-faced policeman appeared from below, holding an elderly Chinaman by the scruff of the neck.

"He's got the key," he explained laconically.

A moment later the door was thrown open. Light was searched for and found, and the garishly decorated place revealed.

It was permeated by a curious odor of stale incense wafted in their direction by a draught from a window overhanging the street. Tackle lay upon the floor; a pulley had been rigged to one of the beams which crossed the ceiling. It was to this spot that escape had been made from the top story of Wu King's building.

The Tong temple was empty from wall to wall. . . .

26 *THE SILVER BOX*

IN HIS TOWER STUDY Dr. Fu Manchu spoke softly.

Two points of light glowed upon the switchboard on the table.

"It was well done, my friend, but the rest is merely a question of time. Base 3 must be vacated. It is regrettable that the representative from Egypt should have been arrested, but steps have been taken to ensure his release. Of Wu Chang's silence we are certain; other representatives are safe. You are short of helpers, therefore many splendid specimens must be sacrificed. But make good your own escape, leaving nothing behind that might act as a clue for the enemy."

"I hear, Master," the voice of old Sam Pak replied as though he stood in the room. "I shall see to these matters."

"Instinct is greater than wit," the guttural voice of Dr. Fu Manchu continued. "By instinct Enemy Number One has smelled us out. I hear you hiss, my friend. We shall see. I have a plan."

"Do you desire, Marquis, that the way be made easy?"

"Such is my wish. Give them this hollow triumph: it will blind their eyes. Base 3 is of no further service: move in this matter, my friend."

Long fingers manipulated switches. The two lights became extinguished, but another appeared upon the board.

"Report," Dr. Fu Manchu directed, "of Number covering Base 3."

"Report to hand," the Teutonic tones of the Memory Man replied, "timed 11.36. Wu King's Bar was raided at 11.05 and everyone on the premises, including Wu King and members of his family, arrested by police. Emergency exit is also in their hands; many other arrests—some forty in all. The barricades have been raised, and everything is normal except that the area is being heavily patrolled. Government agent in charge of operations tonight identified as Captain Mark Hepburn, U.S.M.C. Captain Hepburn has left the area—covered. Report ends. From Number 37."

There was a moment of silence; the long fingers resting upon the lacquered table were so still that they might have been wrought of smoked ivory.

"Report," the voice directed, "of Number responsible for protection of representatives."

"Report of Protection Bureau to hand," the Memory Man replied, "timed 11.50. All are safely returned to their hotels or places of residence, with the exception of Egyptian representative. He was arrested at Entrance 4 together with one Wu Chang who was in his company. This arrest was the subject of an earlier report."

"Latest report of Number covering Exit 4."

"To hand, time 11.38. The raiding party believed to be in charge of Police Captain Corrigan has withdrawn, leaving men estimated at seven to nine covering the point. Report ends. This from Number 49."

"Prepare coast-to-coast reports. I shall require you to relay them in the order received, in one hour."

Amber light prevailed again in the domed room where the man of miraculous memory worked upon his endless task of fashioning that majestic Chinese head. And at the moment that the light reappeared, the long bony fingers of Dr. Fu Manchu reached out to the silver box. Raising the lid, he extracted the delicate equipment for opium smoking which this receptacle contained.

2

"What's the idea, Hepburn?" rapped Nayland Smith.

The New York *Times* propped up against a coffee pot, he was sitting at a frugal breakfast as Hepburn came into the sitting room. Save for a suggestion of shadows beneath his keen eyes, there was little in that bronzed face to show the state of sustained nervous tension in which Nayland Smith had been during the past forty-eight hours. Automatically filling his pipe, he stared at Hepburn.

The mustache and beard had vanished. Mark Hepburn was again his clean-shaven self. He smiled in his almost apologetic way.

"Wasn't it your friend Kipling who said that women and elephants never forget?" he asked. "I guess he might have included Dr. Fu Manchu. Anyway, I was shot at twice last night!"

Nayland Smith nodded.

"You're right," he said rapidly. "I had forgotten momentarily that he saw you at the window. Yes, the bearded newspaperman must disappear."

Fey entered from the kitchenette bearing silver-covered dishes upon a tray; an appetizing odor accompanied him.

Fey's behaviour was that of a well-trained servant in a peaceful English home.

"I am making fresh coffee, sir," he said to Hepburn. "It will be ready in a moment."

He uncovered the dishes and withdrew.

"I am rapidly coming to the conclusion," said Nayland Smith while Hepburn explored under the covers, "that we have outstayed our welcome here. It's only a question of time for one or both of us to be caught either going out or coming in."

Hepburn did not reply. Nayland Smith struck a match, lighted his pipe and continued:

"So far we have been immoderately lucky, although both of us have had narrow squeaks. But we know that this place is covered night and day. It would be wise, I think, if we made other arrangements."

"I am disposed to agree with you," said Mark Hepburn slowly.

"The papers—" Nayland Smith indicated a score of loose sheets upon the carpet beside him—"are reticent about our abortive raid. A washout, Hepburn! Impossible to hold either of the prisoners. We have no evidence against them."

"I know it."

Fey entered with coffee and then withdrew to his tiny sanctum.

"It is merely a question of time," Smith went on, unconsciously echoing the words of Dr. Fu Manchu, "for us to find this Chinese rabbit warren. I attended the lineup this morning, but it's a waste of breath to interrogate a Chinaman. This fact undoubtedly accounts for the survival of torture in their own country. Wu King, as I anticipated, fell back on the story of Tong warfare. Centre Street is beginning to regard me as a tiresome fanatic. Yet—" he brought his palm sharply down upon the table—"I was right about the Chinatown base. It's there, but by the time we find it it will be deserted. An impasse, Hepburn, and our next move in doubt."

He pointed to the newspaper propped up against the coffee pot.

"I begin to see the hand of Fu Manchu everywhere. Although I wore glasses and my clerical dress (upon which you have complimented me) I nearly came to grief on the corner right outside here this morning."

"What happened?"

"A heavy lorry, ignoring signals, drove at me hell-for-leather! Only the skill of my driver saved me. The man said

153

his brakes had failed. . . . The lorry belonged to the Lotus Corporation."

"But Smith——"

"We must expect it. Our enemy is a man of genius. Our small subterfuges probably amuse him! Consider what's at stake! Have you glanced at the Abyssinian situation, for instance? Dr. Fu Manchu's triumph here would mean the end of Italy's ambition."

"You think so?"

Hepburn looked up sharply.

"I know it," Nayland Smith returned. "The map of the world is going to be altered, Hepburn, unless we can check what is going on in this country. Have you given due thought to the fact that almost overnight Paul Salvaletti has become a national figure?"

"Yes; I can't fit him into the picture."

"There is one very curious point . . ."

"To what do you refer?"

"Lola Dumas is with Salvaletti. She is frequently in the news with him."

"Is that so strange? She has always been associated with the League of Good Americans."

"The League of Good Americans is merely another name for Dr. Fu Manchu," rapped Nayland Smith, standing up and beginning to pace the floor. "It is a point of very great interest: it implies that Dr. Fu Manchu is backing Salvaletti; in other words, that Salvaletti is not an opportunist who has sprung into the breach——"

"Good heavens!" Hepburn laid down his fork, "the breach was *prepared* for him?"

"Exactly."

"Is it possible!"

"The pattern begins to become apparent. We have been looking too closely at one small piece of it. I have read the report upon Salvaletti. Even now it is far from complete, but it would appear that his training throughout has tended inevitably in one direction. Thank heaven that Abbot Donegal is safe. I have said it before, I say it again: that priest's life is valuable. He may yet be called upon to stem the tide. Look at the papers . . ."

In his restless promenade he stirred the loose sheets with his foot.

"The grave problems facing the Old World are allotted but little space. The nervous collapse (as such it is accepted) of Orwin Prescott merely occurs as a brief bulletin from Weaver's Farm. The several murders which have decorated

154

the Doctor's visit to the United States are falling into the background. Even our Chinatown raid is granted scanty honors. No, Harvey Bragg, the Martyr, continues to dominate the news—his name now coupled with that of Paul Salvaletti. And—a significant fact, as I have said—Lola Dumas is creeping in."

There was a short silence interrupted only by the buzzing of the telephone, the subdued voice of Fey answering in an adjoining room. Evidently none of the messages was of sufficient importance to demand the presence of Nayland Smith or Hepburn. But Fey would be making careful notes. Smith, staring out of the window, saw that all trace of fog had disappeared; that icily clear visibility which sometimes characterizes New York City in the winter months was prevailing.

"Are you looking at the Stratton Building, Smith?" Hepburn asked.

"Yes," snapped Smith. "Why?"

"You remember what I told you about the strange man who lives up there at the top—as reported by Robbie Adair?"

"Yes."

"Perhaps——I admit maybe because it is associated with Mrs. Adair, I am very curious about this man. I put inquiries in hand late last night and I have a report this morning. There's rather a queer thing about the Stratton Building."

"What is it?"

Nayland Smith turned and looked at Hepburn.

"This—so far as the report goes; it's by no means complete:—The whole of the building is occupied by offices of concerns in which the late Harvey Bragg was interested."

"What!"

"The New York headquarters of the League of Good Americans is there; the head office of the Lotus Transport Corporation; even the South Coast Trade Line has an office in the building."

Nayland Smith came forward, resting his hands upon the table; bending down, he stared keenly into Mark Hepburn's eyes.

"This is very interesting," he said slowly.

"I think so. It's odd, to say the least. Therefore I arranged early this morning to inspect the lightning conductors—by courtesy of the Midtown Electric Corporation. I may discover nothing, but at least it will give me access to a number of the rooms in the building."

"You interest me keenly," said Nayland Smith, returning to the window and staring up at the Stratton Building.

"The League of Good Americans, eh? You must realize, Hepburn, that the great plot doesn't end with the control of the United States. It embraces Australia, the Philippines, and ultimately Canada! Middle Western farmers, crippled by mortgages, are being subsidized by the league and sent to Alaska, where unconsciously they are establishing a nucleus of Fu Manchu's future domination!"

"In heaven's name where does all the money come from?"

"From the Si-Fan, the oldest and most powerful secret society in the world. If the truth about the League of Good Americans—'America for every man and every man for America'—reached the public, I shudder to think what the reaction would be! But to return to personal matters—What are your plans in regard to Mrs. Adair?"

"I have none." Mark Hepburn spoke slowly, his voice sounding even more monotonous than usual. "I have told you everything I know about her, Smith. And I think you will agree that the situation is one of great danger."

"It is—for both. I assume that you are leaving it to Mrs. Adair to communicate with you?"

"I must."

Nayland Smith stared hard for a moment, and then:

"She may be a trump card, Hepburn," he said, "but frankly, I don't know how to play her."

3

"Saw my funny man last night, Goofy," said Robbie Adair, laying down his porridge spoon and staring up wide eyed at Nurse Goff. "Funny man who makes heads."

"I believe he's just a dream of yours, child," Nurse Goff declared. "I have never seen him."

But Robbie was very earnest on the point, and was not to be checked. According to his account, the mysterious madman who hurled models of human heads from his lofty studio had appeared on the previous night. Robbie had awakened very late; he knew it had been very late " 'cause of the way the sky looked." He had gone to the window and had seen the man hurl a plaster head far out over the dome.

"I never heard such a silly tale in my life," Nurse Goff declared. "God bless the child—he's dreaming!"

"Not dreaming," Robbie declared stoutly. "Please can I have some jam? Is Mum coming today?"

"I don't know, dear; I hope so."

"Are we going to the garden?"

"If it's fine, Robbie."

Robbie dealt with bread and jam for some time, and then:

"Will Uncle Mark be there?" he inquired.

"I don't think so, dear."

"Why not? I like Uncle Mark—all 'cept his whiskers. I like Yellow Uncle, too, but he never comes."

Nurse Goff suppressed a shudder. The man whom the boy had christened "Yellow Uncle" terrified her as her dour Scottish nature had never been terrified before. His existence in the life of Mrs. Adair, whom she respected as well as liked, was a mystery beyond her understanding. Rare though his visits were, that he was Mrs. Adair's protector she took for granted. But how Mrs. Adair, beautiful and delicately nurtured, ever could have begun this association with the dreadful Chinaman was something which Mary Goff simply could not understand. The affection of Robbie for this sinister being was to her mind even a greater problem.

"Give me an auto on my birfday," Robbie added reminiscently; "Yellow Uncle did."

"*Gave* you an auto, Robbie. God bless the boy! I don't know where you get these words. . . ."

When, an hour later, his "auto" packed behind in the big Rolls driven by Joe, the cheerful Negro chauffeur, lonely little Robbie accompanied by Nurse Goff set out for his Long Island playground, a "protection" party in a Z-car was following.

Far in the rear, keeping the Z-car in sight, a government car in charge of Lieutenant Johnson brought up the rear of the queer procession.

27 *THE STRATTON BUILDING*

MARK HEPBURN, in blue overalls and wearing a peaked cap, crept out from a window onto a dizzy parapet. Two men similarly attired followed him. One was an operative of Midtown Electric, the firm which had installed the lightning conductors; the other was a federal agent. They were on the forty-seventh floor of the Stratton Building. The leaded dome swept up above them; below the New York hive buzzed ceaselessly.

"This way," said Hepburn, and headed along the parapet.

He constantly looked down into a deep gutter which formed their path until, at a point commanding an oblique view of the gulley which was Park Avenue, he pulled up sharply.

Storm clouds were gathering and sweeping over the city. To look upward was to derive an impression that the towering building swayed like a ship. Mark Hepburn was looking downward. He suppressed an exclamation of satisfaction.

Fragments of clay littered the gutter; on some of the larger pieces might be seen the imprint of a modeler's work. The madman of the Stratton Building was no myth, but an actuality!

Hepburn glanced up for a moment. The effect of the racing clouds above the tower of the building was to make him dizzy. He felt himself lurching and closed his eyes quickly; but he had seen what he wanted to see.

Above the slope of the leaded dome was an iron gallery upon which two windows opened. . . .

"Steady-oh, Captain!" said the government man, seeing him sway. "It's taken a long time to get up, but it wouldn't take long to fall down!"

Hepburn, the moment of nausea past, stared again at the fragments at his feet.

"All right," he replied; "I was never a mountaineer."

He knelt down and examined the pieces of hard clay with keen curiosity. They surely formed part of a modeled head, possibly of more than one modeled head; but no one of them was big enough to give any indication of the character of the finished work. Over his shoulder:

"Gather all these pieces together," he directed, "and bring them away."

The man from the electric firm watched the two agents in respectful silence.

"Ha! what's this?" Hepburn exclaimed.

He had come upon a wired frame to which portions of crumbling clay still adhered. But what had provoked his words when he picked the thing up had been the presence upon the wooden frame, fixed by two drawing pins, of what resembled a tiny colored miniature of a human face, framed around with white paper.

He detached this curious object from the wood and examined it more closely. Raising the mount he stared for a long time at that which lay beneath.

It was a three-cent Daniel Webster stamp, dated 1932, gummed upside down upon a piece of cardboard, then framed by the paper in which a pear-shaped opening had been cut. The effect, when the frame was dropped over the stamp, was singular to a degree.

It produced a hideous Chinese face!

Mark Hepburn took out his notecase and carefully placed this queer discovery in it. As he returned the case to his pocket a memory came of hypnotic green eyes staring into his own—a memory of the unforgettable features of Dr. Fu Manchu as he had seen them through the broken window on the night of the Chinatown raid. . . .

Yes, the fact was unmistakable: inverted and framed in this way, the Daniel Webster stamp presented a caricature, but a recognizable caricature, of Dr. Fu Manchu!

A problem for Nayland Smith's consideration: no more false moves must be made. But here was a building occupied, so far as he knew, entirely by persons associated directly, or indirectly, with the activities of the League of Good Americans. At the top it seemed a madman resided; a madman who modeled clay heads, and who apparently had possessed and thrown away this queer miniature. Definitely there was a link here which must be tested, but tested cautiously.

Thus far he had every reason to believe that his investigation had been carried out without arousing suspicion. He had penetrated to a number of offices on many floors, craning out of windows in his quest of the supposed flaw in the lightning conductors. He had observed nothing abnormal anywhere, and had been civilly treated by a Mr. Schmidt in an office on the street floor, to whom, with his two companions, he had first applied. It remained to be seen if any obstruction would be offered to his penetrating the mysterious apartment which crowned the dome.

Five minutes later he climbed through the window into a room used apparently as a store by the firm leasing this suite of offices on the forty-seventh. He could not restrain a sigh of relief as, quitting the swaying parapet, he reached the security of a rubber laid floor. Mr. Schmidt, representing the owners of the building, waited there as Hepburn's companions in turn climbed in through the low window.

"Everything seems to be in order up to this floor," said Hepburn. "How do we get to the top of the dome? The fault must be there."

Mr. Schmidt stared hard for a moment.

"There's no way up," he replied curtly. "The elevators don't go beyond this floor. There's a staircase to the flagstaff, but the door's been boarded up. Orders of the Fire

Department, I guess. There's nothing up there. It's just ornamental."

"Then how do I carry out the inspection? It will cost plenty to rig ladders. Cheaper to break through to the staircase, wouldn't it be?"

"That doesn't rest with me," Mr. Schmidt replied hastily; "I shall have to ask you to give me time to consult directors on the point."

Mark Hepburn surreptitiously nudged the representative of Midtown Electric, and:

"When can you let us know, Mr. Schmidt?" the electrician inquired. "We have to make a report."

"I'll call you in the morning," Mr. Schmidt replied.

Mark Hepburn experienced an inward glow of satisfaction. Apart from the testimony of Robbie Adair, he himself had seen lighted windows above the dome of the Stratton Building—and today they had found conclusive evidence to show that the rooms were occupied!

28 *PAUL SALVALETTI*

LOLA DUMAS, concealed behind a partly drawn curtain, looked down upon the crowded terraces. Palm trees were silhouetted against an evening sky; there was a distant prospect of steel-blue sea. The crowds below were so dense that she thought of a pot of caviar. Here was humanity, seemingly redundant, but pulsing with life so vigorous that its vibrations reached her on that high balcony.

They were cheering and shouting, and through all the excited uproar, like an oboe motif in an orchestral score, rose the name of Salvaletti.

Salvaletti!

This was merely the beginning of a triumphal progress which unavoidably should lead to the White House. Lola Dumas clutched the curtain nervously, her delicate fingers, on which she wore too many jewels, quivering with the tension of the moment. And they were still shouting and calling for Salvaletti when at the faint sound of an opening door Lola turned sharply.

Paul Salvaletti had entered the room.

Adulation, long awaited success had transformed the man

160

into a god. His pale face was lighted up, inspired; the dark eyes reminded her of hot velvet. His habitual stoop was tonight discarded. He stood upright, commanding, triumphant. She looked now not upon the secretary of the late Harvey Bragg, but upon Caesar.

"Paul!" She took a step forward. "This is triumph. Nothing can stop you."

"Nothing," he replied, and even in speaking that one word the music of his voice thrilled her. "Nothing!"

"Salvaletti for the South!" A cry rose above the uproar below.

A wild outburst of cheering followed. Then came a series of concerted calls:

"Salvaletti! Salvaletti!"

The man plucked out of complete obscurity to be thrust upon a cloudy pinnacle, smiled.

"Lola," he said, "this was worth waiting for!"

She moved towards him, her graceful bare arms extended, and with a low cry of almost savage delight he clasped her. The world was at his feet—fame, riches, beauty. In silence he held her while, more and more insistent, the demand rose up from the terraces:

"Salvaletti! Salvaletti! America for every man. Every man for America!"

The phone bell rang.

"Answer, Lola," Salvaletti directed; "I shall speak to no one tonight but to you."

Lola Dumas glanced at him sharply. The heady wine of success had somewhat intoxicated him. He spoke with an arrogance the very existence of which hitherto he had successfully concealed. She crossed the room and took up the telephone.

A moment she listened; her attitude grew tense; and, ever increasing in volume, the cry "Salvaletti!" swelled up from below. Lola placed the receiver on the table and turned.

"The President," she said.

Those two words wrought a swift change in Salvaletti.

"What!" he whispered.

For a second he hesitated, then, crossing with his characteristic catlike tread, he took up the phone.

"Paul Salvaletti here."

"I am watching you closely," came the imperious, guttural voice. "At this stage, you must not make one mistake. Listen now to my orders. Go out upon the balcony of the room in which you stand. Do not speak, but acknowledge the people. Then bring Lola Dumas out onto the balcony, that all may see her. Move in this matter."

The line was disconnected.

For three, five, ten seconds, as he hung up, Salvaletti's sensitive nostrils remained distended. He had heard the crack of the whip, had resented it.

"What?" Lola asked.

"An order," Salvaletti replied, smiling composedly, "which I must obey."

He crossed, drew the curtains widely apart, and stepped out to the balcony. A roar of excited voices acclaimed him, and for a while he stood there, a pale, impressive figure in the moonlight. He bowed, raised his hand and, turning, beckoned to Lola Dumas.

"You are to join me," he said. "Please come."

He drew her onto the balcony beside him; and the woman associated for so long with Harvey Bragg, founder of the League of Good Americans, potential savior of his country, received an almost hysterical ovation. . . .

Back in the room, the curtains drawn, Lola Dumas sank down on a cushioned settee, beckoning to Salvaletti with her eyes and with her lips. He stood beside her looking down.

"Paul," she said, "did the President give those orders?"

"He did."

"You see, Paul," she said very softly, "he has chosen for you. Are you content?"

29 *GREEN MIRAGE*

MARK HEPBURN AWOKE; sat up. He found himself to be clammy with nervous perspiration, and the dream which had occasioned it was still vivid in his mind. It was this:

He had found himself in an apparently interminable tunnel (which he could trace to Nayland Smith's account of the attempt to explore the East River water-gate). For a period which seemed to span many hours he walked along this tunnel. His only light was a fragment of thick, wax candle, resembling an altar candle. There were twists and turns in the tunnel, and always in his dream he had hoped to see daylight beyond. Always he had been disappointed.

Some great expediency drove him on. At all costs he must reach the end of this subterranean passage. A stake greater than his life was at hazard. And now, gaping blackly, crossways appeared in the tunnel; it became a labyrinth. Every passage revealed by the flickering light of the candle resembled another. In desperation he plunged into one which opened on his right. It proved to be interminable. An opening offered on the left. He entered it. Another endless tunnel stretched before him.

The candle was burning very low; his fingers were covered with hot grease. Unless he could win freedom before that fragment of wick and wax gave up the ghost and plunged him into darkness, he was doomed to wander forever, a lost soul, in this place deep below the world of living men. . . .

Blind panic seized him. He began to run along tunnel after tunnel, turning right, turning left, crying out madly. His exertions reduced the fraction of candle almost to disappearing point. He ran on. In some way it came to him that the life of Nayland Smith was at stake. He must gain the upper air or disaster would come, not to Nayland Smith alone, but to all humanity. The candle, now a tenuous disk, became crushed between his trembling fingers. . . .

It was at this moment that he awoke.

The apartment was very still. Save for the immutable voice of the city-which-never-sleeps, there was no sound.

Hepburn groped for his slippers. There were no cigarettes in the room. He decided to go into the sitting room for a smoke and a drink. That ghastly dream of endless tunnels had shaken him.

The night was crystal clear; a nearly full moon poured its cold luminance into the rooms. Without turning on any of the lights—for he was anxious to avoid wakening Nayland Smith, a hair-trigger sleeper—he found his way to the sitting room. There were cigarettes on the table by the telephone. He found one, but he had no means of lighting it.

As he paused, looking around, he saw through an open door the moon-bathed room beyond. It was the room which he had fitted up as a temporary laboratory; from its window he could just see the roof of the hotel where Moya Adair lived. He remembered that he had left matches there. He went in, crossed and stared out of the window.

His original intention was forgotten. He stood there, tense, watching. . . .

From a window of an out-jutting wing of the Regal-Athenian, one floor below and not twenty yards away, Dr. Fu Manchu was looking up at him!

Some primitive instinct warned him to reject the chimera —for that the man in person could be present he was not prepared to believe. This was a continuation, a part, of his uncanny dream. He was not awake. Brilliant green eyes gleamed in the moonlight like polished jade. He watched fascinatedly.

His impulse—to arouse Smith, to have the building surrounded—left him. Those wonderful eyes demanded all his attention. . . .

He found himself busy in the laboratory—of course he was still dreaming—preparing a strange prescription. It was contrary to all tradition, a thing outside his experience. But he prepared it with meticulous care—for it was indispensable to the life of Nayland Smith. . . .

At last it was ready. Now, he must charge a hypodermic syringe with it—an intravenous injection. It was vital that he should not awake Smith. . . .

Syringe in hand, he crept along the corridor to the second door. He listened. There was no sound.

Very quietly, he opened the door and went in.

Nayland Smith lay motionless in bed, his lean brown hands outside the coverlet. The conditions were ideal, it seemed to Mark Hepburn in his dream. Stealthily he stole across the room. He could not hope to complete the injection without arousing Smith, but at least he could give him some of the charge.

Lightly he raised the sleeve of his pajama jacket. Smith did not stir. He pressed the needle point firmly home. . . .

2

Mark Hepburn felt himself seized from behind, jerked back and hurled upon the floor by unseen hands!

He fell heavily, striking his head upon the carpet. The syringe dropped from his fingers, and as Nayland Smith sprang upright in bed the predominant idea in Hepburn's mind was that he had failed; and so Smith must die.

He twisted over, rose to his knees . . . and looked up into the barrel of a revolver held by Fey.

"Hepburn!" came sharply in Nayland Smith's inimitable voice. "What the devil's this?"

He sprang out of bed.

Fey, barefooted and wearing pajamas, looked somewhat disheveled in the glare of light as Nayland Smith switched on lamps: spiritually he was unruffled.

"It's a mystery, sir," he replied, while Hepburn, slowly

rising to his feet and clutching his head, endeavored to regain composure. "It was the tinkling of the bottles that woke me."

"The bottles?"

Mark Hepburn dropped down into a chair.

"I was in the laboratory," he explained dully. "Frankly, I don't know, now, what I was doing there."

Nayland Smith, seated on the side of the bed, was staring at him keenly.

"I got up and watched," Fey continued, "keeping very quiet. And I saw Captain Hepburn carefully measuring out drugs. Then I saw him looking about as if he'd lost something, and then I saw him go to the window and stare out. He stayed there for a long time."

"In which direction was he staring?" snapped Nayland Smith.

Hepburn groaned, continuing to clutch his head. The memory of some strange, awful episode already was slipping from his mind.

"I thought, at a window down to the right and below, sir. And as he stood there so long, I slipped into the sitting room and looked out from there." He paused and cleared his throat. "I was still looking when I heard Captain Hepburn come out. I shouldn't have behaved as I did, sir, but I had seen Captain Hepburn's eyes. . . ."

"What do you mean?"

"Well, sir, it might have been that he was walking in his sleep! And so, when I heard him coming, I ducked into a corner and watched him go by. I followed him right to your door. He opened it very quietly. I was close behind him when he crossed to the bed——"

Now, suddenly, in a stifled voice:

"The syringe!" Hepburn cried, "the syringe! My God! did I *touch* you?"

He sprang up wildly, his glance questing about the floor.

"Is this what you mean, Hepburn?" Nayland Smith asked. He picked up a *fountain pen*, at the same time glancing down at his left arm. "My impression is that you jabbed the *nib* into me!"

Mark Hepburn stared at the fountain pen, fists clenched. It was a new one bought only that day; his old one had been smashed during operations in the Chinatown raid. So far as he could remember he had never filled it. The facts, the incredible facts, were coming back to him. . . . He had prepared a mixture: of what it was composed he hadn't at this moment the slightest idea. But he had imagined or had dreamed that he charged a hypodermic syringe with it. He must have charged the fountain pen, for he had no hypo-dermic syringe in his possession!

Nayland Smith's penetrating regard never left the troubled face, and then:

"Was I dreaming," Hepburn groaned, "or was I hyp-notized? By heaven! I remember—I went to the window and saw his eyes! *He* was watching me."

"Who was watching you?" Smith asked quietly.

"I don't know who it was, sir," Fey interrupted with an apologetic cough, "but he had one of the most dreadful faces I have ever seen in my life. The moonlight was shining on him. I saw his green eyes."

"What!"

Nayland Smith sprang to his feet. From out of his varied experience an explanation of the strange incident, phantom-esque, arose. He stared hard again at Mark Hepburn.

"Dr. Fu Manchu is the most accomplished hypnotist alive," he said harshly. "During those few moments that you watched him from the window above Wu King's he must have established partial control." He pulled on a dressing gown which lay across the foot of the bed. "Quick, Fey, get Wyatt! He's on duty in the lobby."

Fey ran out.

Nayland Smith turned, threw up the window and craned forward. Over his shoulder:

"Which way, Hepburn?" he snapped.

Mark Hepburn, slowly recovering control of his normal self, leaned on the sill and pointed.

"The wing on the right, third window from the end, two floors below this."

"There's no one there, and the room is dark." The wail which tells that the Fire Department is out, a solo rarely absent from New York's symphony, rose, ghostly, through the night. "I have had an unpleasantly narrow escape. Be-yond doubt you were acting under hypnotic direction. Fey's evidence confirms it. A daring move! The Doctor must be desperate." He glanced down at the fountain pen which lay upon a little table. "I wonder what you charged it with," he murmured meditatively. "Dr. Fu Manchu assumed too much in thinking you had hypodermic syringes in your possession. You obeyed his instructions—but charged the fountain pen; thus probably saving my life."

It was only a few moments later that Wyatt, the govern-ment agent in charge below, found the night manager and accompanied by two detectives was borne up to the thirty-eighth floor of the hotel wing in which the suspected room was located.

"I can tell you there's no one there, Mr. Wyatt," the manager said, twirling a large key around his forefinger. "It was vacated this morning by a Mr. Eckstein, a dark man, possibly Jewish. There's only one curious point about it——"

"What's that?" Wyatt asked.

"He took the door key away. . . ." Mr. Dougherty smiled grimly; his Tipperary brogue was very marked. "Unfortunately, it often happens. But in this case there may have been some ulterior motive."

The bedroom, when they entered, was deserted; the two beds were ready for occupation by incoming guests. Neither here nor in the bathroom was there evidence pointing to a recent intruder. . . .

The detectives were still prowling around and Nayland Smith on the fortieth floor of the tower was issuing telephone instructions when a tall man, muffled in a fur topcoat —a man who wore glasses and a wide-brimmed black hat— stepped into an elevator on the thirtieth floor and was taken down to street level. . . .

"No one is to leave the building," rapped Nayland Smith, "until I get down. Don't concentrate on the tower; post men at every elevator and every exit."

Wyatt, the night manager, and the two detectives stepped out of the elevator at the end of the huge main foyer. The tall man in the fur coat was striding along its carpeted center aisle. The place was only partially lighted at that late hour. There was a buzz of vacuum cleaners. He descended marble steps to the lower foyer. A night porter glanced up at him, curiously, as he passed his desk.

A man came hurrying along an arcade lined by flower shops, jewelers' shops and other features of a luxury bazaar, but actually contained within the great hotel, and presently appeared immediately facing the elevator by which Wyatt and his party had descended. Seeing them he hurried across, and:

"No one is to leave the building!" he cried. "Post men at all elevators and all entrances."

The tall visitor passed through the swing doors and descended the steps to the sidewalk. A Lotus cab which had been standing near by drew up; opening the door, he entered. The cab moved off. It was actually turning the Park Avenue corner when detectives, running from the westerly end of the building, reached the main entrance and went clattering up the steps. One, who seemed to be in charge, ran across to the night porter. Federal Agent Wyatt was racing along the foyer towards them.

"Who's gone out," the detective demanded, "in the last five minutes? Anybody?

But even as the startled man began to answer, the Lotus cab was speeding along almost deserted streets, and Dr. Fu Manchu, lying back in the corner, relaxed after a dangerous and mentally intense effort which he had every reason to believe would result in the removal of Enemy Number One. Nayland Smith's activities were beginning seriously to interfere with his own. The abandonment of the Chinatown base was an inconvenience, and reports received from those responsible for covering the Stratton Building suggested that further intrusion might be looked for. . . .

30 *PLAN OF ATTACK*

GRAY MORNING LIGHT was creeping into the sitting room.

"Last night's attempt," said Nayland Smith (he wore a dressing gown over pajamas) "is not uncharacteristic of the Doctor's methods."

"Poor consolation for me," Hepburn replied, speaking from the depths of an armchair in which, similarly attired, he was curled up.

"Don't let us worry unduly," said Nayland Smith. "I have known others to suffer from the insidious influence of Fu Manchu; indeed, I have suffered myself. Physical fear has no meaning for the Doctor. Undoubtedly he was here in person, here in the enemy's headquarters. He walked out under the very noses of the police officers I had dispatched to intercept him. He is a great man, Hepburn."

"He is."

"There is no evidence that you were drugged in any way last night, but we cannot be sure, for the Doctor's methods are subtle. That he influenced your brain while you were sleeping is beyond dispute. The dream of the interminable labyrinth, the conviction that my life depended upon your escape—all this was prompted by the will of Fu Manchu. You were dreaming, although even now you doubt it, when you thought you awoke. He only made one mistake, Hepburn. He postulated a hypodermic syringe which was not in your possession!"

"But I loaded a fountain pen with some pretty deadly drugs which now it is impossible to identify."

"You carried out your hypnotic instructions to the best of your ability. The power of Fu Manchu's mind is an awful thing. However, by an accident, a pure accident, or an oversight, he failed—thank God! Let us review the position."

Mark Hepburn reached out for a cigarette; his face was haggard, unshaven.

"We are beginning to harass the enemy." Nayland Smith, pipe fuming furiously, paced up and down the carpet. "That there is a staircase below Wu King's with some unknown exit on the street is certain. At any moment I expect a report that the men have broken in there. Its construction has been carried out from the point that I call the water-gate; hence Finney's ignorance of its existence. Once we have reached it, with the equipment at our disposal we can break through. It doesn't matter how many iron doors obstruct us. The entrance from the sewers we have been unable to trace. But penetration to the Chinatown base is only a question of time."

He puffed furiously, but his overworked pipe had gone out. He laid it in an ash tray and continued to walk up and down. Mark Hepburn, laboring under a load of undeserved guilt, watched him fascinatedly.

"What Mrs. Adair knows which would be of value to us is problematical. According to Lieutenant Johnson's report, it would seem to be perfectly feasible to obtain possession of the boy, Robbie, during one of his visits to Long Island."

"The owner of the house and his family are at the coast," Mark Hepburn said monotonously. "He is, as you will have noted, a co-director with the late Harvey Bragg of the Lotus Transport Corporation."

"I had noted it," Smith said dryly; "but he may nevertheless be innocent of any knowledge of the existence of Dr. Fu Manchu. That's the devilish part of it, Hepburn. The other points are: (a) Can Mrs. Adair afford us any material assistance; (b) Is it safe to attempt it?"

"The Negro chauffeur," Hepburn replied, "may have orders, for all we know to the contrary, to shoot the boy in the event of any such attempt. Frankly, I don't feel justified."

"Assuming we succeeded . . ."

"Her complicity would be fairly evident—she would suffer?"

Nayland Smith paused in his promenade and, turning, stared at Hepburn.

"Unless we kidnaped *her* at the same time," he snapped.

Mark Hepburn stood up suddenly, dropping his recently lighted cigarette in a tray.

"By heaven, Smith," he said excitedly, "that may be the solution!"

"It's worth thinking about, but it would require a very careful plan. I am disposed at the moment without imperiling the lives of Mrs. Adair and her son, to concentrate upon the Stratton Building. Your experience there was definitely illuminating."

He crossed to the big desk above which the maps were pinned, and looked down at a number of clay fragments which lay there.

"I feel disposed, Hepburn—if necessary with the backing of the Fire Department—to pursue your inquiry into the flaw in the lightning conductors. An examination could be arranged after office workers had left. But I think it would be unwise to give any warning to this Mr. Schmidt whom you have mentioned, of our intention. Do you agree with me?"

"Yes," Hepburn replied slowly; "that is what I had planned myself. But, Smith . . ."

Smith turned and regarded him.

"Do you realize how I feel? In the first place you know —I haven't disguised it—that I am becoming really fond of Moya Adair. That's bad enough—she's one of the enemy. In the second place, it seems that I am such a poor weakling that this hellish Chinaman can use me as an instrument to bring about your murder! How can you ever trust me again?"

Nayland Smith stepped up to him, grasped both his shoulders and stared into his eyes.

"I would trust you, Hepburn," he said slowly, "as I would trust few men. You are human—so am I. Don't let the hypnotic episode disturb your self-respect. There is no man living immune from this particular power possessed by Dr. Fu Manchu. There's only one thing: Should you ever meet him again—avoid his eyes."

"Thank you," said Mark Hepburn. "It's kind of you to take it that way."

Smith grasped the outstretched hand, clapped Hepburn on the shoulder and resumed his restless promenade.

"In short," he continued, "we are beginning to make a certain amount of headway. But the campaign, as time goes on, grows more and more hectic. In my opinion our lives, as risks, are uninsurable. And I am seriously worried about the Abbot of Holy Thorn."

"In what way?"

"His life is not worth—that!"

He snapped his fingers.

"No." Mark Hepburn nodded, selecting a fresh cigarette and staring rather haggardly out of the window across the roofs of a gray New York. "He is not a man one can gag indefinitely. Dr. Fu Manchu must know it."

"Knowing it," snapped Nayland Smith, "I fear that he will act. If we had a clear case, I should be disposed to act first. The thing is so cunningly devised that our lines of attack are limited. Excluding an unknown inner group surrounding the mandarin, in my opinion not another soul working for the League of Good Americans has the remotest idea of the ultimate object of that League, or of the source of its revenues! All the reports—and I have read hundreds—point in the same direction. Many thousands of previously workless men have been given employment. Glance at the map." He pointed. "Every red flag means a Fu Manchu advance! They are working honorably at the tasks allotted to them. But every one, when the hour comes, will cry out with the same voice: every one, north, south, east and west, is a unit in the vast army which, unknowingly, is building up the domination of this country by Dr. Fu Manchu, through his chosen nominee——"

"Salvaletti!"

"Salvaletti; it seems at last to become apparent. It is clear that this man has been trained for years for his task. I even begin to guess why Lola Dumas is being associated with him. In another fortnight, perhaps in a week, the following of Paul Salvaletti will be greater than that of Harvey Bragg ever was. Nothing can stop him, Hepburn, nothing short of a revelation—not a statement, but a *revelation*, of the real facts. . . ."

"Who can give it? Who would be listened to?"

Nayland Smith paused over by the door, turned, staring at the shadowy figure in the armchair.

"The Abbot of Holy Thorn," he replied. "But at the risk of his life. . . ."

31 *PROFESSOR MORGENSTAHL*

THE MEMORY MAN worked industriously on his clay model. Pinned to the base of the wooden frame was a photographic enlargement of the three-cent stamp with the white paper mask. He was engrossed in his task. The clay head was assuming a grotesque semblance of the features of Dr. Fu Manchu—a vicious caricature of that splendid, evil face.

Incoming messages indicated a feverish change of plan in regard to the New York area. The names of Nayland Smith and Captain Hepburn figured frequently. These two apparently were in charge of counteroperations. Reports from agents in the South, identifiable only by their numbers, spoke of the triumphant progress of the man Salvaletti. Occasional reports from far up in Alaska indicated that the movement there was proceeding smoothly. The only discordant note came from the Middle West, where Abbot Donegal, a mere name to the Memory Man, seemed to be a focus of interest for many agents.

It all meant less than nothing to the prisoner who had memorized every message received since the first hour of his captivity. Sometimes, in the misery of this slavery which had been imposed upon him, he remembered happier days in Germany; remembered how at his club he had been challenged to read a page of the Berlin *Tageblatt*, and then to recite its contents from memory; how, without difficulty, he had succeeded and won his wager. But those were the days before his exile. He knew now how happy they had been. In the interval he had died. He was a living dead man. . . . Busily, with delicate fingers, he modeled the clay. His faith in a just God remained unshaken.

Without warning the door by which he gained access to his private quarters opened. Wearing a dark coat with an astrakhan collar, an astrakhan cap upon his head, a tall man came in. The sculptor ceased to toil and sat motionless —staring at the living face of Dr. Fu Manchu, which so long he had sought to reproduce in clay!

"Good morning, Professor Morgenstahl."

Dr. Fu Manchu spoke in German. Except that he over-stressed the gutturals, he spoke that language perfectly. Professor Morgenstahl, the mathematical genius who had upset every previous conviction respecting the relative distances of the planets, who had mapped space, who had proved that lunar eclipses were not produced by the shadow of the earth, and who now was subjugated to the dreadful task of a one-man telephone exchange, did not stir. His great brain was a file, the only file, of all messages received at that secret headquarters from the whole of the United States. Motionless, he continued to stare at the man who wore the astrakhan cap.

That hour of which he had dreamed had come at last! He was face to face with his oppressor. . . .

The muscles of his powerful body responded to the urge of his brain. At whatever cost to himself, he was determined to kill this man who stood before him.

Vividly before his eyes those last scenes arose: his expulsion from Germany almost penniless, for his great intellect which had won world-wide recognition had earned him little money; the journey to the United States, where no man had identified him as the famous author of *Interstellar Cycles*, nor had he sought to make himself known. He could even remember his own death—for certainly he had been dead—in a cheap lodging in Brooklyn; his reawakening in the room below (with this man, this devil incarnate, standing over him!); his enslavement, his misery.

Yes, living or dead—for sometimes he thought that he was a discarnate spirit—he must at least perform this one good deed: the dreadful Chinaman must die.

"No doubt you weary of your duties, Professor," the guttural voice continued. "But better things are to come. A change of plan is necessitated. Other quarters have been found for you, with similar facilities."

Professor Morgenstahl, sitting behind the heavy table with its complicated mechanism, recognized that he must temporize.

"My books," he said, "my apparatus——"

"Have been removed. Your new quarters are prepared for you. Be good enough to follow me."

Slowly, Professor Morgenstahl stood up, watched by unflinching green eyes. He moved around the corner of the table, where the nearly completed model stood. He was estimating the weight of that tall, gaunt figure; and to ounces, his estimate was correct. But in the moment when, clear of the heavy table, he was preparing to strangle with his bare hands this yellow-faced horror who had rescued

173

him from the grave, only to plunge him into a living hell, the watching eyes seemed to grow larger; inch by inch they increased—they merged—they became a green lake; he forgot his murderous intent. He lost identity. . . .

32 *BELOW WU KING'S*

"LAY OFF THERE," shouted Inspector Finney.

The roar of the oxyacetylene blowpipe ceased. They were working on the third door below Wu King's premises, from a tunneled staircase of the existence of which Wu King blandly denied all knowledge. Turning upward:

"What's new?" Finney shouted.

"We've got the street door open!"

Leaving the men with the blowpipe, Finney ran up. The air was stifling, laden with acrid fumes. An immensely heavy door, an iron framework to the outer side of which the appearance of a wall had been given by cementing half-bricks into the hollow of the frame, stood open. A group of men sweating from their toils examined it. Outside, on the street, two patrolmen were moving on the curious sightseers.

"So that was the game," Finney murmured.

"No wonder we couldn't find it," said one of the men, throwing back a clammy lock of hair from his damp forehead. "It looks like a brick wall and it sounds like a brick wall!"

"It would," Finney commented dryly: "it *is* a brick wall, except it opens. Easy to guess now how they got it fixed. They did their building from the other end, wherever the other end is. Now just where do we stand?"

He stepped out onto the street, looking right and left. The masked door occupied the back of a recess between one end of Wu King's premises and the beginning of a Chinese cigar merchant's. Its ostensible reason was to accommodate a manhole in the sidewalk. The manhole was authentic: it communicated with an electric main—Inspector Finney knew the spot well enough. Tilting back his hard black hat, he stared with a strange expression at the gaping opening where he had been accustomed for many years to see a brick wall.

"Well, I'll be damned!" he muttered.

"This lets Wu out, I guess," said one of the men. "If *we* didn't know the darned thing was here, he can claim he didn't."

"He'll do it," Finney replied. "And he'll probably get by with it. . . . There must be a bell some place: we traced the cable."

"We found it. Forced it out blowing through the iron. The brickwork's made to look kind of old, and there was posters stuck to it. I guess the push was under the posters; that's how it looks."

Inspector Finney went inside again, first glancing sharply right and left at the expressionless faces of a number of Chinamen who, from a respectful distance, were watching operations. There was an elaborate lock to this ingenious door, electrically controlled—but where from, remained to be discovered. . . .

Ten minutes later the third door was forced, and Inspector Finney found himself in a rectangular saloon curiously appointed but showing evidence of long neglect. The place, now, smelled like an iron foundry.

"This looks like an old dope joint to me," said one of the party, "but it's plain it hasn't been used for a long while."

"Strip all the walls," Finney ordered; "we're not through yet."

A scene of whole-hearted wrecking followed upon which the Fire Department could not have improved. Nevertheless, nearly an hour had elapsed before a cunningly hidden fourth door was discovered.

"Go to work, boys," said Finney.

The sweating workers got busy, bringing down the blow-pipe and rigging it for further operations. Finney stared speculatively at a patch of scarred wall. He did not know, indeed never learned, that beyond that very piece of wall upon which his gaze was fixed a spiral staircase led from a point below to the top floor of Wu King's building. Since only by measurements and never by sounding could the shaft in which it ran be discovered, it was not unnatural that Inspector Finney should concentrate the whole of his attention upon the fourth iron door recently discovered.

These iron doors made him savage. At the present moment he was recalling a recent conversation with the government agent, Hepburn; he remembered boasting that no such door could be fitted in the Chinatown area without his becoming aware of the fact. It was a bitter pill, for here were four!

He reflected with satisfaction, however, that no man

175

knows everything. At least he could congratulate himself upon the finding of this secret staircase. Between the eastern end of Wu King's premises and the western end of that adjoining, measurements had shown a space unaccounted for. Operating from inside Wu King's, floor boards had been torn up and a thick party wall brought to light. Through this Finney had caused a way to be broken; and they had found themselves on the first stair below street level.

That was good work! He resettled his hard hat upon his hard head and lighted a cigarette. . . .

Nevertheless, from the time that operations had commenced in early morning, up to the moment when the fourth door succumbed, many weary hours of toil had been spent by the party under Inspector Finney. He was up on the street wondering what all this secret subterranean building really meant when:

"We're through!" came a cry, hollow, from the acrid depths.

A minute later he stood on the lowest step, directing the ray of his torch upon oily, dirty-looking water.

"I guess that's tidal level," a voice said, "but sometime these steps went deeper."

Inspector Finney flashed his light across the unwholesome-looking waters of the well. At the further end he saw a square opening two to three feet above the surface.

"There is or was another iron door," he growled, "but it's open. I wonder what's on the other side."

He was short and stocky himself. He turned to one of the men who had been working on the forcing of the doors.

"What's your height, Ruskin?" he asked.

"Six one-and-a-quarter, Inspector."

"You swim well, don't you?"

"Not so bad."

"If the stone steps carry on down below water level," Finney explained, "you won't have to swim. I figure you could keep your feet, hold a torch above your head and see what's beyond there. What do you say?"

"I'll try it."

Ruskin partly stripped for the endeavor and then, a torch held in his right hand, he began, feeling his way with care, to descend the stone steps. The group on the landing watched in silence. The water, on top of which all sorts of fragments floated, was just up to Ruskin's shoulders when he announced:

"I'm on the level now."

"Go easy," Finney warned. "If you lose foothold strike up to the surface and swim back."

Ruskin did not reply: he walked on, the torch held above his head. He passed under the square opening and stood there for a moment, then:

"Good God!" he screamed.

His torch disappeared—he had dropped it. There was a wild splashing and churning. Finney cast hat and coat aside and went plunging down the steps, another man behind him.

"Show those lights!" he shouted to the men who still remained upon the landing.

In the rays of the torches Ruskin's face showed above the surface. Finney grabbed him, and presently he was hauled up the steps. He lay there pointing down, shaken and gasping. . . .

"There's a great wide space of water back there," he panted—"and there's some awful thing lives in it—a monster! I saw its eyes shining!"

The temple of the seven-eyed goddess had been flooded by Sam Pak, but the head of its presiding deity remained just above the surface. . . .

33 *THE BALCONY*

MR. SCHMIDT, representing the Stratton Estates, stepped out of the elevator on the top floor of the Stratton Building. Two men followed. One, wearing overalls and having a leather bag carried on a strap across his left shoulder, represented Midtown Electric. Mr. Schmidt recognized him as one of the pair who had been on the job before. The other, a tall, lean man wearing glasses and a brusque military mustache, came from the Falcon Imperial Insurance Corporation, which carried the fire risk of the Stratton Building.

A man in the uniform of the Fire Department, who was seated on a chair before a green baize-covered door, stood up as the party came out of the elevator.

"It was really unnecessary, Mr. Englebert," said Schmidt, addressing the gray-mustached man, "to notify the Fire Department. The door which you see was formerly boarded up so that no door showed. The Fire Department has stripped it, in accordance, I suppose, with your instructions, and has seen fit to post a guard over it throughout the whole of the day. Quite unnecessary!"

Mr. Englebert nodded.

"My directors carry a heavy responsibility on this building, Mr. Schmidt," he replied, "and in view of the phenomenal electric storms recently experienced in the Midwest, we must assure ourselves of the efficiency of the lightning conductors."

"That's all agreed, Mr. Englebert. I have the keys of the staircase to the flagstaff, but you have put us to quite some trouble."

Few of the hundreds of windows in the great building showed any light. The office workers engaged by firms occupying premises in the Stratton Building had departed for home. Only a few late toilers remained at their desks. In the three streets which embayed the tall structure, there was nothing to indicate that a cordon had been thrown around the building. Mr. Schmidt himself, who, indeed, was perfectly innocent of any complicity apart from the duties which he owed to the League of Good Americans, remained to this moment unaware of the fact that an office opening on the top floor, the staff of which had left at six o'clock, was now packed with police.

"All clear, sir," said the fireman.

Mr. Schmidt produced a bunch of keys, fumbled for a while, finally selected one, and not without difficulty opened the baize-covered door. He turned.

"I may say here and now," he remarked, "that I have never been in the dome: I have never known it to be opened during the time I have acted for the Stratton Estates. There are rooms up there, I know, which were formerly occupied by the late Mr. Jerome Stratton. . . ." He shrugged his shoulders. "Of course, he was very eccentric. As there was no proper means of escape in the event of fire, they were closed some years ago. I'll lead the way. I have a torch. There are no lights."

He went in, shining the ray of his torch ahead. The man from Midtown Electric followed. Mr. Englebert paused at the threshold; and to the fireman:

"You have your orders," he snapped.

"Sure."

Nayland Smith, his facial disguise that which he employed for the Salvation Army officer, his dress that of a business man, followed Mark Hepburn—representing Midtown Electric—into the darkness illuminated only by Mr. Schmidt's torch. Hepburn supplemented it by the light of another.

They were in a curious, octagonal room in which, facing south, were three windows. There were indications that furniture at some time had stood against the walls. Now the room was bare.

"I guess we'll push right on to the top," said Hepburn. Mr. Schmidt studied a rough plan which he carried.

"The door is on this side, I think," he said vaguely. "One of the late Mr. Stratton's eccentricities."

He walked to a point directly opposite the central window, stood fumbling there awhile, and then inserted a key in a lock and opened the hitherto invisible door.

"This way."

They went up an uncarpeted staircase at the top of which another door was opened. They entered a second octagonal room appreciably smaller than that which they had just quitted, but also destitute of any scrap of furniture; there was an empty alcove on one side.

"You see," said Schmidt, flashing his light about, "there's a balcony to this room, outside the French windows there. . . ."

"I see," muttered Nayland Smith, staring keenly about him.

"From that gallery," said Mark Hepburn in his monotonous voice, "is it possible I could see the cable to the flagstaff."

"The window," Schmidt replied, "appears to be bolted only. I think you can get out there without any difficulty."

Nayland Smith turned suddenly to the speaker.

"There is still another floor above?"

Mark Hepburn had shot back a bolt and opened one of the heavy windows.

"Yes, so I understand. A small domed room immediately under the flagstaff. The door, I believe—" he hesitated— "is directly facing the windows, again. Let us see if I can open it."

He crossed as Hepburn stepped out onto the gallery— that gallery which Professor Morgenstahl had paced so often in the misery of his captivity. . . .

"Here we are!" Schmidt cried triumphantly.

"I see," said Nayland Smith, regarding the newly opened door. "I should be obliged, while we complete our inspection, if you would step down and tell the fireman on duty that he is not to leave without my orders."

"Certainly, Mr. Englebert; then I'll come right back."

Mr. Schmidt crossed and might be heard descending the stair.

As he disappeared:

"Hepburn!" Nayland Smith called urgently.

Hepburn came in from the balcony.

"This place has been hurriedly stripped—and only a matter of hours ago! But, all the same, our last hope is the top floor."

He led the way, shining light ahead. It was a short stair —and the door above was open. Hepburn at his heels, he burst into the room. Small, domed, and surrounded by curious amber-paned Gothic windows which did not appear to communicate with the outer air, it was stripped—empty!

"We are right under the flagstaff," said Hepburn quite tonelessly. "He's been too clever for us. I was marked on my first visit."

Nayland Smith's hands fell so that the ray from his torch shone down upon the floor at his feet.

"He wins again!" he said slowly. "That baize door has been covered all day. There's another way in—and another way out: the cunning, cunning devil." And now, his diction changed as that dauntless spirit recovered from the check: "Come on, Hepburn, downstairs again!" he snapped energetically.

But in the apartment below, with its bedroom alcove and tiny bathroom, formerly the quarters of the eccentric millionaire who had lived in semiseclusion here, Nayland Smith stared about him in something like desperation.

"We have clear evidence," he said, "that this room certainly was occupied forty-eight hours ago. We are not defeated yet, Hepburn."

"I am anxious to study the view from the balcony," Hepburn replied.

"I know why you are anxious."

Undeterred by the note of raillery perceptible in Nayland Smith's voice, Mark Hepburn stepped out onto the iron-railed balcony: Smith followed.

"Where does the boy live, Hepburn?"

"I am trying to identify it. Wait a moment—I have seen these windows lighted from our own apartment. So first let's locate the Regal-Athenian."

"Easily done," rapped Nayland Smith, and pointed. "There's the Regal Tower, half-right."

"Then the penthouse lies somewhere west of where we stand. It must, because I know it isn't visible from our windows."

"That's a pity," said Nayland Smith dryly.

"I'm not thinking the way you believe, Smith, at all. I'm trying to work out a totally different idea. It seems to me . . ."

The sound which checked his words was a very slight sound, yet clearly audible up there where the Juggernaut hymn of New York was diminished to a humming croon, the song of a million fireflies dancing far below.

Nayland Smith turned as though propelled by a spring.

The open French window had been closed and bolted. Visible in the eerie light of a clouded moon, Dr. Fu Manchu stood inside watching them!

He wore a heavy coat with an astrakhan collar, an astrakhan cap upon his head. His only visible protection was the thickness of the glass. . . .

"Hepburn!" Nayland Smith reached for his automatic. *Don't look into his eyes!*

Those strange eyes glittered like emeralds through the panes of the window.

"A shot would be wasted, Sir Denis!" The cold, precise voice reached them out there upon the balcony as though no glass intervened. "The panes are bullet-proof—an improvement of my own upon an excellent device invented by an Englishman."

Nayland Smith's finger faltered on the trigger. He had never known Dr. Fu Manchu to tell a lie. But this was a crisis in the Doctor's affairs. He took a step back and fired obliquely.

The bullet ricocheted as from armor plate, whistling out into space! Dr. Fu Manchu did not stir a muscle.

"My God!" (and it sounded like a groan) came from Mark Hepburn.

"You can hear me clearly through the ventilators above the window," the Asiatic voice continued. "I regret that I should have given you cause, Sir Denis, to doubt my word."

Hepburn turned aside; he was trying desperately to think coolly. He stared downward from the balcony. . . .

"You are one of the few men whom I have encountered in a long life," Dr. Fu Manchu continued, "of sufficient strength of character to look me in the eyes. For this I respect you. I know by what self-abnegation you have achieved this control, and I regret the necessity which you have thrust upon me. Our association, if at times tedious, has never been dishonorable."

He turned aside, placing a small globular lamp upon the bare floor of the room: within it a bright light sprang up. He took a step back towards the window.

181

"I am not prepared to suffer any human hindrance in this hour of destiny. I have chosen Paul Salvaletti to rule at the White House. Here, in the United States, I shall set up my empire. Time and time again you have checked me—but this time, Sir Denis, you arrive too late. You are correct in your surmise that there is another means of entrance to these apartments, formerly occupied by Professor Morgenstahl (whose name will be familiar to you) and by myself."

"Smith," Hepburn whispered—"there's one chance . . ."

But Nayland Smith did not turn; he was watching Dr. Fu Manchu. The superhuman Chinaman was winding what appeared to be a watch. He placed it on the floor beside the lamp, turned, and spoke:

"I bid you good-bye, Sir Denis; and—I speak with sincerity —not without regret. Your powers of pure reasoning are limited: your gifts of intuition are remarkable. In this respect I place you among the seven first-class brains of your race. Captain Hepburn has excellent qualities. He is a man I should be glad to have in my service. However, he has chosen otherwise. The small apparatus which I have placed upon the floor (a hobby of the late Lord Southery, a talented engineer whom I believe you knew) contains a power which, expanding from so small a center, will, I am convinced, astound you. I have timed it to explode in one hundred and twenty seconds. Its explosion will entirely obliterate the dome of the Stratton Building. I must leave you."

He turned, and in the glare of the globular light upon the floor crossed to the door and disappeared.

Nayland Smith, fists clenched, glared in through the bulletproof glass.

"Hepburn," he said, "I have been blind and mad. Forgive me."

"Smith! Smith!" Hepburn grasped his arm. "I have been trying to tell you! . . . You know what we're supposed to be here for?"

"The lightning conductor. What the hell does it matter now!"

"It matters everything. Look!"

Hepburn pointed downwards. Nayland Smith stared in the direction indicated.

The cable of a lightning conductor attached from point to point passed down immediately beside the balcony to a dim parapet below. . . .

"God help us!" Smith whispered, "will it bear a man's weight?"

34 *"THE SEVEN"*

"THE HISTORY OF AMERICA," said the Abbot of Holy Thorn, "has acquired several surprising chapters since our last meeting, Sir Denis."

Nayland Smith, standing at the window of the abbot's high-set study staring out at a sun-bathed prospect, turned slightly and nodded. Every detail of his former visit had recurred in his memory. And at this hour, while the fate of the United States hung in the balance, he was really no nearer to success than on the night when first he had entered the room! His briar pipe was fuming like a furnace. Abbot Donegal lighted another cigarette. . . .

The explosion at the Stratton Building in New York was already ancient history. Amid the feverish excitement now sweeping the country, a piece of news must be sensational indeed to survive for longer than forty-eight hours.

Fragments of the dome had fallen at almost incredible distances from the scene of the explosion. The huge building had rocked upon its foundations, great gaps appearing in the masonry. The firemen, faced with a number of problems unique in their experience, had worked like demons. The total loss was difficult to compute, but, miraculously, there had been few serious casualties.

Their descent of the dome by means of the lightning conductor was a thing to haunt a man's dreams, but Smith and Hepburn had accomplished it. Then had come that race along the narrow parapet to the window of the office occupied by the police party: finally, a wild dash down the stairs—for the elevator could not accommodate all. . . .

The mystery of the origin of the explosion had not been publicly explained to this day.

"Those amazing financial resources controlled by Salvaletti," said the abbot, "have enabled him to make heavy inroads. He has stolen many of my converts: the Brotherhood of National Equality has suffered. My poor friend Orwin Prescott, as you know, has set out upon a world cruise. This most damnable campaign, this secret poisoning, unlike anything the world has known since the days of the Borgias, has wrecked that fine career. The other victims

183

are countless: I doubt, Sir Denis, if even you know their number."

"On several occasions," Smith replied grimly, "I have narrowly escaped being added to their number. You also, Dom Patrick, have had an unpleasant experience, of which I need not remind you. Your reference on the radio last night to certain secret stirrings in the Asiatic colonies throughout the States created a profound sensation. It resulted in my presence here today. . . ." He rested his hands on the table, looking into the upraised eyes of the abbot. "Only because you have been silent have you remained immune so long."

"That silence had to be broken," said the priest sternly.

"I should have preferred that you awaited the word from me," rapped Nayland Smith, standing upright and beginning to pace the floor. "I have insufficient men at my disposal for the work of protection they are called upon to do. Washington, you know as well as I, is an armed camp. The country is in a state of feverish unrest, unparalleled even in war time. Big names, now, are deserting to the enemy!"

"I am painfully aware of the fact, Sir Denis," the abbot replied sadly. "But I am informed that the circumstance under which some of these desertions took place have been peculiar."

He stared in an odd way at Nayland Smith.

"Your information is correct! Cruel forms of coercion have been employed in many instances. And the purpose of my visit is this—" he paused before the desk at which the abbot was seated: "You intimated that you intended to touch upon this phase of the campaign in your next address on Wednesday night. You implied that other revelations were to follow. As a result of those words, Dom Patrick Donegal, your life at this moment is in grave danger. I ask you as man to man: How much do you know? What do you intend to say?"

The abbot, his chin resting on an upraised hand, stared unseeing before him. He resembled the figure of some medieval monk who out of the reluctant ether sought to conjure up the Great Secret. Nayland Smith watched him silently.

He had real respect for Patrick Donegal, and despite the slightness of their acquaintance something resembling friendship. His sincerity, if he had ever doubted it, he doubted no longer: he was deeply read, fearless, unshakable in his faith. And that the abbot had sources of information denied to the Department of Justice, Nayland Smith knew quite well.

"I know," said the abbot, at last, speaking very slowly and with a studious distinctness, "the character of the man who, remorselessly and over many murdered bodies, has driven Paul Salvaletti forward to the place which he holds. I do not know his name. He is a member of a very old Chinese family, and a man of great culture. He controls, or at least he has a voice in the councils of a secret society based in Tibet, but represented in all parts of the world where Eastern nationals are to be found."

"Do you know the name of this society?" Nayland Smith asked.

"I do not. Our missionaries in the East, who sometimes refer to it as 'The Seven,' regard it as the power of Satan manifested in evil-minded men. The Maffia in Italy was for generations a thorn in the side of the Church. An old friend of mine working in Japan tells me that the Society of the Black Dragon exercises a firmer hold over the imagination of the people than any religion has ever secured. But . . . 'The Seven' . . ." He paused and glanced up.

Nayland Smith nodded.

"Their wealth is incalculable, I am told. Men in high places, wielding great social and political influence, are among the members. And all their resources have been rallied to support this attack among the Constitution of the United States. You see, Sir Denis—" he smiled—"my inquiries have made great headway!"

"They have!" rapped Nayland Smith, and again paced the floor.

The Intelligence Department of Abbot Donegal's Church went up a notch higher. Never before this hour had he realized that the Rock of St. Peter was behind him in his fight against the powers of Dr. Fu Manchu.

"Satan in person is on earth," said the priest. His face bore the rapt look of the mystic—his voice rose upon a note of inspiration. "His works are manifest. Ours are the humble hands chosen to cast him down!"

Abruptly his expression changed; he became again the practical man of the world.

"We are together in this," he said, smiling—"Federal Agent 56! Now I am prepared to listen to your advice; I do not undertake to accept it."

Nayland Smith stared out of the window. Far away to the right, through crystal-clear air, he could catch a glimpse of a wide river. He twitched at the lobe of his ear and turned.

"I never waste advice," he said rapidly. "You have set your course; I am powerless to alter it. But if, as you say, we work together, there are certain things upon which I must insist."

He rested his hands on the desk; steely eyes pierced into guarded recesses of the abbot's mind.

"I am responsible for your personal safety. You must help me. Your life from now onward is dedicated to our common cause. I shall make certain arrangements for your protection; the conditions will be onerous . . . but you must accept them. I will add to your knowledge of this vast conspiracy. You, alone, can stem the tide. I will give you *names*. Upon the result our final success depends."

"Success or failure in human affairs invariably hangs upon a thread," the abbot replied. "The engagement of Paul Salvaletti and Lola Dumas has been given publicity greater than any royal wedding in the Old World ever obtained in America. In this the satanic genius who aims to secure control of the United States proves himself human—for it is human to err."

"I see!" snapped Nayland Smith; his eyes glittered with repressed excitement. "You have information touching the private life of Salvaletti?"

"Information, Sir Denis, which my conscience demands I should make public. . . ."

35   *THE LEAGUE OF GOOD AMERICANS*

"IT IS ESSENTIAL, my friend, to our success, even at this hour," said Dr. Fu Manchu, "indeed essential to our safety, that we silence this pestilential priest."

The room in which he sat appeared to contain all those appointments which had characterized his former study at the top of the Stratton Building. The exotic tang of incense was in the air, but windows opened onto a veranda helped to sweeten the atmosphere. Beyond a patch of lawn terminated by glass outbuildings a natural barrier of woods rose steeply to a high skyline. The trees, at the call of Spring, were veiling themselves in transparent green garments, later magically to be transformed into the gorgeous vestments of Summer. The Doctor's ever-changing headquarters possessed the virtue of variety.

From the point of view of the forces controlled by Nayland

Smith, he had completely disappeared following the explosion at the Stratton Building. The cave of the seven-eyed goddess had given up none of its secrets. Sam Pak, the much sought, remained invisible. A state-to-state search had failed to produce evidence to show that Dr. Fu Manchu was still in the country.

Only by his deeds was his presence made manifest.

Salvaletti was the idol of an enormous public. His forthcoming marriage to Lola Dumas promised to be a social event of international importance. An almost frenzied campaign on the part of those saner elements who recognized that the League of Good Americans was no more than a golden bubble, was handicapped at every turn. Men once hopeless and homeless who find themselves in profitable employment are not disposed to listen to criticisms of their employers. A policy of silence had been determined upon as a result of many anxious conferences in Washington. It was deemed unwise to give publicity to anything pointing to the existence of an Asiatic conspiracy behind the league. Substantial evidence in support of such a charge must first be obtained, and despite the feverish activity of thousands of agents all over the country, such evidence was still lacking. The finances of the league could not be challenged; they stood well with the Treasury: there were no evasions. Yet, as Sir Denis had proved to a group of financial experts, the League of Good Americans, at a rough estimate, must be losing two million dollars a week!

How were these losses made good?

He knew. But the explanation was so seemingly fantastic that he dared not advance it before these hard-headed businessmen whose imaginations had been neglected during the years that they concentrated upon solid facts.

Then, out of the blue, had come the Voice of the Holy Thorn. It had disturbed the country, keyed up to almost hysterical tension, as nothing else could have done. Long-awaited, the authoritative voice of the abbot had spoken at last. Millions of those who had awaited his call had anticipated that despite his known friendship for the old regime he would advocate acceptance of the new.

That Paul Salvaletti's program amounted to something uncommonly like dictatorship Salvaletti had been at no pains to disguise. His policy of the readjustment of wealth, a policy which no honest man in the country professed to understand, nevertheless enjoyed the cordial support of all those who had benefited by it. The agricultural areas were becoming more and more thickly dotted with league farms.

Their produce was collected and disposed of by league distributors: there were league stores in many towns. And this was no more than the skeleton of a monumental scheme which ultimately would give the league control of the key industries of the country.

Salvaletti had realized some of the promises of Harvey Bragg—promises which had been regarded as chimerical. . . .

Where a ray of sunlight touched his intricately wrinkled face, old Sam Pak crouched upon a stool just inside the windows, his mummy-like face grotesque against the green background of the woods.

"What has this priest learned, Master, which others had not learned before? Dr. Orwin Prescott knew of our arrival in the country. . . ."

"His source of information was traced—and removed. . . . Orwin Prescott served his purpose."

"True."

No man could have said if Sam Pak's eyes were open or closed as the shriveled head was turned in the direction of that majestic figure behind the table.

"Enemy Number One has been unable to obtain evidence which would justify his revealing the truth to the country." Dr. Fu Manchu seemed to be thinking aloud. "He has hindered us, harried us, but our great work has carried on and is nearing its triumphant conclusion. Should disaster come now—it would be his gods over ours. For this reason I fear the priest."

"The wise man fears only that which he knows," crooned old Sam Pak, "since against the unknown there can be no defense."

Dr. Fu Manchu, long ivory hands motionless upon the table before him, studied the wizened face.

"The priest has sources of information denied to the Secret Service," he said softly. "He has a following second only to our own. Salvaletti, whom I have tended as the gardener tends a delicate lily, must be guarded night and day."

"It is so, Marquis. He has a bodyguard five times as strong as that which formerly surrounded Harvey Bragg."

Silence fell for some moments. Dr. Fu Manchu, from his seat behind the lacquer table, seemed to be watching the woodland prospect through half-closed eyes.

"Some reports indicate that he evades his guards." Fu Manchu spoke almost in a whisper. "These reports the woman, Lola Dumas, has confirmed. My Chicago agents are ignorant and obtuse. I await an explanation of these clandestine journeys."

188

Sam Pak slowly nodded his wrinkled head.

"I have taken sharp measures, Master, with the Number responsible. He was the Japanese physician, Shoshima."

"He *was?*"

"He honorably committed hara-kiri last night. . . ."

Silence fell again between these invisible weavers who wrought a strange pattern upon the loom of American history. This little farmstead in which, unsuspected, Dr. Fu Manchu pursued his strange studies, and from which he issued his momentous orders, stood remote from the nearest main road upon property belonging to an ardent supporter of the League of Good Americans. He was unaware of the identity of his tenant, having placed the premises at the disposal of the league in all good faith.

Dr. Fu Manchu sat motionless in silence, his gaze fixed upon the distant woods. Sam Pak resembled an image: no man could have sworn that he lived. A squirrel ran up a branch of a tree which almost overhung the balcony, seemed to peer into the room, sprang lightly to a higher branch, and disappeared. The even-song of the birds proclaimed the coming of dusk. Nothing else stirred.

"I shall move to Base 6, Chicago," came the guttural voice at last. "The professor will accompany me; his memory holds all our secrets. It is essential that I be present in person on Saturday night."

"The plane is ready, Marquis, but it will be necessary for you to drive through New York to reach it."

"I shall leave in an hour, my friend. On my journey to Base 6 I may pay my respects to the Abbot Donegal." Dr. Fu Manchu spoke very softly. "Salvaletti's address on Saturday means the allegiance of those elements of the Middle West hitherto faithful to the old order. We must silence the priest. . . ."

36 *THE HUMAN EQUATION*

MARK HEPBURN could not keep still: impatience and anxiety conspired to deny him repose. He stood up from the seat in Central Park overlooking the pond and began to walk in the direction of the Scholar's Gate.

Smith had started at dawn by air to reach the Abbot Donegal, whose veiled statements relative to the man and the movement attempting to remodel the Constitution of the country had electrified millions of hearers from coast to coast. A consciousness of defeat was beginning to overwhelm Hepburn. No charge, unless it could be substantiated to the hilt, could check the headlong progress of Paul Salvaletti to the White House. . . .

And now, for the first time in their friendship, Moya Adair had failed to keep an appointment. Deep in his heart Hepburn was terrified. Lieutenant Johnson had traced Robbie's Long Island playground, but Moya had begged that Mark would never again have the boy covered.

She had been subjected to interrogation on the subject by the President! Apparently her replies had satisfied him—but she was not sure.

And now, although a note in her own hand had been conveyed to him by Mary Goff, Moya was not here.

If he should be responsible for any tragedy occurring in her life he knew that he could never forgive himself. And always their meetings took place under the shadow of dreadful, impending harm. He walked on until he could see the gate; but Moya was not visible. His restlessness grew by leaps and bounds. He turned and began to retrace his steps.

He had nearly reached the familiar seat which had become a landmark in his life when he saw her approaching from the opposite direction. He wanted to shout aloud, so great was his joy and relief. He began to hurry forward.

To his astonishment Moya, who must have seen him, did not hasten her step. She continued to stroll along looking about her as though he had not existed. His heart, which had leaped gladly at sight of her, leaped again, but painfully. What did it mean? What should he do? And now she was so near that he could clearly see her face . . . and he saw that she was very pale.

An almost imperceptible movement of her head, a quick lowering of her lashes, conveyed the message:

"Don't speak to me!"

His brow moist with perspiration, he passed her, looking straight ahead. Very faintly the words reached him:

"There's someone following. Keep him in sight."

Mark Hepburn walked on to where the path forked. A short, thick-set man passed him at the bend but did not pay any attention to him. Hepburn carried on for some ten or twelve paces, then dodged through some bushes, skirted a boulder and began to retrace his steps.

The man who was covering Moya was now some twenty yards ahead. Hepburn kept him in view, and presently he bore right, following a path which skirted the pond. In the distance Moya Adair became visible.

A book resting on her knee, she was watching a group of children at play.

The man passed her, making no sign. And in due course Hepburn approached. As he did so, Moya bent down over her book. He went on, keeping the man in sight right to the gate of the park. When he saw him cross towards the plaza, Mark Hepburn returned.

Moya looked up. She was still very pale; her expression was troubled.

"Has he gone?" she asked rather wearily.

"Yes, he has left the park."

"He has gone to make his report." She closed her book and sighed as Mark Hepburn sat down beside her. "I seem to be under suspicion. I think the movements of everybody in the organization are checked from time to time. There has been some tremendous upset. Probably you know what it is? Frankly—I don't. But it has resulted in an enormous amount of mechanical work being piled up on my shoulders. I receive hundreds of messages, apparently quite meaningless, which I have to take down in shorthand and repeat if called upon."

"To whom do you repeat them, Moya?"

"To someone with a German accent. I have no idea of his identity." Her gloved fingers played nervously with the book. "Then there is the Salvaletti-Dumas wedding. Old Emmanuel Dumas and myself have been made responsible for all arrangements. Lola, as you know, is with Salvaletti. It's terribly hard work. Of course, it's sheer propaganda and we have plenty of assistance. Nothing is being neglected which might help Salvaletti forward to the Presidency."

"The murder of Harvey Bragg was a step in that direction," said Hepburn grimly; "but——"

He checked his words. A party operating under his direction had located Dr. Fu Manchu and the man known as Sam Pak in a farmhouse in Connecticut! Even now it was being surrounded. Lieutenant Johnson was in charge. . . .

Moya did not answer at once; she sat staring straight before her for a while and then:

"That may be true," she replied in a very quiet voice. "I give you my word that I don't know if it is true or not.

And I'm sure you realize—" she turned to him, and he looked into her beautiful, troubled eyes—"that if I had known I should not have admitted it."

He watched her for a while in silence.

"Yes, I do," he said at last, in his unmusical, monotonous voice. "You play the game, even though you play it for the most evil man in the world."

"The President!" Moya forced a wan smile. "I sometimes think he is above good or evil—he thinks on a plane which we simply can't understand. Has that ever occurred to you, Mark?"

"Yes." Mark Hepburn nodded. "It's Nayland Smith's idea, too. It simply means that he's doubly dangerous to the peace of the world. You are such a dead straight little soul, Moya, that I can't tell you what I have learned about the man you call the President. It's a compliment to you, because I think if you were asked what I had said, you would feel called upon to answer truthfully."

Moya glanced at him, then looked aside.

"Yes," she replied slowly, "I suppose I should. But—" she clenched her hands—"quite honestly, I don't care very much today who gets control of the country. In the end, all forms of government are much alike, I believe. I am frightfully, desperately worried about Robbie."

"What's the matter, Moya?"

Hepburn bent to her. She continued to look aside; there were tears on her lashes.

"He's very ill."

"My dear!" In the most natural way in the world his arm was around her shoulders; he held her to him. "Why didn't you tell me at first? What's wrong? Who is attending him?"

"Dr. Burnett. It's diphtheria! He contracted it on his last visit to the garden. I have heard, since, there's a slight epidemic over there."

"But diphtheria, in capable hands——"

"Something seems to have gone wrong. I want another opinion. I must hurry back now."

Mark Hepburn cursed himself for an obtuse fool, for Moya knew that he was a doctor of medicine.

"Let me see him!" he said eagerly. "I know that sounds egotistical; I mean, I'm a very ordinary physician. But at least I have a deep interest in the case."

"I wanted you to see him," Moya answered simply. "Really, that was why I came today. I only learned last night what was the matter. . . ."

Nayland Smith hurried down from the plane and ran across the flood-lighted dusk of the flying ground to a waiting car. The door banged; the car moved off. To the other occupant:

"Who is it?" he snapped.

"Johnson."

"Ah, Johnson, a recruit from the navy, I believe, as Hepburn is a recruit from the army? I have been notified that Dr. Fu Manchu and the man, Sam Pak, have been traced to a farmhouse in Connecticut. The latest news?"

"Dr. Fu Manchu left by road a few minutes ago, before I and my party could intercept him."

"Damnation!" Nayland Smith drove his right fist into the palm of his left hand. "Too late—always too late!"

"He was heading for New York. Every possible point en route is watched. I returned by air to meet you."

"However disguised," said Smith, "his height alone makes his a conspicuous figure. Tell me where to drop you. Keep in touch with the Regal."

A police car preceded them on the lonely road and another brought up the rear. But a third car, showing no lights and traveling at sixty-five to seventy, passed.

A torrent of machine-gun bullets rained upon them! A violent explosion not five yards behind told of a wasted bomb!

The murder party roared away ahead—a Z-car, with Rolls engines built for two hundred miles per hour. . . .

The heavy windows had splintered in several places—but not one bullet had penetrated!

Johnson sprang out onto the roadside as they pulled up.

"Everything right in front?"

"O.K., sir."

Men were running to them from the leading car and jumping out of that which followed, when, leaning from the open door:

"Back to your places!" Nayland Smith shouted. "We stop for nothing. . . ."

In the covered car park of the Regal-Athenian, Smith alighted and ran in. The door was still swinging when Wyatt, a government man, came out from the reception office.

"I have a message from Captain Hepburn," he said.

Nayland Smith, already on his way to the elevator, paused, turned.

"What is it?"

"He does not expect to be here at the time arranged, but asks you to wait until he calls you."

Upstairs, in their now familiar quarters, Fey prepared a whisky.

"What's detaining Captain Hepburn?" Nayland Smith demanded. "Do you know?"

"I don't, sir, but I think it's something to do with the lady."

"Mrs. Adair?"

"Yes, sir. Mary Goff—a very excellent woman who has called here before—brought a note for Captain Hepburn this morning, just after you left, sir. Captain Hepburn has been out all day, but he returned an hour ago, collected up some things from his laboratory, and went out again."

Nayland Smith set down his glass and irritably began to load his pipe.

This was a strange departure from routine, and Mark Hepburn was a man of routine. Smith did not understand. Admittedly he was ahead of time, but he had counted upon finding Hepburn here. In such an hour of crisis as this, the absence of his chief of staff was more than perturbing. Every minute, every second, had its value. Dr. Fu Manchu had thwarted them at point after point. Despite their sleepless activity that cold, inexorable genius was carrying his plans to fruition. . . .

The phone bell rang. Fey answered. A moment he listened, then, looking up:

"Captain Hepburn, sir," he said.

3

"How is he, Dr. Burnett?"

Moya's voice was breathlessly anxious—her eyes were tragic. Dr. Burnett, a young man with charming manners and a fashionable practice, shook his head, frowning thoughtfully.

"There's really nothing to worry about, Mrs. Adair," he replied. "Nevertheless I am not entirely satisfied."

Moya turned as Mark Hepburn came into the sitting room. His intractable hair was more than normally untidy. He was acutely conscious of the danger of the situation, for he knew now that his presence would be reported by those mysterious watchers whose eyes missed nothing. He had made a plan, however. If Moya should be in peril, he would declare himself as a federal agent who had forced his way in to interrogate her.

"Dr. Burnett," said Moya, "this is—" for the fraction of a

second she hesitated—"Dr. Purcell, an old friend. You don't mind if he sees Robbie?"

Dr. Burnett bowed somewhat frigidly.

"Not at all," he replied; "in fact, I was about to suggest another opinion—purely in the interests of your peace of mind, Mrs. Adair. I had thought of Dr. Detmold."

Dr. Detmold had the reputation of being the best consulting physician in New York, and Mark Hepburn, as honest with himself as with others, experienced a moment of embarrassment. But finally:

"The boy's asleep," said Dr. Burnett, "and I am anxious not to arouse him. But if you will come this way, Dr.—er—Purcell, I shall be glad to hear your views."

In the dimly lighted bedroom, Nurse Goff sat beside the sleeping Robbie; her appearance indicated, correctly, that she had known no sleep for the past twenty-four hours. She looked up with a gleam of welcome in her tired, shrewd eyes as Hepburn entered.

He beckoned her across to the open window, and there in a whisper:

"He looks very white, nurse. How is his pulse?"

"He's failing, sir! The poor bairn is dying under my eyes. He's choking—he can swallow nothing! How can we keep him alive?"

Mark Hepburn crossed to the bed. Gently he felt the angle of the boy's jaw: the glands were much enlarged. Slight though his touch had been, Robbie awoke. His big eyes were glassy. There was no recognition in them.

"Water," he whispered. "Froat . . . so sore!"

"Poor bonnie lad," murmured Mary Goff. "He's crying for water, and every time he tries to swallow it I expect him to suffocate. Oh, what will we do! He's going to die!"

Hepburn, who had hastily collected from the Regal those indispensable implements of his trade, a stethoscope, a thermometer and a laryngeal mirror, began to examine the little patient. It was a difficult examination, but at last it was completed. . . .

Although painfully aware of her danger, he hadn't the heart to deter Moya when, her face a mask of sorrow, she crossed to the boy's bed. He beckoned to Dr. Burnett, and outside in the sitting room:

"I fear the larynx is affected," he said; "I am not equipped for a proper examination in this light. But what is your own opinion?"

"My opinion is, Dr. Purcell, that the woman Goff, although she is a trained nurse, has a sentimental attachment

195

to the patient and is unduly alarming Mrs. Adair. The action of the antitoxin, admittedly, has been delayed, but if normal measures are strictly carried out I can see no cause for alarm."

Mark Hepburn ran his fingers through his untidy hair.

"I wish I could share your optimism," he said. "Do you know Dr. Detmold's number? I should like to speak to him."

4

"The human equation—forever incalculable," muttered Nayland Smith.

He hung up the telephone and crossing, stared out of the window.

The night had a million eyes: New York's lights were twinkling. . . . Admittedly the situation was difficult; he put himself mentally in Hepburn's place: and Hepburn had asked only to be allowed to remain until the famous consultant arrived.

Nayland Smith stared at the decapitated trunk of the Stratton Building. There were lighted rooms on the lower floors, but the upper were in darkness. The great explosion at the summit had wrought such havoc that even now it was possible the entire building would be condemned. That explosion had been the personal handiwork of Dr. Fu Manchu!

Their escape from the catastrophe prepared for them fell nearly within the province of miracles. Yet to this very hour Dr. Fu Manchu remained at large, his wonderful brain weaving schemes beyond the imagination of normal men. . . .

Could anything, short of the destruction of that apparently indestructible life, prevent the triumph of Paul Salvaletti? The puzzle was maddeningly insoluble. The League of Good Americans began frankly to assume the dimensions of a Fascisti movement, with the dazzling personality of Salvaletti at its head. On Wednesday next, at eight o'clock (if he lived), Abbot Donegal would tell the country the truth. What would the reaction be?

Dr. Fu Manchu was buying the United States with gold!

Once, in Nayland Smith's presence, he had said: "Gold! I could drown mankind in gold!" That secret, to the discovery of which so many alchemists had devoted their lives, was held by the Chinese Doctor. Smith had known for a long time that gigantic operations in gold were being carried on. Indeed, although few had even suspected, it was these secret operations which had created the financial chaos from which every nation of the world suffered to this day.

Tonight the end seemed to him inevitable. There, alone, staring out at the lights of New York, Nayland Smith fought a great fight.

Could he hope to check this superman who fought with weapons not available to others; who had the experience of unimaginable years; who wielded forces which no other man had ever controlled? There was one certain way, and one only: that which Dr. Fu Manchu himself doubtless would have chosen.

The death of Paul Salvaletti would bring his mighty structure crashing to the earth. . . .

But, even though the fate of the country, perhaps of the Western world, hung in the scales, assassination was not a weapon which Nayland Smith could employ.

There was perhaps another way: the destruction of Dr. Fu Manchu. That subtle control removed, the gigantic but fragile machine would be lost; a rudderless ship in a hurricane.

A bell rang. Fey came in and crossed to the telephone.

"Lieutenant Johnson, sir."

Nayland Smith took up the receiver.

"Hullo, Johnson."

"Touch and go again!" came Johnson's voice on a note of excitement. "Dr. Fu Manchu was recognized by one of our patrols, but his car developed tremendous speed, and our men couldn't follow. They called through to the next point. The car was intercepted. It was empty—except for the driver! We've got the driver."

"Anything more?"

"Yes: a report that two men were seen to change cars in Greenwich. Descriptions tally. Second car sighted just over the line. But description now passed on to all patrols. Speaking from Times Building."

"Stand by. I'll join you."

Nayland Smith hung up.

"Fey!" he shouted.

Fey reappeared silently.

"Captain Hepburn is at the second address under the name of Adair in the notebook on the telephone table. We have no number for this address. If I want him you will send a messenger."

"Very good, sir."

"I shall keep in touch. I am going out now."

"As you are, sir?"

"Yes." Nayland Smith smiled grimly. "My attempted change of residence was a fiasco, and I don't propose to give further amusement to the enemy by wearing funny disguises."

37 THE GREAT PHYSICIAN

"I HAVE CALLED Dr. Detmold," said Mark Hepburn, "and have told him to bring—" he hesitated —"the necessary remedies."

Moya clutched him convulsively. For the first time in their strange friendship he found her in his arms.

"Does that mean—" she was watching him with an expression which he was never to forget—"that——"

"Don't worry, Moya—my dear. It will be all right. But I'm glad I came."

"Mark," she whispered, "I never realized until now how I wanted—someone I could count on."

Mark Hepburn stroked her hair—as many times he had longed to do.

"You know you can count on *me?*"

"Yes—I know I can."

Hepburn tried to conquer the drumming in his ears, which was caused by the acceleration of his heart. When he spoke, his voice was even more toneless than normally.

"I'm not a very wonderful bargain, Moya; but when all these troubles are past—because it isn't fair to ask you now . . ."

Moya raised her eyes to his: they were bright with stifled tears. But in them he read that which made further, ineloquent words needless.

All the submerged poetry in his complex character expressed itself in that first ecstatic kiss. It was a passionate sacrament. As he released Moya he knew, deep in his buried self, that he had found his mate.

"Moya, darling."

Her head rested on his shoulder. . . .

"Mark, dear, messages from this apartment are tapped," she said. "It's quite possible that your conversation with Dr. Detmold will be reported elsewhere."

"If you will excuse me for a moment," he muttered, "I shall declare myself and put you all under arrest."

Moya gently freed herself and stepped away as Dr. Burnett joined them.

"In certain respects," said Burnett, "the patient's condition, admittedly, is not favorable. My dear Mrs. Adair—" he patted her shoulder—"he is in very good hands. Dr. Detmold is coming?"

"Yes," Hepburn replied.

"I am sure he will endorse my opinion. The symptoms are not inconsistent with the treatment which I have been following."

Mark Hepburn entirely agreed. Robbie's survival of the treatment was due to a splendid constitution.

"If you will excuse me for a moment," he muttered, "I should like to look at the patient."

In the silence of the sick room he bent over Robbie. There was agony now in the eyes of Nurse Goff. The boy had had a choking fit in which he had narrowly escaped suffocation. He was terribly exhausted. His fluttery pulse was alarming. Walking on tiptoe, Hepburn crossed to the open window, beckoning Nurse Goff to follow him.

There he held a whispered consultation. Presently the door opened, and Dr. Burnett came in with Moya; the reassuring tone of his voice died away as he entered the room. He looked in a startled manner at his patient.

A change for the worse, which must have been apparent even to a layman, had taken place. Dr. Burnett crossed to the bed. There came a sound of three dull blows on the outer door, as if someone had struck it with a clenched hand. . . .

"Dr. Detmold!" Moya whispered brokenly, and ran out.

The two men were bending anxiously over the little sufferer when a suppressed cry from the vestibule, a sound of movement, brought Hepburn upright. He turned at the moment that a tall figure entered the bedroom.

It was that of a man in a long black overcoat having an astrakhan collar, who wore an astrakhan cap of a Russian pattern. Mark Hepburn's heart seemed to miss a beat—as he found himself transfixed by the glance of the green eyes of Dr. Fu Manchu!

For a moment only he was called upon to sustain it. The situation found him dumbfounded. Dr. Fu Manchu, removing his cap and throwing it upon a chair, turned to Dr. Burnett.

"Are you attending the patient?"

He spoke in a low voice, sibilant but imperative.

"I am. May I ask who you are, sir?"

Dr. Burnett glanced at a leather case which the speaker had placed upon the floor. Ignoring the inquiry, Dr. Fu

Manchu bent over Robbie for a moment, then stood upright, and turned as Moya came in.

"Why was I not notified earlier?" he demanded harshly.

Moya clutched at her throat; she was fighting back hysteria.

"How could I know, President," she whispered, "that——"

"True." Dr. Fu Manchu nodded. "I have been much preoccupied. Perhaps I am unjust. I should have prohibited the boy's last visit. I was aware that there was diphtheria in that neighborhood."

Something in his unmoving regard seemed to steady Moya.

"Your only crime is that you are a woman," said Dr. Fu Manchu quietly. "Even to the last you have done your duty to me. I must do mine. I guaranteed your boy's safety. I have never failed to redeem my word. From small failures great catastrophes grow."

"And I must protest," Dr. Burnett interposed, speaking indignantly but in a low voice. "At any moment we are expecting Dr. Detmold."

"Detmold is a dabbler," said Dr. Fu Manchu contemptuously, and crossing to the bed he seated himself in a chair, staring down intently at Robbie. "I have canceled those instructions."

"This is preposterous," Burnett exclaimed. "I order you to leave my patient."

Dr. Fu Manchu moved a gaunt yellow hand in a fanlike movement over Robbie's forehead, then, stooping, parted his lips with the second finger and the thumb of his left hand, and bent yet lower.

"When did you administer the antitoxin?" he demanded.

Dr. Burnett clenched his teeth, but did not reply.

"I asked a question."

The green eyes became suddenly fixed upon Dr. Burnett, and Dr. Burnett replied:

"At eleven o'clock last night."

"Eight hours too late. The diphtheritic membrane has invaded the larynx."

"I am dispersing it."

Moya's hands closed convulsively upon Mark Hepburn's arm.

"God help me!" she whispered. "What am I to do?"

Her words had reached the ears of Dr. Fu Manchu.

"You are to have courage," he replied, "and to wait in the sitting room with Mary Goff until I call you. Please go."

For one moment Moya glanced at Hepburn. Then Nurse

Goff, her face haggard with anxiety, put an arm around her and the two women went out. Dr. Fu Manchu stood up.

"Surgical interference is unavoidable," he said.

"I disagree!" Burnett in his indignation lost control, raising his voice unduly. "Until I have conferred with Dr. Detmold I forbid you to interfere with the patient in any way. Even if you are qualified to do so—which I doubt—I refuse to permit it."

Dr. Burnett found himself transfixed by a glance which seemed to penetrate to his subconscious mind. He became aware of an abysmal incompetence which he had successfully concealed even from himself throughout a prosperous career. He had never experienced an identical sensation in the whole of his life.

"Leave us," said the guttural voice. "Captain Hepburn will assist me."

As Dr. Burnett, moving like an automaton, went out of the room, the fact crashed in upon Hepburn that Dr. Fu Manchu had addressed him by his proper name and rank!

And, as if he had read his thoughts:

"My presence here tonight," said Dr. Fu Manchu, "is due to your telephone message to Sir Denis Nayland Smith. It was intercepted and relayed to me on my journey. To this I am indebted for avoiding a number of patrols whose positions you described. Be good enough to open the case which you will find upon the carpet at your feet. Disconnect the table lamp and plug in the coil of white flex."

Automatically, Mark Hepburn obeyed the order. Dr. Fu Manchu took up a mask to which a lamp was attached.

"We shall operate through the cricoid cartilage," he said. "But——"

"I must request you to accept my decisions. I could force them upon you but I prefer to appeal to your intelligence."

He moved his hands again over the boy's face; and, slowly, feverish bright eyes opened, staring upward.

Something resembling a tortured grin appeared upon Robbie's lips.

"Hello . . . Yellow Uncle," came a faint, gasping whisper. "I's glad . . . you come . . ."

He choked, became contorted, but his eyes remained open, fixed upon those other strange eyes which looked down upon him. Gradually the convulsion passed.

"You are sleepy." Fu Manchu's voice was a crooning murmur. The boy's long lashes began to flicker. "You are sleepy . . ." His lids drooped. "You are very sleepy . . ." Robbie's eyes became quite closed. "You are fast asleep."

"A general anesthetic?" Hepburn asked hoarsely.

"I never employ anesthetics in surgery," the guttural voice replied. "They decrease the natural resistance of the patient."

Nayland Smith, seated in the bullet-proof car, a sheaf of forms and other papers upon his knee, looked up at Johnson, who stood outside the open door.

"What are we to make of it, Johnson? An impasse! Here is the mysterious message received by Fey half an hour after I left: a request from Hepburn that under no circumstances should we look for evidence at the apartment he had visited, as someone lay there critically ill. No hint regarding his own movement, but the cryptic statement: 'Keep in touch with Fey and have no fear about my personal safety. *I make myself responsible for Dr. Fu Manchu!*'"

"Fey is sure it was Hepburn who called him," said Johnson. . . .

"But that was early last night," snapped Smith; "it is now 3.15 in the morning! And except for the fact that our latest reports enabled us to draw a ring on the map of Manhattan, where are we? Dr. Fu Manchu is almost certainly inside that ring. But since we cannot possibly barricade the most fashionable area of New York, how are we to find him?"

"It's a deadlock sure enough," Johnson agreed. "One thing's certain: Hepburn hasn't come out since he went in! A mouse couldn't have got out of that building. There are lights in the top apartment . . ."

And even as these words were being spoken, Mark Hepburn, in a darkened room, was watching the greatest menace to social order the world has known since Attila the Hun overran Europe, and wondering if Nayland Smith would respect his request.

He had witnessed a feat of surgery unique in his experience. Those long yellow fingers seemed to hold magic in their tips. Smith's assurance became superfluous. Dr. Fu Manchu, the supreme physician, was also the master surgeon. He was, as Hepburn believed (for Nayland Smith's computation he found himself unable to accept), a man of over seventy years of age. Yet with unfailing touch, exquisite dexterity, he had carried out an operation in a way which Hepburn's training told him to be wrong. It had proved to be right. Dr. Fu

Manchu had performed a surgical miracle—under hypnosis!

But it had left the little patient in a dangerously weak condition.

The night wore on, and with every hour of anxiety, Moya came nearer and nearer to collapse. Except for the ceaseless, hoarse voice of New York, the sick room was silent.

That strange, supercilious gesture of Fu Manchu before he began the operation was one Hepburn could never forget; it had a sort of ironic grandeur.

"Call your headquarters," the Chinese Doctor had directed, "at the Regal Tower. Ensure us against interference. Allay any doubts respecting your own safety: I shall require you here. Conceal the fact that I am present, but accept responsibility for handing me over to the law. I give you—personally—my parole. Instruct the exchange that no calls are to be put through tonight. . . ."

Nurse Goff was on duty again, although it was amazing how the weary woman kept awake. She sat by the open window, her hands clasped in her lap, her eyes fixed not upon the deathly face of Robbie, but on the gaunt profile of the man who bent over him. Moya was past tears; she stood just inside the open door, supported by Hepburn.

For five hours Dr. Fu Manchu had sat beside the bed. Some of the restorative measures which he had adopted were those that any surgeon would have used; others were unfamiliar to Hepburn, who could not even guess what was contained in the phials which he opened. Once, in the first crisis, Fu Manchu had harshly directed him to charge a hypodermic syringe. Then, bending over the boy and resting his hands upon his head, he had waved him aside. Now, as Hepburn's training told him, the second, the grand crisis, was approaching.

Moya had not spoken for more than an hour. Her lips were parched, her eyes burning: she quivered as he held her against him.

A new day drew near, and Hepburn, watching, saw (and read the portent) beads of moisture appearing upon the high yellow brow of Dr. Fu Manchu. At four o'clock, that zero hour at which so many frightened souls have crossed the threshold to take their first hesitant steps upon the path beyond, Robbie opened his eyes, tried to grin at the intent face so near to his own, then closed them again.

It came to Mark Hepburn as a conviction that that lonely little spirit had wandered beyond recall even by the greatest physician in the world, who sat motionless at his bedside. . . .

38 WESTWARD

Dim gray light was touching the most lofty buildings, so that they seemed to emerge from sleeping New York like phantoms of lost Nineveh; later would come the high-flung spears of sunrise to break golden upon the towers of those temples of Mammon. As Blücher might have remarked, "What a city to loot!"

Nayland Smith rang a bell beside a glazed door with iron scrollwork. Park Avenue is never wholly deserted day or night, but at this hour its fashionable life was at lowest ebb, and every possible precaution had been taken to avoid attracting the attention of belated passers-by. It was necessary to ring the bell more than once before the door was opened.

A sleepy night porter, his hair touseled, confronted them. Nayland Smith stepped forward, but the man, an angry gleam coming into his eyes, barred the way. He was big and powerfully built.

"Where do you think you're going?" he demanded.

"Top floor," rapped Nayland Smith. "Don't argue."

The man had a glimpse of a gold badge, and over the speaker's shoulder saw that he was covered by an automatic held by Lieutenant Johnson.

"What's the fuss?" he growled. "I'm not arguing."

But actually, although he was only a very small cog in the wheel, he knew that the occupants of the penthouse apartment at the top of the building were closely protected. He had secured his appointment through the League of Good Americans, and he had had orders from the officers of the league, identifiable by their badges, scrupulously to note and report anyone who visited that apartment.

In silence he operated the elevator. At the top:

"Go down again," Nayland Smith ordered, "and report to the officer in charge in the vestibule."

As the elevator disappeared he looked about him: they were a party of four. Anxiety for Hepburn's safety had driven him to make this move. Belatedly he had remembered a letter once received from Orwin Prescott—and in Prescott's handwriting. It had been written automatically, under hypnotic direction. He remembered that Hepburn quite

204

recently had succumbed to that uncanny control which Dr. Fu Manchu possessed the power to exercise. . . . Hepburn's message to Fey might be no more than an emanation from that powerful, evil will!

"Be ready for anything," he warned sternly, "but make no move without orders from me."

He pressed the bell.

A moment of almost complete silence followed. He had been prepared to wait, perhaps to force the door. He was about to ring a second time when the door opened.

Mark Hepburn faced him!

Amazement, relief, doubt, alternately ruled Nayland Smith's mind. The situation was beyond analysis. He fixed a penetrating stare on Hepburn's haggard face: his hair was disheveled, his expression wild, and with a queer note almost of resentment in his tone:

"Smith!" he exclaimed.

Nayland Smith nodded and stepped in, signaling to his party to remain outside.

Crossing a small vestibule, he found himself in a charmingly appointed sitting room, essentially and peculiarly feminine in character. It was empty.

"I'm sorry about all this seeming mystery," said Hepburn in a low voice; "and I understand your anxiety. But when you know the facts you will agree, I think, there was no other way."

"You undertook a certain responsibility," Nayland Smith said grimly, "in a message to Fey——"

"Not so loud, Smith! I stand by it. . . . It's hard to explain——" he hesitated, his deep-set eyes watching Nayland Smith—"but with all his crimes, after tonight——I'm sorry. Moya—Mrs. Adair—collapsed when she heard the news——"

"What, that the boy was dead?"

"No—that he will live!"

"I am glad to hear it. Largely as a result of your discovery of the Connecticut farm," said Nayland Smith, continuing intently to watch Hepburn, "we have narrowed down our search to an area surrounding this building. Your long, inexplicable absence following that message to Fey has checked us. I should be glad, Hepburn, if you would inform me where you believe Fu Manchu to be——"

The door opened, and Dr. Fu Manchu came in.

Smith's hand plunged to his automatic, but Fu Manchu, frowning slightly, shook his head. His usually brilliant eyes were dully filmed. He wore a black suit and beneath his coat a curious black woolen garment with a high collar. In some strange way he resembled a renegade priest who had abandoned Christianity in favor of devil worship.

"Melodrama is uncalled for, Sir Denis," he said, his guttural voice expressing no emotion whatever. "We are not in Hollywood. I shall be at your service in a moment." He turned to Hepburn. "My written instructions are on the table beside the bed: you will find there also the name of the physician I have selected to take charge of the case. He is a Jew practicing in the Ghetto; a man of integrity, with a sound knowledge of his profession. I do not imply, Sir Denis, that he is in the class of our mutual friend, Dr. Petrie (to whom I beg you to convey my regards), but he is the best physician in New York. I desire, Captain Hepburn, to be arrested by Sir Denis Nayland Smith, who has a prior claim. Will you be good enough to hand me over to him?"

Hepburn spoke hoarsely.

"Yes . . . Smith, this is your prisoner."

Fu Manchu bowed slightly. He took up a leather case which at the moment of entering he had placed upon the carpet beside him.

"I desire you, Captain Hepburn," he said, "to call Dr. Goldberg immediately, and to remain with the patient until he arrives. . . ."

All but imperturbable as he had trained himself to be, Nayland Smith at this moment almost lost contact with reality. At the eleventh hour, with counsels of desperation becoming attractive, Fate rather than his own wit had delivered this man into his hands. Swiftly he glanced at Hepburn and read in the haggard face mingled emotions of which he himself was conscious. He had never dreamed that triumph achieved after years of striving could be such deadsea fruit. The dimmed green eyes were fixed upon him, but there was nothing hypnotic in their regard; rather they held an ironical question. He stepped aside, indicating with his hand the vestibule in which the three men waited.

"Precede me, Dr. Fu Manchu."

Fu Manchu, carrying the case, walked with his cat-like tread out into the vestibule, three keen glances fixed upon him, three barrels covering his every movement.

"Ring for the elevator," rapped Nayland Smith.

One of the men went out through the front door, which had been left open.

Dr. Fu Manchu set his case upon the floor beside a chair.

"I assume, Sir Denis," he said, his voice very sibilant, "I am permitted to take my coat and my cap?"

He opened a paneled cupboard and looked inside. Momentarily the opened door concealed him as a heavy black topcoat with an astrakhan collar was thrown out onto the back of the chair. Ensued an interval of not more than five seconds . . . then Nayland Smith sprang forward.

The leather case stood beside the chair, the black coat was draped across it; but the cupboard was empty!

Dr. Fu Manchu had disappeared.

2

"I am growing old, Hepburn," said Nayland Smith. "It is high time I retired."

Mark Hepburn, studying the crisp graying hair, bronzed features and clear eyes of the speaker, laughed shortly.

"No doubt Dr. Fu Manchu wishes you would," he said.

"Yet he fooled me with a paltry vanishing-cabinet trick, an illusion which was old when the late Harry Houdini was young! Definitely, Hepburn, my ideas have become fixed. I simply cannot get used to the fact that New York City is a former stronghold of the most highly organized and highly paid underworld group which Western civilization so far has produced. That penthouse apartment, as we know now, was once occupied by Barney Flynn, the last of the big men of bootlegging days. The ingenious door in the hat cupboard was his private exit, opening into another building—a corresponding apartment which he also rented."

"Moya didn't know," said Hepburn.

"I grant you that. Nor was the apartment one of her own choosing. But she remembers (although in her disturbed state at the time she accepted the fact) that Fu Manchu *appeared* in the vestibule—although no one had opened the door! Had I realized that he had given you his parole, I might have foreseen an attempt to escape."

"Why?"

Nayland Smith turned to Hepburn; a faint smile crossed his lean features.

"He insisted that you should formally hand him over to *me*. You did so—and he promptly disappeared! Dr. Fu Manchu is a man of his word, Hepburn. . . ." He was silent awhile, then: "I am sorry for Mrs. Adair," he added, "and granting the circumstances, I think she has played fair. I hope the boy is out of danger."

Hepburn sat, pensive, looking down from the plane window at a darkling map of the agrarian Middle West.

"According to all I have ever learned," he said presently,

"that boy should be dead. Even now, I can't believe that any human power could have saved him. But he's alive! and there's every chance he will recover and be none the worse. You know, Smith—" he turned, his deep-set, ingenuous eyes fixed upon his companion—"that's a miracle. . . . I saw surgery there, in that room, that I'll swear there isn't another man living could have performed. That incompetent fool, Burnett, had lost the life of his patient: Dr. Fu Manchu conjured it back again."

He paused, watching the grim profile of Nayland Smith.

Dr. Fu Manchu had successfully slipped out of New York. But police and federal agents, urged to feverish activity by emergency orders from Washington, had made one discovery: Fu Manchu was headed West.

Outside higher police commands and the Secret Service, the intensive scrutiny of all travelers on Western highways by road or rail was a mystery to be discussed by those who came in contact with it for many years afterwards. Air liners received federal orders to alight at points not scheduled; private planes were forced down for identification; a rumor spread across half the country that a foreign invasion was imminent.

Despite Nayland Smith's endeavors, a garbled version of the facts had found currency in certain quarters; Abbot Donegal's words had given color to rumors. There had been riots in Asiatic sections: in one instance a lynching had narrowly been averted. The phantom of the Yellow Peril upreared its ugly head. But day by day, almost hour by hour, more and more adherents flocked to the standard of Paul Salvaletti; who represented, had they but known, the only real Yellow Peril to which the United States ever had been exposed.

"I'm still inclined to believe," Mark Hepburn said, "that I'm right about the object of the Doctor's journey. He's heading for Chicago. On Saturday night Salvaletti addresses a meeting on the result of which rests the final tipping of the scales."

Nayland Smith twitched the lobe of his left ear.

"The Tower of the Holy Thorn is not far off his route," he replied; "and Dom Patrick addresses the whole of the United States *tonight!* The situation is serious enough to justify the Doctor's taking personal charge of operations to check the voice of the abbot. . . ."

That the priest's vast audience even at this eleventh hour could split the Salvaletti camp was an admissible fact. Even now it was thought that the former Chief Executive would be returned to office; but the league faction would make that office uneasy.

"Salvaletti's magnificent showmanship," said Smith, "the sentimental appeal in his pending marriage, are the work of a master producer. The last act shows a brilliant adventurer assuming control of the United States! It is not impossible, nor without precedent. Napoleon Buonaparte, Mussolini, Kemal have played the part before. No, Hepburn! I doubt if Fu Manchu will passively permit Abbot Donegal to steal the limelight. . . ."

39 *THE VOICE FROM THE TOWER*

ALL APPROACHES to the Tower of the Holy Thorn would have reminded a veteran of an occupied town in war time. They were held up four times by armed guards. . . .

When at last the headlamps of the road monster which had been waiting at the flood-lit flying ground shone upon the bronze door, so that that thorn-crowned Head seemed to come to meet them in the darkness, Nayland Smith sprang out.

"Is Garstin there?" Hepburn called.

A man came forward.

"Captain Hepburn?"

"Yes. Anything to report?"

"All clear, Captain. It would need a regiment with machine guns to get through!"

Mark Hepburn stared upward. The tower was in darkness right to the top; the staff which dealt with the abbot's enormous mail had left. But from its crest light beaconed as from a pharos.

And as Mark Hepburn stood there looking up, Nayland Smith entered the study of Dom Patrick Donegal.

"Thank God I see you safe!" he said, and shot out a nervous brown hand.

Patrick Donegal grasped it, and stood for a moment staring into the eyes of the man who had burst into his room.

"Thank God indeed. You see before you a chastened man, Sir Denis." The abbot's ascetic features as well as his rich brogue told that he spoke from his heart. "Once I resented

209

your peremptory orders. I have changed my mind; I know that they were meant for my protection and for the good of my country. You see—" he pointed—"the broadcasting corporation has equipped me with a microphone. Tonight I speak in the safety of my own study."

"You have followed my instructions closely?"

Nayland Smith was watching the priest with almost feverish intentness.

"In every particular. You may take it—" he smiled— "that I have not been poisoned or tampered with in any way! My address for tonight I wrote with my own hand at that desk. None other has touched it."

"You have included the facts which I gave you—and the figures?"

"Everything! And I am happy to have you with me, Sir Denis; it gives me an added sense of security. At any moment now, the radio announcer will be here. I trust that you will stay?"

Nayland Smith did not reply. He was listening—listening keenly to a distant sound. Although he was barely aware of the fact, his gaze was set upon a reproduction of Carpaccio's St. Jerome which hung upon the plastered wall above a crowded bookcase.

And now the abbot was listening, too. Dim cries came from far below; shouted orders. . . .

A drone of airplane propellers drew rapidly nearer. Smith crossed to the window. A searchlight was sweeping the sky. A moment he watched, then turned, acted—and his actions were extraordinary.

Seizing the abbot bodily, he hurled him in the direction of the door! Then, leaping forward, he threw the door open, extended a muscular arm, and dragged him out. On the landing, Dom Patrick staggered; Smith grasped his shoulder.

"Down!" he shouted, "down the stairs!"

But now the priest had appreciated the urgency of the case. Temporarily shaken by this swift danger, as a man of courage he quickly recovered himself. On the landing below:

"Lie flat!" cried Smith, "we must trust to luck!"

The noise of an airplane engine grew so loud that one could only assume the pilot deliberately to be steering for the tower. Came a volley of rifle fire. . . .

They were prone on the marble-paved floor when a deafening explosion shook the Tower of the Holy Thorn as an earthquake might have shaken it. Excited cries followed, crashing of fallen debris; an acrid smell reached their nostrils: the drone of propellers died away.

Abbot Donegal rose to his knees.

"Wait!" cried Smith breathlessly. "Not yet!"

The air was pervaded by a smell resembling iodine. He distrusted it, and stood there staring upward towards the top landing. The crown of the elevator shaft opposite the abbot's door was wrecked. He could detect no sign of fire. The abbot, head bowed, gave silent thanks.

"Smith!" came huskily, "Smith!"

An increasing clatter of footsteps arose from the stairs below, and presently, pale, breathless, Mark Hepburn appeared.

"All right, Hepburn!" said Nayland Smith. "No casualties!"

Hepburn leaned heavily against a handrail for a moment; he had outrun them all.

"Thank God for that!" he panted. "It was an aerial torpedo—we saw them launch it!"

"The plane?"

"Will almost certainly be driven down."

"What d'you make of this queer smell?"

Mark Hepburn sniffed suspiciously, and then:

"Oxygen," he replied. "Liquid ozone electrically discharged, maybe. For some reason" (he continued to breathe heavily) "the Doctor wanted to avoid fire. . . ."

Cautiously they mounted the stair and looked into the dark wreckage which had been Dom Patrick's study. There were great holes in the roof through which one could see the stars, and two entire walls of the room had disappeared. All lights had gone out. Nayland Smith started as a hand touched his shoulder.

He turned. Abbot Donegal stood beside him, pointing.

"Look!" he said.

One corner of the study remained unscathed by the explosion. In it stood the microphone installed that day, and from the plaster wall above, St. Jerome looked down undisturbed. . . .

"A sign, Sir Denis! God in His wisdom has ordained that I speak tonight!"

2

Lola Dumas lay curled up on a cushioned settee; she wore a rest gown and slippers, but no stockings. And in the dimly lighted room the curves of her slender, creamy legs created highlights too startling in their contrast against the blue velvet to have pleased a portrait painter. Stacks of crumpled newspapers lay upon the carpet beside her. Her elbows buried in the cushions, chin resting in cupped hands, Lola stared across the darkened room, her somber eyes speculative, almost menacing.

On the front page of the journal which crowned the litter a large photograph of Lola appeared. It appeared in nearly all the others as well. She was the most talked-about woman in the United States. Drawings of the dresses to be worn by her bridesmaids had already been published in the fashion papers. It was to be a Louis XIII wedding: twenty tiny pages dressed as Black Musketeers, with Lola herself wearing the famous diamond brooch upon the recovery of which Dumas' greatest romance is based. An archbishop would perform the cermony, and not less than two bishops would be present. A cardinal would have been more decorative; but since the rites of the Church of Rome had been denied to Lola following her first divorce, she had necessarily abjured that faith.

Moya Adair in the Park Avenue apartment, assisted by extra typists called in for the occasion, had sent out thousands of polite refusals to more or less important people who had applied for seats in the church. None were left.

Lola was to be married from her father's Park Avenue home. Five hundred invitations had been accepted for the reception; the Moonray Room of the Regal-Athenian had been rented, together with the services of New York's smartest band.

So keen was the interest which the magnetic rise of Paul Salvaletti had created throughout the world that despite the disturbed state of Europe, war and the rumors of war, special commissioners were being sent to New York by many prominent European newspapers to report the Salvaletti-Dumas wedding. In fact this wedding would be the master stroke of the master schemer, setting the seal of an international benediction upon the future President. Love always demands the front page.

But in the somber eyes of Lola Dumas there was no happiness. She lived for what she called "love" and without admiration must die. In fact, after her second divorce, the circumstances of which had not reflected creditably upon her, she had proclaimed that she intended to renounce the vanities of the world and take the veil. Perhaps fortunately for her, she had failed to find any suitable convent prepared to accept her as a novice.

There came a discreet rap on the door.

"Come in," Lola called, her voice neither soft nor caressing.

She sat upright, slender jeweled fingers clutching the cushions as Marie, her maid, came in.

"Well?"

Marie pursed her lips, shrugged and nodded vigorously.

"You are sure?"

"Yes, madame. He is there again! And tonight I have found the number of the apartment—it is Number 36."

Lola swung her slippered feet to the floor and clenching and unclenching her hands began to walk up and down. In the semidarkness she all but upset a small table upon which a radio was standing. Marie, fearing one of the brainstorms for which Lola was notorious, stood just inside the door, watching fearfully. Of course, Lola argued, Paul's mysterious absences (which since they had been in Chicago had become so frequent) might be due to orders from the President. But if this were so, why was she not in Paul's confidence?

It was unlikely, too, for on many occasions before, and again tonight, he had slipped away from his bodyguard and had gone alone to this place. Tonight, indeed, it was more than ever strange: the Abbot Donegal was broadcasting, and almost certainly his address would take the form of an attack.

Any man who admired her inspired Lola's friendship, but Paul Salvaletti had been the only real passion of her life. There were many who thought that she had been Harvey Bragg's mistress. It was not so; a circumstance for which Harvey Bragg deserved no blame. Given knowledge of all the facts, his harshest critic must have admitted that Harvey had done his best. Always it had been Paul, right from the first hour of their meeting. She had recognized him; had known what he was destined to become. Her other duties, many of them exacting and tedious, which the President compelled her to undertake, she had undertaken gladly with this goal in view.

The intrusion of the woman Adair had terrified her, followed as it had been by her own transfer to nurse's duties (which she understood) in Chinatown. She hated the thought of this Titian blonde's close association with Paul. Mrs. Adair was cultured, too, the widow of a naval officer, a woman of good family . . . and always the plans of the President were impenetrable.

Abruptly, long varnished nails pressed into her palms; she pulled up in that wildcat walk right in front of the radio.

"What's the time, Marie?" she demanded harshly.

213

"It is after eight o'clock, madame."

"Fool! Why didn't you tell me!"

Lola dropped down onto one knee; she tuned in the instrument. Nothing occurred but a dim buzzing. She knelt there manipulating the control, but could get no result. She looked up.

"If this thing has gone wrong," she said viciously, "I'll murder somebody in this hotel."

Suddenly came a voice:

"This is a National Broadcast . . ." Formalities followed, and then: "I must apologize for the delay. It was caused by an accident to the special microphone, but this has been adjusted. You are now about to hear Dom Patrick Donegal, speaking from the Tower of the Holy Thorn."

Lola Dumas threw herself back upon the settee, curling her slim body up, serpentine, among the cushions. She was striving with all her will to regain composure. The beautiful voice of the priest helped to calm her; she hated it so intensely, for in her heart of hearts Lola knew that the Abbot of Holy Thorn was a finer orator than Paul Salvaletti. Then her attention was arrested:

"A torpedo of unusual design," the abbot was saying coldly, "fired from an airplane, wrecked my study and delayed this broadcast. I am now going to tell you, and I ask you to listen with particular attention, by whom that torpedo was fired into my study."

With the judgment of a practiced speaker he paused for a moment after this sensational statement. Hourly, Lola had expected an attempt to be made to silence the abbot. It had been made—and had failed! She began to listen intently. This man, this damnable priest, was going to wreck their fortunes!

When he resumed, Patrick Donegal, with that unfailing art in which Cicero had been his master, struck another note:

"There are many of you, I know, who, day after weary day, have returned from a tireless and honorable quest of work, to look into the sad eyes of a woman, to try to deafen your ears to that most dreadful of all cries coming from a child's lips: 'I am hungry.' The League of Good Americans, formerly associated with the name of Harvey Bragg, has—I don't deny the fact—remedied much of this. There are hundreds of thousands, it may be millions, of men, women and children in this country who today have won that meed of happiness which every human being strives to earn, through the offices of the league. But I am going to ask you to consider a few figures—figures are more eloquent than words."

In three minutes or less, the abbot proved (using Nayland

Smith's statistics) that over the period with which he dealt, alone, some twenty million dollars had been expended in the country through various activities of the league which, even admitting the possibility of anonymous donations from wealthy supporters, could not have come out of national funds!

"You may say, and justly so, This is good: it means that unearned wealth is coming into the United States. I ask you to pause—to think . . . Is there such a thing as unearned wealth? Even a heritage carries its responsibilities. What are the responsibilities you are incurring by your acceptance of these mysterious benefits? I will tell you:

"You are being bought with alien money!" the abbot cried, "you are becoming slaves of a cruel master. You are being gagged with gold. The league and all its pretensions is a chimera, a hollow mockery, a travesty of administration. You are selling your country. Your hardships are being exploited in the interests of an alien financial genius who plans to control the United States. And do you know the nationality of that man? He is a *Chinaman!*"

Lola's jeweled fingers were twitching nervously upon the cushions, her big eyes were very widely opened. Marie, uninvited, had taken a seat upon a chair just inside the door. This was the most damning attack which anyone had delivered: its possible consequences outsped the imagination. . . .

"Who is this man who tonight attempted to murder me in my own room? This callous assassin, this ravisher of a nation's liberty? By the mercy of God my life was spared that I might speak, that I might tell you. He is an international criminal sought by the police of the civilized world; a criminal whose evil deeds dwarf those of any home-grown racketeer. His name will be known to many who listen: it is Dr. Fu Manchu. My friends, Dr. Fu Manchu is in America— Dr. Fu Manchu tonight attempted my assassination—Dr. Fu Manchu is the presiding genius of the League of Good Americans!"

A moment he paused, then:

"This is the invisible President whom you are being bribed to send to the White House!" he said in a low, tense voice, "not in his own person but in the person of his servant, his creature, his slave—Paul Salvaletti! Paul Salvaletti, who stands upon the bloody corpse of Harvey Bragg . . . for I am going to tell you something else which you do not know: Harvey Bragg was assassinated to make way for Paul Salvaletti."

Even in the silence of that room where Lola Dumas
215

crouched among the cushions it was possible to imagine the sensation which from coast to coast those words had created.

"The wedding of the man Salvaletti promises to be an international event, a thing for which distinguished people are assembling. I say it would be an offense for which this country would never be forgiven," he thundered, "to permit that sacrilegious marriage to take place! I say this for three reasons: first, that Paul Salvaletti is merely the shadow of his Chinese master; second, that Paul Salvaletti is an unfrocked priest; and third, that he is already married."

Lola Dumas sprang to the floor and stood rigidly upright.

"He married an Italian girl—she was just sixteen—Marianna Savini, in a London registry office on March the 25th, 1929. She accompanied him secretly when he came to the United States; she has been with him ever since—she is with him now. . . ."

3

"It was a good shot," said Captain Kingswell, "although at such close range that row of lighted windows offered a fine target. But it isn't the gunner, it's the pilot I want to meet. The way he dipped to the tower was pretty work."

"Very pretty," said Nayland Smith. "As I happened to be inside the tower, I fully appreciated its excellence. You were chasing this plane, I gather?"

Captain Kingswell, one of many army aviators on duty that night, nodded affirmatively.

"I should have caught him! It was the maneuver by the tower that tricked me. You see, I hadn't expected it."

The big armored car sped through the night, its headlights whitening roads and hedges.

"It is certain that they were driven down?"

"Lieutenant Olson, who was covering me on the left, reports he forced the ship down near the river somewhere above Tonawanda."

"Is there any place around there," Mark Hepburn asked slowly, "where they might have landed?"

"I may as well say," the pilot replied, smiling, "it's a section I don't pretend to be familiar with. Landing at night is always touch and go, even if the territory is familiar. It's only halfway safe on a proper flying ground. Hullo! there's Gilligham!"

The headlights picked up a distant figure, arms outstretched, wearing army air uniform. This was an agricultural district where folks were early abed; the country roads were deserted. As the car pulled up the aviator ran to the door:

"What news, Gilligham?" cried Captain Kingswell.

"We're shorthanded to surround the area where they crashed," replied Gilligham, a young fresh-faced man, immensely excited; "at least, it's ten to one they crashed. But I've done my best, and search parties are working right down to the riverbank."

"How far to the river?" jerked Nayland Smith.

"As the crow flies, from this spot a half mile."

Smith jumped out, followed by Hepburn. A crescent moon swam in a starry sky. Directly above their heads as they stood beside the car outflung branches of two tall elms, one on either side of the narrow, straight road, met and embraced, to form a deep stripe of shadow.

"This is the frontier?"

"Yes, the opposite bank's in Canada."

Through the silence, from somewhere far off, came a sound like that of a ceaseless moan; at times, carried by a light breeze, it rose weirdly on the night, as though long-dead gods of the redman, returning, lamented the conquest of the white.

Nayland Smith, his eyes bright in the ray of the headlamp, turned to Hepburn questioningly.

"The rapids," said Mark. "The wind's that way."

As the breeze died, the mournful sound faded into a sad whisper. . . .

"Hullo!" Smith muttered, "what are those lights moving over there?"

"One of our search parties," Gilligham replied. "We expect to locate the wreck pretty soon. . . ."

But half an hour had elapsed before the mystery plane was found. It lay at one end of a long, plowed field: the undercarriage had been damaged, but the screw, wings and fuselage remained intact. Again the work of a clever pilot was made manifest. There was no sign of the occupants.

"This is a Japanese ship," said Captain Kingswell, on a note of astonishment. "Surely can't have crossed right to here in the air? Must have been reassembled somewhere. Looks like it carried four of a crew: a pilot, a reserve (maybe he was the gunner) and two others."

He had climbed up and was now inside.

"Here's a queer torpedo outfit," he cried, "with three reserve tubes. This is a fighting ship." He was prowling around enthusiastically, torch in hand. "We'll overhaul every inch of it. There may be very interesting evidence."

"The evidence I'm looking for," rapped Nayland Smith

irritably, "is evidence to show which way the occupants went. But all these footprints—" he flashed his torch upon the ground—"have made it impossible to trace."

He turned and stared towards where a red glow in the sky marked a distant town. Away to the east, half masked by trees, he could see outbuildings of what he took to be a farm.

"Tracks over here, mister!" came a hail from the northern end of the meadow. "Not made by the search party!"

Nayland Smith, his repressed excitement communicating itself to Hepburn, set out at a run.

The man who had made the discovery was shining a light down upon the ground. He was a small, stout, red-faced man wearing a very narrow brimmed hat with a very high crown.

"Looks like the tracks of three men," he said: "two walkin' ahead an' one followin' along."

"Three men," muttered Nayland Smith; "there's the possibility there were four in the plane. Let me see . . ."

He examined the tracks, and:

"I must congratulate you," he said, addressing their discoverer. "Your powers of observation are excellent."

"That's all right, mister. In these per'lous times a man has to keep his eyes skinned—'specially me; I'm deputy sheriff around here: Jabez Siskin—Sheriff Siskin they call me."

"Glad to have you with us, Sheriff. My name is Smith—federal agent."

Two sets of imprints there were which admittedly seemed to march side by side. The spacing indicated long strides; the depth of the impressions, considerable weight. The third track, although made by a substantial-sized shoe, was lighter; there was no evidence to show that the one who had made it had crossed the meadow at the same time as the other two.

"Move on!" snapped Nayland Smith. "Follow the tracks but don't disturb them."

From point to point the same conditions arose which had led the local officer to assume that the third traveler had been following the other two; that is, his lighter tracks were impressed upon the heavier ones. But never did either of the heavier tracks encroach upon another. Two men had been walking abreast followed by a third; at what interval it was impossible to determine.

Right to a five-barred gate the tracks led, and there Deputy Sheriff Siskin paused, pointing triumphantly.

The gate was open.

Nayland Smith stepped through onto a narrow, wheel-rutted lane.

"Where does this lane lead to?" he inquired.

"To Farmer Clutterbuck's," Sheriff Siskin replied; "this is all part of his land. The league bought it back for him. The farm lays on the right. The river's beyond."

"Come on!"

It was a long, a tedious and a winding way, but at last they stood before the farm. Clutterbuck's Farm was an example of the work of those days when men built their own homesteads untrammeled by architectural laws, but built them well and truly: a rambling building over which some vine that threatened at any moment to burst into flower climbed lovingly above a porch jutting out from the western front.

Their advent had not been unnoticed. A fiery red head was protruded from an upper window above and to the right of the porch, preceded by the barrel of a shotgun, and;

"What in hell now?" a gruff voice inquired.

"It's me, Clutterbuck," Deputy Sheriff Siskin replied, "with federals here, an' the army an' ev'rything!"

When Farmer Clutterbuck opened his front door he appeared in gum boots. He wore a topcoat apparently made of rabbit skin over a woolen nightshirt, and his temper corresponded to his fiery hair. He was a big, bearded, choleric character.

"Listen!" he shouted—"It's you I'm talkin' to, Sheriff! I've had more'n enough o' this for one night. Money ain't ev'rything when a man has to buy a new boat."

"But listen, Clutterbuck——"

Nayland Smith stepped forward.

"Mr. Clutterbuck," he said—"I gather that this is your name—we are government officers. We regret disturbing you, but we have our duty to perform."

"A boat's a boat, an' money ain't ev'rything."

"So you have already assured us. Explain what you mean."

Farmer Clutterbuck found himself to be strangely subdued by the cold authority of the speaker's voice.

"Well, it's this way," he said. (Two windows above were opened, and two heads peered out.) "I'm a league man, see? This is a league farm. Can't alter that, can I? An' I'm roused up tonight when I'm fast asleep—that's enough to annoy a man, ain't it? I think the war's started. Around these parts we all figure on it. I take my gun an' I look out o' the window. What do I see? Listen to me, Sheriff—what do I see?"

"Forget the sheriff," said Nayland Smith irritably; "address your remarks to me. What did you see?"

"Oh, well! all right. I see three men standin' right here outside—right here where we stand now. One's old, with white whiskers an' white hair; another one, some kind of a colored man, I couldn't just see prop'ly; but the third one—him that's lookin' up—" he paused—"well . . ."

"Well?" rapped Nayland Smith.

"He's very tall, see? as tall as me, I guess; an' he wears a coat with a fur collar an' he wears a fur cap. There's a sickle moon, an' his eyes—listen to this, Sheriff—his eyes ain't brown, an' his eyes ain't blue, an' they ain't gray: they're green!"

"Quick, man!" Nayland Smith cried. "What happened? What did he want?"

"He wants my motorboat."

"Did he get it?"

"Listen, mister! I told you I'm a league man, didn't I? Well, this is a league official, see? Shows me his badge. He buys the boat. I didn't have no choice, anyway—but I'd been nuts to say no to the price. Trouble is, now I got no boat; an' money ain't ev'rything when a man loses his boat!"

"Fu Manchu knows the game's up. They had a radio in the place!" said Smith to Hepburn in a low tone vibrant with excitement.

"Then God help Salvaletti!"

"Amen. We know he has agents in Chicago. But by heaven we must move, Hepburn: the Doctor is making for Canada!"

4

At roughly about this time, those who had listened to Patrick Donegal and who now were listening to radio topics received a further shock. . . .

"Tragic news has just come to hand from Chicago," they heard. "A woman known as Mrs. Valetti occupied Apartment 36 in the Doric Building on Lakeside. She was a beautiful brunette, and almost her only caller was a man believed to be her husband who frequently visited there. About 8.30 this evening, Miss Lola Dumas, whose marriage to Paul Salvaletti has been arranged to take place next month, came to the apartment. She had never been there before. She failed to get any reply to her ringing but was horrified to hear a woman's scream. At her urgent request the door was opened by the resident manager, and a dreadful discovery was made.

"Mrs. Valetti and the man lay side by side upon the day bed in the sitting room. On the woman's arms and on the man's neck there were a number of blood-red spots. They were both dead, and a window was wide open. Miss Dumas collapsed on recognizing the man as her fiancé, Paul Salvaletti. She is alleged to have uttered the words, 'The Scarlet Bride' —which the police engaged on the case believe to relate to the dead woman. But Miss Dumas, to whom the sympathy of the entire country goes out in this hour of her unimaginable sorrow, is critically ill and cannot be questioned.

"The crisis which this tragedy will create in political circles it would be impossible to exaggerate. . . ."

40 *"THUNDER OF WATERS"*

"THEY'RE JUST LANDING!" cried the man in the bows of the Customs launch—"at the old Indian Ferry."

"Guess those Canadian bums showed 'emselves," growled another voice. "We had 'em trapped, if they'd gone ashore where they planned."

Nayland Smith, standing up and peering through night-glasses, saw a tall, dark figure on the rock-cut steps. It was unmistakable. It was Dr. Fu Manchu! He saw him beckon to the second passenger in the little motorboat; and the other, a man whose hair shone like silver in the moonlight, joined him on the steps. A third remained in the boat at the wheel. Dr. Fu Manchu, arms folded, stood for a moment looking out across the river. He did not seem to be watching the approaching Customs craft so swiftly bearing down upon him, but rather to be studying the shadowed American bank, the frontier of the United States.

It came to Nayland Smith, as they drew nearer and nearer to the motionless figure, that Dr. Fu Manchu was bidding a silent farewell to the empire he had so nearly won. . . .

Just as words of command trembled on Smith's lips Fu Manchu spoke to the occupant of the boat, turned, and with his white-haired companion strode up the steps—steps hewn by the redman in days before any white traveler had seen or heard "The Thunder of Waters."

The motorboat spluttered into sudden life and set off downstream.

"Stop that man!" rapped Nayland Smith.

Dr. Fu Manchu and the other already were lost in the shadow.

"Heave to—federal orders!" roared a loud voice.

Farmer Clutterbuck's motorboat was kept on its course. "Shall we let him have it?"

"Yes—but head for the steps."

Three shots came almost together. Raising the glasses again, Nayland Smith had a glimpse of a form crouching low over the wheel . . . then a bluff which protected the Indian Ferry obscured the boat from sight. As they swung in to the steps:

"What was that move?" somebody inquired. "I guess we missed him anyway."

But Nayland Smith was already running up the steps. He found himself in a narrow gorge on one side completely overhung by tangled branches. He flashed a light ahead. Three federal agents came clattering up behind him.

"What I'm wondering," said one, "is, where's Captain Hepburn?"

Nayland Smith wondered also. Hepburn, in another launch, had been put ashore higher up on the Canadian bank, armed with Smith's personal card upon which a message had been scribbled. . . .

Dr. Fu Manchu and his companion seemed to have disappeared.

But now, heralded by a roar of propellers, Captain Kingswell came swooping down out of the night, and the first Very light burst directly overhead! Nayland Smith paused, raised his glasses, and stared upward. Kingswell, flying very low, circled, dipped, and headed downriver.

"He's seen them!" snapped Smith.

Came a dim shouting . . . Hepburn was heading in their direction. A second light broke.

"By God!" Nayland Smith cried savagely, "are we all blind? Look at Kingswell's signals. They have rejoined the motorboat at some place below!"

Two more army planes flew into view. . . .

"Back to the launch!" Smith shouted.

But when at last they set out again, the batlike maneuvers of the aviators and the points at which they threw out their flares indicated that the cunning quarry had a long start. It seemed to Nayland Smith, crouched in the bows, staring ahead, that time, elastic, had stretched out to infinity. Then he sighted the motorboat. Kingswell, above, was flying just ahead of it. He threw out a light.

In the glare, while it prevailed, a grim scene was shown. The man at the wheel (probably the same who had piloted the plane) lay over it, if not dead, unconscious; and the silver-haired passenger was locked in a fierce struggle with Dr. Fu Manchu!

Professor Morgenstahl's hour had come! In the stress of that last fight for freedom the Doctor's control, for a matter of seconds only, had relaxed. But in those seconds Morgenstahl had acted. . . .

"This is where we check out!" came a cry. "Hard over, Jim!"

Absorbed in the drama being played before him—a drama the real significance of which he could only guess— Nayland Smith had remained deaf to the deepening roar of the river. Suddenly the launch rolled and swung about.

"What's this?" he shouted, turning.

"Twenty lengths more and we'd be in the rapids!"

The rapids!

He craned his head, looking astern. Somewhere, far back, a light broke. Three planes were flying low over the river . . . and now to his ears came the awesome song of Niagara, "The Thunder of Waters."

An icy hand seemed to touch Nayland Smith's heart. . . .

Dr. Fu Manchu had been caught in the rapids; no human power nor his own superlative genius could prevent his being carried over the great falls! The man who had dared to re-model nature's force had been claimed at last by the gods he had outraged.

THE END

I f you have enjoyed this book, you will want to read other inexpensive Pyramid best-sellers. You will find them wherever paperbacks are sold or you can order them direct from the publisher. *Yours For The Asking:* a free, illustrated catalogue listing more than 700 books published by Pyramid. Write the publisher: PYRAMID BOOKS, Dept. K-99, 9 Garden Street, Moonachie, N. J. 07074.